The
Hindmost

The Hindmost

Barry Kennedy

Doubleday Canada Limited

Canadian Cataloguing in Publication Data
Kennedy, Barry (Barry G. J.)
  The hindmost
ISBN 0-385-25730-9
I. Title.
PS8571.B62725H56 1998   C813' 54   C98-930093-5
PR9199.3K46H56 1998

Front cover photograph by Wally Moss
Cover design and back cover photograph by Kevin Connolly
Text design by Heidy Lawrance Associates
Printed and bound in the USA

Published in Canada by
Doubleday Canada Limited
105 Bond Street
Toronto, Ontario
M5B 1Y3

BVG 10 9 8 7 6 5 4 3 2 1

For Gordon

It had been a good wedding, even though most people normally don't like winter weddings.

Monigan was blowing in on the wind from the northeast, navigating along the path in the small inner-city park. The swirling snow was embroidering the ground around his feet. His new shoes didn't allow him much purchase on the slick spots. Next time he'd steal a pair with good treads.

Monigan rubbed a hip that was sore from one of the earlier falls and stopped to pat himself down for a cigarette. No luck. As well, he was freezing. If he had grabbed a coat from the cloakroom as he dashed out he wouldn't be so cold. He glanced up at the sky that was veined through the tangle of naked tree limbs overhead. He spat.

His large fists barely fit in the pockets of his tuxedo pants, but he rammed them deeper and hunkered his head down. He didn't notice he'd wandered off the path till the snow was almost to his knees, and when he twisted around, trying to locate the proper route, he lost his balance and dropped. He decided to take a breather. A little work formed two concave scoops that supported him, and he sat there as if on a sleeping bench in an igloo. He couldn't feel his feet very well, so he groped to make sure his shoes were still on, then leaned forward, dug the tails of the tux out from underneath himself, spread them flat to the sides and rear and sat there comfortably, looking like a beetle with a split carapace, ready to fly.

It had been a good wedding. Not as good as his own, but that had been so long ago that he suspected he might be selectively remembering the sweet spots and spitting out the bad. His wife claimed theirs was the worst wedding she had ever attended, though Monigan couldn't get a handle on logic like that. Any time Monigan was the focus of attention it meant things were going his way. The caterers hadn't shown up and there was a fight or two, but he was the groom and she was the bride and they hadn't run out of booze. The rest was nit-picking. He'd tell her that the next time he ran into her, though the last time he'd seen her was four years past.

But Monigan saw no sense in living in anything but the present, particularly now that he was freezing his ass off. He had almost made it through the reception that afternoon, an accomplishment of sorts. He was content.

It had been a good wedding, except for the master of ceremonies, who had stood to the side of the head table telling off-color jokes with women present. That's something Monigan would never do. Not at a wedding. No problem if he was just with the guys, or a woman he was going out with, or one he didn't like, or if he was in a mood not to care, or if he was drinking and got carried away, or if he forgot. But not in front of a bride. And he'd never fight at a wedding. Unless he had to fight, and then he took it outside. At his own wedding Monigan had been forced into dealing with his wife's brother, but he did it properly and took him outside. And once the man was down Monigan hadn't put the boots to him. Not at a wedding.

But the emcee today had been close to taking what Monigan called his six-incher. Not one of those wild roundhouse swings they call a hook these days. The old style, when you miss with a right hand then drop the left from the elbow as you turn. The weight shift does it all, so the hook travels six inches and it's over. Walk your sister home. But it was Saturday, Monigan's peaceful day, so the emcee escaped justice. Six-incher and walk your sister home. All it would have taken.

It had been a good wedding, but the mistake they made was opening the bar before the buffet. Had Monigan been able to get some food in his stomach he might have bluffed his way through. But throwing down drinks with the boys at the bar had forced him to make small talk, and they soon discovered he didn't even know the bride's name. They had been polite about it. When he snatched up the meatballs and the bottle of champagne they had chased him some, but you can hardly blame them for that. And they hadn't chased him far.

Despite the cold, his sleeping bench was starting to melt. He could feel the water soaking through his long underwear. But he was feeling okay. He had long ago established Saturday as his peaceful day, and he was usually able to keep it that way.

He looked down and noticed his tux was grubby. He'd put it in with Katlyn's laundry when he took it over for her Monday morning. He liked doing things for Katlyn, the only person he felt like doing anything at all for these days. The thought of her allowed him a small smile. He wished he had hooked up with a woman like Katlyn years back. And he was more or less right. Even now, if he could meet an older version of her it might drag him out of his gloomy cycle, at least for a time. Then the inevitable bitching and nagging and dictating would begin, on both sides, and he would be off. And Monigan realized it. He was constitutionally unable to kid himself and knew full well every relationship and every job and anything else he turned his hand to ruptured with time. But if he had met someone like Katlyn back then, who knows? If he had rooted his bad habits out early enough he might not be sitting in the snow with no cigarettes. Then again, the thought of still being married with a good job and a roof he owned himself over his head almost made him sick. He rubbed his chin and realized he hadn't shaved. That's partly what had given him away, even before the reception.

The wind grew more insistent. Monigan didn't mind to a certain point. He liked the cold and the wind and the rain and the snow. It was all part of why he appreciated Toronto, at least his small part of it. The grit and the grayness, the concrete and the stone, the rough urban guts of it all. He tried to rise but his hands broke through the snow and he flopped idiotically onto his back. The snow had refrozen around his lower legs and held him like a doomed mastodon, and, as he needed a drink and a cigarette, he shifted onto one elbow, looking for help of any type. He shielded his eyes from the blowing snow. There appeared to be a man out there, but he was barely moving.

Up the diagonal pathway, Bill was having a hell of a go of it. He couldn't have weighed more than a hundred pounds, so as best he could he slid his feet along, sliding without stepping because every time he lifted a leg clear of the ground a gust would claim it and shake him furiously. His eyes were brimming, from the cold, he figured. If he hadn't cried at the funeral then it must be the cold making his eyes wet.

Monigan's shout brought Bill to a halt and he bobbled around in the wind like a horse with the blind staggers. He wiped his eyes with the back of his sleeve.

"Hey, Kid — gimme a hand here."

Honest mistake on Monigan's part, given Bill's high cheekbones, flat features and large eyes. A face that was quite the incongruity with the lithe, old-man's frame that anchored him to the ground, however unsteadily. His body was designed to survive catastrophe; like an ant, no matter how far the fall, his mass was too insubstantial to snuff him out.

"Got any cigarettes?" Monigan was finally sitting upright.

Bill didn't smoke, but he rooted through his pockets anyway.

"Don't matter," Monigan said. "Only dig around my feet for me, I'm freezing my sack off here."

Bill stepped off the path and was instantly immobilized.

"Beautiful," Monigan said.

Down with a smack went Bill.

"Fuck a duck," Monigan said.

They stared at each other a while till the cop came across them.

The constable didn't say anything at first. Monigan looked vaguely familiar, then he remembered him as the loudmouth from

The Workbench Tavern. Bill was new to him, but he had been at Division for only a month and there were a lot of locals he didn't know yet. Already he longed for the warmth of the patrol car, so he lightly kicked the seat of Bill's pants.

"Hey, Sport," he said.

"If it ain't the cops," Monigan said. "That you, Doyle?"

"How do you know my name?"

"Couldn't be from every time you stick your ugly face in The Workbench, minding somebody else's business, so it must be from the war dispatches. Now come on — get us outta here."

Doyle latched onto Bill's ankles and with one heave had him back on the path. Monigan's weight posed more of a problem. When Doyle almost had him free the cop slipped, and the two of them smashed through the snow bench, fetching up face to face.

"Got any cigarettes?"

Doyle recoiled from Monigan's fetid blast and shoved himself away. Awkwardly, the pair of them eventually made it back to the path.

"What's your name?" Doyle said to the big guy's partner.

"Bill."

A large, frost-covered hand thrust between the men and patted Bill on the back.

"Bill, is it?" Monigan said. "Hell of a try, Bill."

"I'll get to you," Doyle said without taking his eyes off the little guy. "Where do you live, Bill?"

"I can't feel my toes," Monigan said. "Honest to God, I can't feel a thing. Two more minutes I'd of had gangrene. You're a hero, Doyle, that's what you are. The brass'll hear about this."

"Shut up," Doyle said. "Bill, you have to tell me where you live."

"Right in Nathan Phillips Square, they'll be pinning a medal on you while you stand there in your dress uniform."

"What's *your* name?"

Monigan pulled up the jacket, vest and shirt to reveal a grimy T-shirt with his name on it.

"Monigan," Doyle said flatly.

"Where's your cigarettes?"

Doyle withdrew a pack and went through all the stages, as Monigan's fingers were frozen bratwursts by then. Doyle turned back to Bill, whose wobbling was gaining intensity, a rhythmic rotation on his heels, aperiodic but smooth. Doyle lightly held him by the upper arm and the wobbling attenuated till Bill stopped with one last rattle of bones.

"Where do you live, Bill?"

"Jesus," Monigan said. "These are menthol, Doyle."

"I said I'll get to you!"

Monigan spat.

"Have you been drinking, Bill?"

"That's good," Monigan said. "Showing off your schooling."

"Listen," Doyle said. "I just don't want anybody freezing to death out here. Supposed to go down to thirty below tonight."

"I'll see he gets home," Monigan said.

"Sure you guys are okay?"

"Yeah, yeah. Only a couple blocks to go."

"Right," Doyle said. "Right, then."

"Right, then," Monigan said. "You look kinda young, you know that? To be a cop, I mean."

"Mind your own business, Sport."

"Sport. Right, then."

Doyle spun and headed for the car.

"Hey!" Monigan yelled. "Gimme another of them menthols."

Doyle did so then skidded up the path and got in his cruiser. He looked back at the two of them in his mirror, standing there without a care in the world. Having to deal with people like that wasn't why he had joined the force. He started the car and banged it into gear and drove off.

The two men got moving, Monigan falling slightly behind.

"Look at the treads you got on them shoes, Bill. I'd be at The Workbench by now, I had treads like them."

When they hit the street they stopped to rest. Monigan was tiring easily these days. He used to be a hell of an athlete, but that was as long ago as his wedding. He had stopped playing sports when he got married, and that's when the fatigue began to creep in. Then the added pressure of dealing with a family had come close to snuffing out his last spark of life. He was thinking often of his wife these days, try as he might to blind his mind's eye to her image. A lot of his anger and resentment had sloughed away, with the terrifying result that he occasionally found himself missing her. Not enough to do anything about it, for among other things it would mean having to deal with his son, whom he considered to be the ultimate dozey bastard.

Dwayne Feller. Monigan had been talking to Frodo the other day at The Workbench, and the bookie said he had seen Dwayne on stage at a downtown comedy club. Monigan knew precious little about genetics, but he was convinced his sperm had enough strength and moxie not to churn out a goddamn comedian. And Frodo had said the kid wasn't even funny. It made the old man feel free, justified; he had done the right thing by leaving.

Monigan looked down at Bill, who was standing beside him with a vague expression, apparently at ease with whatever was coming his way next. Monigan grinned at him. If there was one thing he was good at it was recognizing people who needed a little direction.

"Plan is, you're coming to the bar with me," Monigan said. "See if the chili pot's on. Couple beers, chili, you'll be fine." He gripped Bill's elbow.

Bill was steadier on his feet now that they were out of the park and on solid, albeit slushy pavement — so Monigan let him go and satisfied himself with occasional taps and pulls to keep him on an even keel. Another few blocks and they'd be at The Workbench. As Monigan said, they'd be fine when they reached there. It was his home. A little sports, couple beers, chili.

"Hey, Bill — you got any money on you?"

TWO

Dwayne Feller was dying. The attack was coming from just below his belt. From his center a liquid flow of evil forced him to lock his knees to keep from pitching forward. His stomach was roiling, his throat constricting, but he willed himself to be strong. Not much time left, he knew that, just as he knew he would triumph. He was determined to show them all, every one of them, the scoffers and the skeptics, the doubters and the rat-faced cynics. No one could doubt after this as long as he kept thinking and talking until he had them on their knees.

But Dwayne could feel himself dying. And so could the crowd, evidenced by their faces, their body language, squirming and shifting in their seats, playing with their drinks. Dwayne could see them avoiding eye contact, embarrassed for him.

Dwayne needed this show. Three years as a standup comic doing five-minute spots on Amateur Night, and finally the owner had promoted him to do a fifteen-minute opening spot on Saturday. Dwayne would be followed by the headliner for the week, and he was desperate to leave an impression. But of course he would. He was funny, wasn't he? He glared at the audience, throttled the microphone and launched back into his act.

At the back of the room the other comics were in fits, hugely enjoying the slaughter.

"Look at him." Harold Arens was almost in tears.

They all were in awe, heads craned forward, drinks untouched, cigarettes burned down to their fingers.

"Too much," Reba Stiles said.

Dwayne was nervous, but that they could understand. Promotion to doing a regular set was a memory they all shared, and no matter how much their talent had developed since, each had his secret place where horror and humiliation abided. So they could empathize with Dwayne, but, in a curious inversion of how normal people behave, could not sympathize. Doing so invariably got in the way of a good laugh.

The past Monday, when they heard the news of Dwayne's promotion, the regular house comics and a sprinkling of amateurs had agreed it was a show not to be missed. Two hours before show time had seen them already entrenched at the back of the room, barricaded behind beer bottles, glasses, extra smokes, chicken fingers and some magician's prop trunk.

Harold had started well as the emcee, hosting the show with flair, nurturing the crowd along to a point where they were warm and eager for more. A stylish couple from New York had been properly savaged about their place of residence, but it was done with taste, and they had taken it in good spirits. A drunken postal worker out with the lads for his birthday had been put in his place; he then passed out so was no further threat. A spry old gal had almost choked to death at Harold's first reference to the sexual act, but quickly got into the swing of things and now was sitting there feeling risqué, wishing it were Tuesday so she could brag about what she had heard to her ceramics class.

The owner of The Laugh Chance, a middle-aged man named Sturgis, had played a hunch and promoted Dwayne to open the show, counting on Harold's ability as the emcee and Reba Stiles's comedic excellence as the headliner to carry the evening. The club Sturgis ruled over was a good room. Up on the second floor, few pillars to block the view, two strong spotlights, a consistent sound system.

The house was still energized as Dwayne delivered his opening remarks. There were some initial laughs at his appearance, but they died out as the audience realized it hadn't been arranged for their enjoyment. Hard to put a finger on, really. Shoulders too narrow for his frame, tall and thin on top yet larded and chunky everywhere else. The whole collection of parts had been assembled improperly; he looked slapped together by aliens with no model from which to work. But after a couple of minutes the crowd had formed a more objective opinion. A feeling of doubt was in the air, chilling the room.

Then suddenly the fan could barely turn, so much shit had hit it. It always started slowly when a joke didn't work. Then, as self-pity mingled with indignation in Dwayne's system, he lashed out. All fury and righteous wrath, berating, browbeating, a frontal assault under a creeping barrage of insults.

And that's what was happening now. Patrons were fleeing for the door as Dwayne heaped invective upon them. The sound and lighting girl was flashing the red warning light at the stage. The waitresses stopped serving and stood transfixed at the bar. The comics turned to look at Reba Stiles, whose spiritual essence was in shock at the prospect of following Dwayne's version of an act.

One of the comics coughed and pointed to the office door as the club owner went into action. Sturgis flung himself at the table, and as the comics tssked and fretted in disapproval while trying to suppress their laughter, he grabbed Harold by the arm and propelled him toward the stage.

Harold bounded on stage and over to the mike, jostling Dwayne aside in the process. "Keep it going for Dwayne Feller!"

The audience complied, literally. They stared.

Harold did his best to win them back, but by this point the crowd hated anyone who even looked like a performer. They would have turned on their uncle's best party gags, beaten their children for knock-knock jokes, flayed their mothers for a pun. A restless hostility had taken root in their hearts and Harold was having no part of it. He introduced Reba Stiles, who was doing her best to appear casual.

Reba approached the mike and cleared her throat. "Dwayne's a tough act to follow," she said. "His day job is strangling unwanted orphans."

This raised a couple of chuckles from the room and a roar from the comics. The boys relaxed — she'd do okay. Sturgis went back into his office, screaming just the once.

Dwayne left the stage and strode down the aisle. He went to the bar and ordered a cranberry juice and Coke. Checked his watch: 2120 hours. He had done his time!

"Good set," Harold said, then went weak with laughter and laid his head on the table.

Harold had no idea what came over Dwayne on stage. Many comics he knew adopted a personality in their acts that had nothing to do with their real life, acting out some bizarre character or other, but with Dwayne it wasn't intentional. Offstage he was full of brag and blather, but Harold knew him well enough to see that in general he was a tormented type with barely a dram of self-esteem. Hitting the boards, however, brought out all his feral impulses. Clearly the process of standup warped Dwayne's judgment.

"Some of that new material needs work," Dwayne admitted.

Harold barked so loudly at the understatement that several people turned and shushed him.

"Maybe just change the order around," Dwayne said.

Harold lost it and fled for the foyer.

Dwayne watched him go then focused on the stage, truly puzzled at the way the audience was responding to Reba. They were laughing! He reasoned that there must be a trick, space somewhere for a lever, a device, a hook, that would enable him to win the crowd's affection. There was a catch to everything, Dwayne figured, though he had never come upon one in anything he had done. He had failed to find the key to his father's popcorn fart of a heart, and felt that's what had driven Monigan away. He was angry at his father for not showing him how to reach in and make contact, but he also believed that his towering intellect should have cleared such a trifling obstacle. The son should have been able to find it. The hook, the catch.

In any event, his father had been gone four years. If only Monigan could see his son now. But Monigan had seen neither Dwayne nor the comic's mother in four years.

Harold was back. As he sat down Dwayne addressed him earnestly. "What did you think of the political material?"

Harold sighed heavily. Dwayne was too complicated a project for him to have taken on. Harold had always been the one. The lone victim at a family gathering trapped in conversation with a drunken in-law; the target for street people eager to share their worldly insights; the solitary figure on the subway to whom the psychotics of the city gravitated. After all, Harold believed, he was a standup comic, so if Toronto's troubled citizens wanted to hear his take on their problems then let them pay a cover charge. But even when he was exasperated beyond measure Harold couldn't raise any anger at Dwayne. The man needed his help, simple as that. Now if only Dwayne would take advice instead of dishing it out . . .

"Here comes Sturgis," one of the comics said.

The owner had the scent and was racing to the back of the room. Reflected light glistened off his suit as his fingers clawed at the collar, loosening the tie, giving him room to breathe. He reached the table and stood looming over Monigan's son, though that might be too strong a phrase, as even seated Dwayne was on eye-level with the owner. After pausing to show his confidence, Dwayne rose to his feet and followed along to the office. He looked at the sign on the door — LAUGH CHANCE COMEDY THEATRE — then chuckled and waved at an aisle table, responding to a compliment he was sure had been directed his way. The short arm of Sturgis grabbed him by the belt and the two of them were alone in the room.

The office was an untidy pen. A long, low desk stood against the side wall, a roll-o chair with an orthopedic backrest sticking out of its knee hole. Most of the back wall was taken up by shelves of video cassettes, comics from all over North America down on tape, ten or fifteen minutes each, entire careers encapsulated in less time than it takes a normal person to apply for a job. What might give them immortality usually earned them dismissal. Charts, calendars and schedules were everywhere, all slashed, edited and scribbled on, palimpsests in the revisionist world of standup comedy.

Sturgis groaned as he lowered himself into the chair and adjusted the ties on the backrest. Dwayne looked around but there was no other chair. Sturgis never socialized purely for the joy of it and thought sitting gave him the advantage in an argument. Given his five-foot stature, it was probably a wise approach.

Dwayne squeezed between the steel filing cabinet and a pile of posters, playbills and menus, and leaned against the wall.

"Change your shirt," Sturgis said.

Dwayne looked down and plucked the thing away from his chest.

"Saturday night and you show up looking like you fell asleep in your dinner." Sturgis sighed. "A comedy club lives on return customers and word of mouth. How many of those people do you think will be back?"

Dwayne stared over his head.

Sturgis swallowed and started in again, slowly. "Fourteen years I've had this club, twenty years in the business."

"Good years."

"Shut up."

Dwayne looked at his shirt again, wondering what the meeting was all about. He hoped Sturgis wanted him to stay and do the late show, too. Dwayne was proud of his political material.

"You chased out over forty customers. You were on your way to clearing the room and the headliner wasn't even on yet. Half an hour into the show and people were streaming out!"

"Listen." Dwayne raised a finger as a roar of laughter collided with the door. "Reba's killing out there. If I hadn't chased out those ungrateful mutants she'd be struggling for her life."

"Reba is funny. You didn't help at all. Don't you listen to the audience when you're up there?"

"Castro said that to die with dignity, one has no need of company."

"Castro?"

"Fidel."

"I know, you idiot. What the hell does that cigar-sucker have to do with your driving my customers into the night?"

"Many are called; few are chosen."

"Ah!" Sturgis vigorously massaged the back of his neck and clasped both hands on top of his head.

"Am I free to go?"

"Yes, just leave."

Dwayne pulled his shirt out a little and fluffed it over his belt. Most men were wearing their shirts stylishly loose these days and Dwayne tried to keep abreast of new trends. He looked up. "Am I still free to come down for Amateur Night on Tuesday?"

Sturgis thought seriously about it. "Oh, Christ. Why not?"

As Dwayne was stumping off a waitress poked her head into the office and told Sturgis that there were at least twelve people downstairs at the front door with complaints about the first show, which had just ended. Sturgis wearily stood up. Accustomed to being the ogre, he suddenly felt unequal to the role. First he had to deal with Dwayne and now he had to face a pack of whiners. The Billy Goats Gruff were laying an ass-whipping on the troll tonight.

The first show was over and the crowd was filtering through the room and out the door. Reba Stiles had done a remarkable job of winning them over, but following an act like Dwayne's put too much pressure on her mental-editing process. Harold Arens gave her a big hug when she got to the back of the room.

"Where's Dwayne?" she asked.

"He just came out of the Star Chamber," Harold said.

Dwayne was standing by the exit to the upstairs foyer, bidding the crowd goodnight. "Thank you . . . thanks for coming out."

People were averting their eyes and moving sideways through the door.

Downstairs, Sturgis was pressing complimentary tickets into the hands of the offended parties. It wouldn't be until the next day that they discovered the tickets were for the Auto Show. Sturgis swore at their backs and climbed the stairs to the second floor, where he came upon Dwayne at the door, glad-handing people. Sturgis cuffed him on the back of the head.

"Hello, Reba," Dwayne said when he got to the back of the room. "Lovely show." He said it as if praising a dog for a good fetch. Over to the bar he went, returning with a cranberry juice and Coke, crashing down across the table.

"Are you in much trouble with Sturgis?" Harold asked.

"No," Dwayne said. "Yes. I don't know." He leaned back and watched the waitresses as they raced around the room, cleaning tables and ashtrays and setting out fresh hurricane candles, rushing to get set up for the second show.

From the office door Sturgis eyed the back tables, angry and envious and altogether pissed off at the pack of comics. He didn't know exactly what to say to them but a good dressing down between shows was obligatory and surely something would pop to mind on the way over. It had been a tough night and he was only halfway through it. He moved sleepily, like an old frog emerging from estivation.

"Here he comes," Harold Arens said. "A face that lunched on a thousand ships."

"Not bad," Sturgis said to Reba. "Now all of you listen up. First, keep your mouths shut when the show's going on. When you're performing you bitch about the noise coming from the back, then the minute you're off you join the party. Second, clean up these back tables at the end of the night. There are enough slobs in here as it is without the staff having to swab down after you pigs."

Sturgis already felt better being back in control, arteries ramming fresh blood to his brain. "And no more bar tabs!" he screamed.

"Third," Harold said.

"What?"

"You didn't use the number. I lose track when you don't use the numbers."

"I'll kill you, Arens."

Harold lit a cigarette.

"No tabs. You guys run them up then bolt without settling up." Sturgis paused for effect. He hadn't been in the business for twenty years without learning something about timing. "Is that clear?"

A chorus of mumbles.

"Personally," Dwayne said innocently, "I'm with Harold. I find the numbers handy, too."

Sturgis gave them all a look that used to be intimidating, but the regulars had seen it too many times. He provided them with a place to strut their stuff, but that was about as far as it went. Their loyalty Sturgis had used as a bargaining chip so often that it was now an abstract concept. They gave him the bare minimum of co-operation, except for the odd bout of brown-nosing to ensure their spots on the roster. So they stared back at Sturgis till the little man spun off to the office.

The crowd was filing in for the second show, and already there was higher energy in the room. The comics had picked up on it.

"Good house," Harold said to Reba. "And don't worry — you don't have to follow Dwayne."

Dwayne hadn't heard. A wonderful idea had occurred to him, so sweeping in the effect it would have on his career that he had to share it with his friends immediately. He was trembling.

"Hey," Harold said. "Are you okay?"

"Tuesday night I'll be transformed," Dwayne proclaimed. There was no response so he continued. "I've decided on a new stage name: Dwayne Goldman."

"Goldman?" Harold asked.

"You're Jewish," Dwayne said.

"Of course I am. So what?"

"The fact that your people have suffered is important to your act. Therein lies much of Jewish humor. Unfortunately my ancestry's fairly clean of slaughter and affronts to its humanity. So, Dwayne Goldman."

"Dwayne, performers change their names all the time to get attention," Harold said. "But you can't get up there and start doing Jewish material."

"Are you claiming some kind of racial copyright?" Dwayne said. "Handed down from a mountain, no doubt?"

"I'm not even going to comment."

"I'd appreciate it if all of you would use my new name in casual conversation, to help me get into character. And Harold, I hope I can count on you to bring me up to speed on some of the Jewish superstitions. The Second Temple, this kosher business, that type of thing. I'm familiar with Hebraic lore from the reading I do, but I want to *feel* it."

"There's something wrong with you," Harold said.

"Nonsense."

Harold looked at Reba for support but only succeeded in making her laugh. The comics admired Harold for his ability and humility, but he was on his own with Dwayne. Harold fell back on old habits and simply changed the subject. "Did your mother enjoy the show?"

They peered through the smoke and haze that was sashaying around the house lights. Alone at a table dead center of the room sat an old woman with a bun of streaked hair.

"My mother always enjoys my act," Dwayne said. "That's why it's so hard to keep her at bay."

"Mrs. Goldman," Harold said.

Dwayne unfolded himself and drained the last of his drink. "I need time to work on my craft. New material is crying out in my head. This has been a benchmark, a turning point. I'm glad you were here to share it with me." He retrieved his trenchcoat from its nesting place on the floor in the corner and made for the rear

staircase door. "If my mother manages to free herself from her tor-
por, tell her I've left."

"Aren't you even going to say goodnight to her?" Reba asked.

"She'll just pester me for money."

"You refuse your own mother money?"

"I intend to pay her back," Dwayne said in a huff.

THREE

"Here we are," Monigan said, leading Bill through the door of The Workbench Tavern. "Get yourself down at the bar while I take a squirt."

"Hi," Katlyn said as Monigan hurried past.

Monigan's new friend Bill surrounded a stool at the bar and after a couple of tries made it on top. Still cold, he pulled his coat tighter.

"What can I get you?" Katlyn asked.

Bill let a gurgle spill over his lips and Katlyn translated it into a draft. "Dollar-fifty."

"That's on me," Monigan said, still doing up his pants. "And drop one here, Katy."

"What's it like out there?" Katlyn asked.

"Cold as a bobsledder's cock."

Katlyn slid over Monigan's beer and automatically reached for a pen.

"Put it on my —"

"Tab," she finished.

Katlyn had trouble keeping a straight face around Monigan. Despite his having twenty-five years on her, he was her best friend, maybe her only real friend. He was always on the verge of flying out of control, but he was a good man. Most of the bar's patrons never gave a straight answer to anything, guarding secrets of their existences, shielding motives, but not Monigan, and that was one of the things she loved about him.

Monigan lived upstairs in a small room on the top floor of the four-storey building. When he was late with his rent or behind in paying his tab Katlyn would let it slide. Somehow he always scrounged enough to get by, and it wasn't as if she were unable to track him down. If he wasn't upstairs he was down in the bar, in her face and on her case. Except Saturday afternoons.

"Wedding end early today?" She smiled, turning her into a little girl.

"Yeah," Monigan said. "Don't know what it is with these kids. Give us a cigarette, will you?"

Katlyn left her pack open in front of him.

"How's the chili coming along?" Monigan lit up and looked at Katlyn through the smoke.

"The range is still broken," she said.

Monigan looked disgustedly at the kitchen area, one low counter with full access from the bar, sporting a portable gas range and a pot. The beer fridge beside it held the supplies, on this day one green pepper, salt and two pounds of hamburger that looked ground from a hoof-and-mouth victim.

"I should report you. Only reason they let you open on Sundays is you gotta serve food."

"It's Saturday."

"None of that's the point." Monigan drew deeply on the butt and coughed. "Cold out there gets right into you and my buddy Bill could use some food. Well, gimme the key, gonna warm up with some pool. Bill, come on and get your coat off, you don't wanna die of the temperature change."

In the time it took Bill to remove his coat and walk to the pool table, Monigan had released the balls with the key — saving four quarters — and had them racked.

"Eight ball. You break."

The Workbench. Katlyn's father had bought the place six years before after hitting a ridiculous Trifecta, in the only bit of financial commitment he had ever displayed. It was a grungy tavern usually patronized by the more bizarre examples of the local fauna, but some nights it was fun. A few film people lived in the area and dropped in, some artists hung around, plus those businessmen who appreciated a place without the cloying pretentiousness of singles bars. A place where you could get the right mixture of relaxation and trouble. Jailhouse tattoos decorated the hands and arms of many of the regulars. Ex-pro athletes like the place because here no one ever forgot what they had accomplished on the rink, the field or the diamond, even if only because they had cost someone a big bet at one time. It was certainly the place to go to pick up various pieces of merchandise that had followed the purveyors home from work or the department store. It was bar, rec room, front porch and caravanserai.

The place was almost empty. Over in a corner booth a man was in mild disagreement with his wife, but neither of them was committed to the argument so their sallies were brief and unable to upset the room's equilibrium. Two younger men were indifferently watching TV in the back. Someone was sitting at the bar reading the *Toronto Sun* classifieds. The overhead fan was tossing the pages around but even that contraption had picked up on the mood in the room and was performing sullenly, wobbling on its axis. The hammered tin ceiling, a monument to nicotine accumulation, hung low over the old pub. A thousand pictures covered the walls: ex-athletes, locals who had had a day in the spotlight for one reason or another, actors who had passed through when a movie called for a scene in a bar of broken hearts. The maroon carpeting was barely surviving and its color could only be determined by searching along the edges where it met the green wood walls, for the rest was worn through to the boards.

Behind the horseshoe bar, under the overhanging glasses, Katlyn grinned at Monigan and started swabbing the coolers. Keeping them clean was an irritation as they were covered with bumper stickers and promotional decals that her father sent back from around the continent:

. . . ROLL TIDE . . . 'GATORS . . . DESERT STORM . . . IF YOU
CAN'T HUNT WITH THE BIG DOGS, STAY ON THE PORCH . . .
LIONS . . . BLUE JAYS REPEAT CHAMPS . . .

Katlyn finished and rinsed and squeezed the bar rag. She raised the
lid on the ice tank, filled a glass with cubes and topped it off with
ginger ale. She pulled up a stool and watched Monigan and Bill play
pool. Not much had been going her way lately, though it seldom did
in January. Maybe it was the weather and the lack of light. Maybe it
was simply the memory of her mother's dying in that month, when
Katlyn was fifteen. Five people came to the funeral, including her
father, who was late. Her father, who then raised her as best he could
for a few years until his vices turned rabid. A gambler who was
unsuccessful at cards, the horses, or anything else he had tried while
still head of a household, he fastened on golf as his game. He was
good enough to make a few bucks here and there, a good hustler,
beating around courses across the continent, playing money games
with jaded business types, suits with reasonably low handicaps and
too much time on their hands. Periodically he'd remember he had a
bar that was losing money in Toronto and, incidentally, a daughter
who managed it. So he'd send a bumper sticker.
    "Jesus Christ in a turtleneck!" Monigan couldn't believe it.
    Bill's break had been feeble, the cue ball barely clearing the other
balls out of their triangle. Monigan put his cigarette down on the
rail and slammed three straight stripes into the pockets, hammering the balls in his usual fashion. That's how he played: balls firing
off the table like grenade shrapnel, rolling under radiators, skipping off tables, slashing through piles of money and ranks of beer
bottles, patrons cursing and throwing the balls back to him on a
line. But then he miscued and scratched on his next shot. Bill
stepped up and calmly cleared the table, not stopping when he
sank the eight ball but shooting till even Monigan's balls were
down. The table sat empty, a fuzzy greensward of felt dully reflect-
ing the neon light from the Labatt sign in the window.

"Hey!" Monigan looked around. "Where'd those guys who were watching TV go? Rustle up some action on the table."

The two men came out of the bathroom, one wiping his nose and the other trying not to sneeze.

"You!" Monigan said. "Yeah, the both of you, what say you dig out them wallets? Partners against me and my friend. Look at the arms on him, he can barely hold a cue, and me, I'm an old guy had too much to drink at a wedding today, you ask anybody."

The men looked at each other, and the lead one unrolled the five-dollar bill he had in his hand. He licked the inside of it then stopped short as the cop came through the door. He plucked his coat from the back of his chair and with his partner fled out the side door.

"Doyle," Monigan said to the cop. "Doyle, Doyle, Doyle — you think you can cost me money like that, chasing out a couple marks? Maybe I won't sign the report gets you that medal."

"I thought you were going to see this guy made it home. Bill, isn't it?"

"Bill's all right, he's Willie Mosconi, who he is."

Doyle cruised around the bar, dishing out the hairy eyeball, but everyone ignored him.

"Hi, Katlyn," Doyle said.

"Hello, Officer."

"No need to call me Officer."

"I got a name for you," Monigan said. "Think I don't?"

"By yourself today?" Katlyn asked. She liked Doyle. They were the same age and he had a good job and all that, but she felt bad for him when he came in the bar and was treated like dirt.

"My partner's off sick," Doyle said.

"Constable Ogilvie?" Katlyn said. "Tell her to get well soon."

"She just has a touch of the 'flu that's going around. Half of Division has it."

"Would you like a coffee?"

Doyle removed his hat and ran his fingers through his hair.

"Can't stop. I've got the cruiser today, so many off sick."

"Come by again."

Doyle replaced his hat, tilted the visor down over his eyes and turned smack into Bill, dropping him to the floor.

"That's the way, is it?" Monigan rushed to help Bill to his feet. "Tit for tat, eye for an eye. You figure you saved my life now you're evening things up by stomping my pal. That medal's gone, Doyle, history."

"Sorry," Doyle said to Bill.

Bill was fine, saved by his insect mass. Monigan took Bill's hands, checking the fingers. "Cabbagetown Fats, that's who you are, Bill. You look after these hands, you wanna be my partner. I can play too, you know."

Doyle was simmering again. He wasn't in the mood to deal with these two again, Monigan and Bill, standing there in tuxedos. "Move aside, Sport."

"I got your sport right here."

Doyle cast one last look around then off he went, back to the cruiser.

"He's okay," Monigan said to Katlyn. "For a cop, I mean."

Katlyn laughed. "Can I get you two another round? On the house."

Monigan dragged Bill to a stool. On the house.

Across the bar an old man with a Blue Jays cap was on the way to the bathroom. He came off his chair bent over ninety degrees at the waist, gradually straightening as each step allowed him greater freedom of movement, so by the time he reached the door he was fully upright. It was like watching hominid evolution in thirty paces.

Katlyn dropped the beer in front of the two resplendent bums.

"Katy," Monigan said. "Call out them wedding announcements from the paper for me. I forgot my reading glasses in the store again."

"Don't you get tired of being thrown out of a reception every week?"

"Weddings are okay, even short ones. That's what you need."

"Me," she said flatly.

"Yes, you."

"How is it that you're such an expert?"

"I know, I know. But I had a good one for a while. I guess technically I even own part of a house. Course, I got a son out of the deal, so that drags it down to a toss-up."

"Dwayne," Katlyn said. "I keep telling you to bring him around some day. There's no harm in just letting me meet him."

Monigan made a face wild with affected terror until Katlyn was reduced to giggling hysteria.

Bill abruptly pitched off his stool, staggered a bit, then wandered over to the pool table, where he picked up a cue and idly rolled it between his fingers.

"What's Bill's story?" Katlyn asked.

"Don't know," Monigan said. "Just ran into him today over by the Riverdale Farm. Goofy looking little guy, eh?"

"I thought you met him at the wedding."

"Nope, I don't know about the tux, what the deal is on that."

Monigan crushed out his butt and dug his fingers into Katlyn's package. "Last one."

"Nice guy."

"Hey, don't you owe me a fin?"

"It's the other way around."

"Okay — drop me another five and I owe you ten."

"Sure, as soon as you pay something on your tab."

"That's mean," Monigan said.

One of the locals came around the bar and on the way to the can caught Monigan's eye. He held the door open and jerked his head.

"I'd rather drop my gear in a Syrian prison," Monigan said and spat on the floor. He looked up, but Katlyn hadn't noticed. Cocaine. He didn't know why that stuff was so popular. Crazies, that's what they were in Monigan's opinion. Jittering, teeth-grinding sleaze bags rocketing around like a bunch of lunatics. Not for Monigan. He'd die of cirrhosis, like a man.

"Here," Katlyn said reluctantly, sliding across a five. "Go get us some smokes."

Monigan grinned. As he passed the pool table a clattering burst forth as the balls fell into the tray below the change slots. Bill bent and started rolling them to the far end of the table.

"How'd you do that without the key?" Monigan asked.

Bill blinked and hitched at his pants "I have a way with stuff," he said.

Monigan looked back at Katlyn and nodded approvingly of his new friend.

The wind had veered farther south and with its long fetch across Lake Ontario had no trouble piercing through Monigan's tux as he crossed the street to the corner store. By the time he got back to The Workbench, Bill was potting the last ball.

"Clear the table?" Monigan asked in a jet of breath as the door closed out the cold.

"I have a way," Bill said.

Monigan reclaimed his stool and dropped a handful of filched pepperoni sticks on the bar. "Could use some chili on a night like this."

"Don't nag. I told you the stove's broken."

A dull *whoomph!* drew their attention to the kitchen area, where Bill had gone after replacing his cue. The old bum stepped back from the stove, the two rings merrily burning.

"I know," Monigan said. "You have a way."

Bill stared at the propane rings, mesmerized. He wondered if Jean was okay, wherever she was. They had lived together in the rooming house, but really they never saw each other for days or weeks at a time. Jean was funny that way, just wander off, no word to anyone. Couple days would go by so Bill would check the pubs and the flops and the parks, but no Jean. She'd come back eventually, a mess, with no recollection of where she'd been, what she'd done. Bill had known Jean should be someplace where she could get help, be looked after, but there was no money. And he couldn't do it, though he tried. He'd fix up a little supper for her, some soup — she liked that canned Habitant pea soup — and some muffins, the ones you could put right in the toaster. She liked her tea clear and strong, but she didn't always drink it. He tried to keep tabs on her near the end, but she had a way of eluding him, always did have one up on him, come to think about it.

Her brother from Buffalo was at the funeral but he couldn't bring his wife. The funeral had been fine.

Bill smoothed the front of his tuxedo. He had looked good for her, people had told him that. You look good for your wife, Bill, people had said that to him. She used to look good, Jean did.

She had been found in Moss Park by two kids sliding down the pile of snow in back of the arena, the shavings that had been scraped off the rink and dumped back there. She hadn't been there very long, the police said, which was good. Bill couldn't find the dress, the floral cotton print he had bought her for Christmas that year he was working in the Eaton's warehouse, but that was okay. She looked fine in the casket. She almost had a smile.

Better go home now. It had been a long walk from the funeral parlor, a long day. Funny, his wife dying like that. They burned her, that was the best thing to do. Where's the door?

"Hold on." Monigan had Bill's coat.

"Where does he live?" Katlyn asked. "We can't let him wander around like that."

"I'll find out," Monigan said. "I'll get him home."

The two men struggled with the coat and finally Bill stood there ready to go, looking healthier with the coat's bulk filling out his bones.

"I'll be back in a bit," Monigan said. "And that chili better be ready now that you've run out of excuses."

The time ground on until everyone who had wandered by over the course of the evening was gone. The neon beer lights reflected off the inside of the windows back into the room. Katlyn pulled their plugs one by one. At the last one, the front Labatt sign by the pool table, she stopped and stood just so, looking at herself in the window, half of her painted in blue neon.

One day two years past Katlyn was walking along Queen Street heading west, slopping along in the slush and the grit. She had just finished work at the consignment clothing shop down the street and wanted to stop at the local used book store. On her mind was some pleasant browsing among the stacks, but so was the young man who worked there during the week. He was a homely, eccentric type but she figured . . . well, she didn't know what she figured. He recognized her and said hello and suddenly she was in a normal conversation. Not a great sharing or abreaction, but polite, normal conversation. Until she fled. A muttered apology and she was out the door and back on the street, blindly splashing along in mortification. She was acutely aware that it wasn't considered normal to find conversation with a stranger so disconcerting. It was how her mother used to act.

That night, alone in her room, she sat down at her dresser and lit a cigarette. When it was done she put it out in the ashtray and looked in the mirror. Brushed her hair, in pain at its thinness, at the limp strands reaching her shoulders. Put on some lipstick, red, but it looked so peculiar she wiped it off with a wad of tissue.

And then it happened, one of those moments of decision that seems trivial to someone used to dealing with crises, but is momentous to a novice. By the time Katlyn reached her father on the phone at the Miami Marriott he was already in bed. By the time she hung up, she was the new manager of The Workbench. True, her father had lost interest in the enterprise, if he ever had any, and furthermore was assuaging his guilt by tossing her a bone, but for once Katlyn had something all her own. Maybe not much, but at least it involved interacting with people. The strange nature of the people was inauspicious, but they were people all the same. She was leaping into the basket, cutting the ground tethers and sailing the balloon away, up and away. She was terrified, but the greater fear of the alternatives carried the day.

With the lights down she could see outside, a jumbled sea of snow and debris on Dundas Street. A streetcar rumbled by. She went back to the bar. After locking the cash in its drawer she poured herself a small Tia Maria from her own bottle in the cooler. She looked at her watch and decided to give Monigan ten more minutes.

FOUR

The back door of The Laugh Chance opened and Dwayne ushered his unshapely bulk out into the cold night air. The alley was empty and well lit so he had no fear of following it out to Church Street. Once there he cut north to Dundas then east for the longest part of his trek. Two streetcars cruised by, but Dwayne was not in the mood for the company of more strangers.

Besides, he liked the harshness of the air, the raw conditions. He liked everything about the winter. The cold made him bundle up in clothes and boots and gloves and hats; the security it provided was almost maternal. Even the darkness was perfect, daylight only encouraging the type of scurrying behavior found in insects and salesmen. Night was when magic became real.

Dwayne stopped at the light on Jarvis Street and looked up. The cold front had torn through and left a clear sky. Only a few stars were visible, light pollution from the city washing out the others. Dwayne felt washed out himself. He had been replaying the show in his mind and couldn't pinpoint quite when he had lost control. If he stuck to his prepared material his sets went fine but he easily lost the ability to focus on one topic or person or event. Then when forced to improvise he panicked and lashed out. He tried to dismiss the crowd from his mind, to blank out the night, but it didn't work, had never worked. He had come to some type of acceptance of that. The show would haunt him till the next one. That and the adrenalin rush kept him awake for hours after a performance.

The corner of Dundas and Sherbourne Dwayne approached with loathing. He always stopped at the family grocery store for supplies, and it was there the local weirdos held court. A dozen of them were there now, bombarding him with catcalls and demands for spare change and offers of crack.

Standup comedy is a long, hard road, but Dwayne had reduced it to the hope of a couple of good shows, as if that's all it would take. A couple of good shows and he'd be headlining. After that a trip to New York to play Caroline's and Catch A Rising Star, guest spot on Letterman, and he'd have it made, could move out of the neighborhood, maybe on his own. He had it well planned and sharply delineated in his mind. He came out of the store with three submarine sandwiches, two quarts of chocolate milk, six pudding cups and a hundredweight of potato chips.

The locals on the corner were small-time pimps, crack wackos and their ilk. It was the stool bikers who terrified Dwayne; big, bearded slobs who would have loved to terrorize people from astride Harleys, but who had been turned down even by that fraternity and now reigned over the burger stand attached to the store. Dwayne weaved his way around and through the idlers, clutching his bag to his chest and avoiding eye contact. Half a block up the street his nerve returned and he glanced back at the corner, relieved he hadn't been forced into using the pro wrestling moves he had learned from TV. When safe and secure in his apartment he frequently hoped someone *would* try to take him on so he could leave a scattering of thrashed and broken bodies on the sidewalk for the police to collect at their leisure. That would certainly gain him a spot on the nightly news, and in show business all exposure is welcome. But that would take effort and skill and in fact an entirely different person.

His feet were sore by the time he reached home. His new winter galoshes were a bit tight and the buckles cut into his legs just above his ankles. He sprang the four deadbolts and entered to the blinding glare of his safety lamps. He kicked off his boots.

Dwayne lived in the basement bachelor suite of his mother's house. The main room held a futon mattress, several boxes of books, a crippled reclining chair heaped high with pizza boxes and research materials, a pine coffee table festooned with candy bars and instant soup cups and other items of his siege rations, a TV and a VCR and, possibly, an indigenous strain of bacteria. Dwayne looked around at it all with keen appreciation.

He could hear his mother padding around upstairs, so she had beaten him home from the club. He couldn't believe what she spent on taxis. Had Dwayne been paying rent for his suite he would consider it an egregious waste of his money. But he wasn't, though now that he was a house comic he hoped to rectify the situation.

The TV came to life at a flick, likewise the VCR. As the tape began to rewind Dwayne started his inspection. The door at the bottom of the stairs leading to the main part of the house seemed secure. He jiggled the combination lock and checked the chain to make sure then peered closely at the top hinge. It looked as if a pinch bar or a chisel had been jammed into the crack from the other side.

His mother had been trying to break in again. As much as he loved her, Dwayne was so studious in his attempt to live the unfettered life of a comedian that the only way his mother could talk to him was over the phone. So she spent the preponderance of her waking hours trying to get into her son's apartment. She was well aware that creativity feeds on leisure time but Dwayne had so much time on his hands, and did so little with it, that she feared for his sanity. There were other reasons why she feared for his sanity, but this one she should be able to root out.

Dwayne had worked up a sweat on the walk home. He took off his outerwear and pawed at his heavy wool trousers, hitching them a foot over his belly. Snacks in hand, he stretched out on the futon and punched at the remote. Here was solid entertainment. Dwayne knew pro wrestling was bogus but there was something so satisfying in the sheer emotion, affected or not. It was like standing beside the tracks as a train races past, cars rattling and swaying, all kinetic energy and power.

The phone rang as he was halfway through the first submarine sandwich. The beef was stringy tonight. He would have a word with the store manager in the morning.

"Hello, Mother."

"How did you know it was me?"

Dwayne didn't have to check his watch. "It's 2330 hours."

"So it is."

"Well?"

"That was a wonderful show tonight, son."

"Have you been trying to break into my apartment again?"

"You didn't answer."

"I walked home. You knew exactly when to expect me."

"I was worried. Don't you read the papers? Stabbings, shootings, Toronto's not safe anyplace these days. Swarming, that's the new thing. Practically an epidemic."

"An epidemic."

"Why do you swear so much on stage when you don't any other time? Your act is wonderful, but it is hard on the ears."

"It's my obligation to be larger than life. People should be shocked, at least people like those tonight. That group should be led in chains to the galleys."

"I just want you to be happy." This was attended by a muffled sob.

Dwayne was used to the histrionics. He looked at his watch: 2346 hours. He decided to start limiting her calls to fifteen minutes. This was monstrous.

Failing to get a rise, his mother sniffed to signify the end of her crying jag. "I'm better now."

"In what sense?" Dwayne scratched his belly.

"That Reba Stiles, I sure like her act."

"Don't start on this again."

"Don't you like her?"

Dwayne let a thimbleful of priapic thoughts trip through his head. "Yes, well enough, I guess."

"Why don't you ask her out on a date?"

"Comics should never date one another. Competition between the sexes is bad enough. Add the professional jealousy she'd feel the day I become a megastar and . . . well, you can see down that road."

"But you never date anyone, son. It would be so nice to see your personal life improve."

"My personal life has been sacrificed for my art."

"I met a nice girl the other day who knows nothing about comedy."

"Please!" Dwayne shuddered. He knew that some anglerfish males are much smaller than the females. They find a mate, bite onto her and fuse to her body. Eventually the male withers away into a lump of tissue with only the gonads remaining intact, leaving the female to live her life carrying this portable sperm supply. No, no. 2352 hours.

"Think about it, that's all I ask."

"I have to go."

"Would you like to go for a walk tomorrow? I know you like to walk."

"I'm devoting the day to my craft."

"You should get more exercise. Look what happened to your father."

"I'm hanging up," Dwayne said. "And tamper with my door at your peril."

He went back to the futon and in his distraction crushed a bag of chips. He dug them out from under himself and flicked the remote. A hairy barbarian went hurtling headfirst through the ropes. Dwayne loosed a sigh.

2400 hours. Dwayne smiled. In retrospect, the show had gone well tonight, enough to make the other comics realize he was a man to be reckoned with. A quart of chocolate milk rushed down his throat as he snuggled into the pillows.

The wrestling match ended just as Harold Arens made the counterintuitive move of phoning Dwayne at home. Harold was in no mood to be trapped in another conversation with Dwayne that night, but his concern won out. As usual with Dwayne, it was no simple matter. The number Harold dialed put him in touch with Dwayne's mother, who complained about the hour before railing on about various earthly woes. Harold finally left his own number and was just about to go to bed when Dwayne called back.

"Sorry, Dwayne. I know it's late."

"Nonsense. We're all in this together. Are you having trouble with a bit? Run it by me and I'll try to polish it up."

"This isn't about my act." Harold fervently hoped not. The day he needed Dwayne's help in comedy they'd be finding his drug-bloated body and a suicide note.

"Okay," Dwayne said.

"It's just that . . . well, you've had a regular spot at the club now —"

"A great feeling. Magnificent!"

"Let me finish." Harold fumbled for words. "As usual after a show I can't sleep —"

"Neither can I."

"Anyhow, I wanted to warn you about something."

Dwayne was getting impatient. And it wasn't all his fault. Harold was a gifted up-and-comer who responded brilliantly on stage to shifting moods and circumstances, but offstage had trouble talking about things without a punchline. Dwayne would have a word with him about it.

"I'm going out for a drink," Harold finally said. "There's a bar right by where you live that's pretty easy on the last-call rules. We can meet if you want."

Dwayne smiled to himself. It was rare that other comics wanted to bond with him. "Why not?"

"It's called The Workbench — see you there in five minutes."

Dwayne felt like he had a mild dose of malaria, alternately freezing and sweating. He knew The Workbench was where his father lived and hung around. Dwayne had been avoiding the place since the old man left home. To Dwayne, a straight-laced if grubby sort, the establishment fairly reeked of evil. But Harold wanted to see him. So disparate are standup comics in their backgrounds and views on life that their cleaving together would be astonishing to anyone unfamiliar with the camaraderie induced by wilfully putting your ass on the line every night. Infantry platoons become a true unit through similar exigencies, but comics do it intentionally.

By the time Dwayne reached The Workbench Harold was already inside. Dwayne could barely see him by peeking through the window, as the place was dark except for the dim play of light over the horseshoe bar. Dwayne knocked and Harold let him in. Dwayne moved carefully, advancing slowly, each step placing him more firmly in the grip of his father's world. He could almost smell the wicked old pisstank.

"Katlyn," Harold said as he returned, "this is Dwayne."

"Hello," Katlyn said.

Dwayne stared, drymouthed. For some reason he found himself thinking of the Spanish Civil War heroine and inspirational rallying cry: *La Pasionaria!*

"Welcome to The Workbench," Katlyn said. She glanced around and laughed. "The end of life as we know it."

"Much like the K-T boundary," Dwayne said. He wasn't much good in social situations and habitually compounded the unease he both felt and created by trying to display his learning. Harold rushed to change the subject but Dwayne skilfully used the flying start to his advantage. "Luis and Walter Alvarez," Dwayne continued, not really knowing why. "They proposed that the mass extinction at the Cretaceous-Tertiary boundary was caused by an asteroid or meteorite impact. Anomalously high levels of iridium in Italian and Danish sediments lend credence to their theory, as do impact-melt spherules and shocked quartz grains found in several locations."

Katlyn looked him calmly in the face and said, "I know."

Harold laughed like hell. Katlyn had known Dwayne for two minutes and could already handle him better than Harold could after three years.

"Would you like a beer?" Katlyn said.

"A cranberry and Coke, please. Cleanses the system."

Katlyn glanced at Harold for support.

"We work together," Harold said. "Dwayne's one of the comics."

"Oh, I see." She didn't see, not in the slightest.

Dwayne was not the most unusual creature she had come across in the bar, not by a long shot, but at that time of night it was always best to keep an eye out. He was odd, but Katlyn could sense a softness under the veneer of bluster. Dwayne sat down and Katlyn slid over his drink.

"Another rough night at the club," Harold said.

"How do they keep it afloat?" Katlyn asked. "Every time you mention it things seem to be going worse down there."

"Mostly by paying us jack," Harold said. "Which reminds me, Dwayne — there's something about Sturgis I want to warn you about."

Dwayne shot a look at Katlyn. He believed strongly that there should be no sharing of club information with civilians.

"Katlyn's okay," Harold said.

"Sorry." Dwayne never apologized for anything but, well . . . there she was.

"Now that you're a regular comic, Sturgis can up the pressure because you have something to lose," Harold said. "He's done it to all of us at one time or another."

"Pressure?"

"He knows we need a home club to work out of, so anything goes. Threats, coercion, whatever it takes. Of course, there's a fine line between getting what he needs and scaring us all off. He has scams and double-deals going from the booze to the health codes."

"But what can the comics do for him?"

"One example," Harold said. "There used to be circus scams around the country until they changed the laws to try and stamp them out. A circus would phone a bunch of local businesses in a small town, say they were coming for a big show. They'd get the corporate sponsors to buy advance tickets to help the kids and local charities. Counting, of course, on the fact that the businessmen wouldn't actually attend, they'd sell the place out a few times over. Hell, sometimes they'd fake the whole operation and never even set foot in the town."

Katlyn shook her head while Dwayne looked for a correlation.

"Sturgis has tried the same thing with the comics," Harold said. "Six months ago he called Reba and I into the office and leaned on us to market club tickets in exactly the same way."

"He could hire someone for that," Katlyn said. "Sounds like it's about control, to me."

"Yeah, yeah, we knew that. But desperation is a pretty strong motivator. We finally refused, then didn't get a spot at the club for two months. I had to borrow money from my dad just to cover rent, and that hurt."

Dwayne chuckled mirthlessly. "A situation I'll never be in. My father's a penniless reprobate."

Katlyn peered at him closely. "Dwayne Feller? Is that your mother's maiden name?"

Dwayne nodded. "Yes. My father lives upstairs. I thought you'd be familiar with the old tosspot."

"Yes, of course . . . Monigan is a friend. A good friend." Katlyn was delighted. "I finally get to meet a member of his family."

"Family."

"Oh, Dwayne . . . he talks about you so much."

"I have a few choice phrases for him as well."

Katlyn dropped her eyes. "I didn't mean to stir anything up."

Now Dwayne felt bad for upsetting her. He turned back to Harold. "In any event, thanks for the information. I'll be careful."

"Refill?" Katlyn asked.

"No," Dwayne said. "I seem to have left home without my wallet."

"On the house," Katlyn said. "It's the least I can do to support the local arts."

Dwayne fidgeted. Charity. He didn't respond well to charity.

"I mean, at least you guys are doing it."

"Sort of."

"Did you see that movie with James Woods the other night? I can't remember the name, but Woods's character just made a bunch of money or something."

"You paid attention to the details," Harold said.

Dwayne scowled at him for interrupting.

"Anyhow, he's acting like a bigshot. Tells his friends at a dinner party that he's going to charter a jet that night and fly them to Vegas to catch Steve Martin's midnight show."

"Never saw it," Harold said.

"All I'm saying is that I would rather be the person doing the show in Vegas than have the money to fly there to see it. You guys are doing it. You're on the pointy end of the stick."

Now there's a fine attitude, Dwayne thought.

"You have a case," Harold said.

"A case," Dwayne snorted. "It's a perfect analysis. You're being simplistic, Harold."

"Whatever you say." Harold could sense Dwayne's rising anger. He had never seen him riled up offstage before, only when Dwayne was foundering in confusion during a show. He glanced at Katlyn then back at Dwayne and instantly realized what was happening here.

As for Dwayne, he found himself in an untenable situation. When he was this worked up at the club he had an outlet, that's what standup was all about. But here was all this emotion trying to breach the surface, and the exertion needed to keep it down was making his eyes bulge and his capillaries engorge. He felt faint and laid his head on the bar.

"Hey," Harold said. "You okay?"

"Yes," Dwayne said. "My mother, that's all. She's been upset lately and I should go home to check on her." He slid off the stool and stood to his full manly height in front of Katlyn. "Wonderful evening. Magnificent."

"It's been fun," Katlyn said, trying to suppress a grin. "Come back anytime. I mean it."

"Harold," Dwayne said formally with a slight bow.

On his friend's exit, Harold made to toss off a joke, but the look on Katlyn's face made him stow it away for a future heckler. He pushed out his glass.

At home and in bed at last, fully dressed, girdled by discarded bags and food wrappers, Dwayne finally rid himself of adrenalin. It was hard for most people to fathom that his father lived less than two blocks away and that Dwayne hadn't seen him in four years. The two of them had a lot of business to clear up, but unfortunately they weren't the type of men who easily address business. Add in the irony that the dump his father lived in was run by a woman Dwayne was taken with and it is easy to see that Dwayne would be hard pressed to hold onto his precious leisure time. He couldn't even think of Katlyn in a lascivious way. She was too virginal. In the strictest sense of the word, Dwayne was even more so, if that's possible. In fact it isn't possible, but Dwayne Feller transcended many accepted worldly truths.

FIVE

Monigan was on his way back to the pub, hustling along the sloppy sidewalk. Bill was safe for the night three blocks away.

After sorting the information out of Bill's ramblings, Monigan had escorted him home and up the stairs. As Bill got his door open and pushed it in, Monigan was assailed by a rolling wave of funk. He fumbled for the light switch. The single overhead bulb cast its yellow light on a scene of domestic squalor. Bill's room was twenty feet long by twelve wide and was littered with piles of clothing, mechanical gadgets and filth. Monigan lived like a pig, was even somewhat proud of it as a display of individuality, but this was out of his league. A small kitchen table stood in the middle of the room. Against the far wall was a mattress in a state of decay normally associated with corpses from Irish bogs. Mounds of material mildewed in place, more than matching in smell and texture the abandoned food on the counter and in the sink. The room was replete with dissolution and heartbreak.

Monigan guided Bill into the room and stood back by the door, swallowing hard, his cranky mood quashed by the sight of his new friend's living conditions.

Bill stood there a moment and looked at the mattress where he and Jean had slept. At least, when she wasn't wandering around. The last time had led to her death from exposure or indifference or the simple accumulation of bad luck. For the first time he felt a stirring of anger at the event, anger at some phantom that stalked the urban landscape preying on his sort.

"What's up?" Monigan said.

"My wife died."

"So that's why the tuxedo."

"I have to get it back tomorrow cause I rented it just for today. I collected bottles for three months. I was going to take her to dinner but then this, so I rented the suit." He plucked at the tux and turned to Monigan. "I have some soup if you're hungry."

"No, that's okay."

"She used to leave and go places but that's all right. I like being by myself."

"Me, too."

"It's nice being by myself. But sometimes it's good to have someone to share it with. When we were together I could still be alone if I wanted."

"Listen — you need anything?"

Bill looked puzzled. "No."

"I guess I gotta go."

"I'm making some tea."

"I gotta go." Monigan shuffled and blinked at the smell, which was almost corporeal. "You like hockey?"

"The game?"

"Leafs got a afternoon game on the tube tomorrow against Detroit. I'll come by about noon, we'll go to The Workbench, get Katy to make up some chili."

"I have to take the tuxedo back."

"They'll be closed tomorrow. We'll do that Monday."

Bill took off his overcoat and dropped it on a pile of clothes, on top of which was a soiled floral print dress.

"Let me have the coat," Monigan said. "I'm about dying in this weather. I'll bring it back tomorrow when I pick you up."

Bill waved. Holding his breath, Monigan entered the room and snatched the thing off the pile, in his haste tripping over the innards of some type of device.

"I'm fixing that," Bill said.

"What is it?" Monigan regained his place in the doorway.

"I don't know, but it's broken."

Monigan nodded and both men jumped as a door slammed in the hallway. A scarred, ravaged man stood in the wan light of the doorway next to Bill's. He stepped out into the hall and wiped his hands on the front of his green work shirt, staggering slightly as he shoved past Monigan and addressed Bill.

"I told you before, I told you. Shut up, you come home late. You and your fucking wife, leaving the door open."

"My wife died."

"One less asshole." He was a large man, dirty and obscene, his narrow squint hostile and mindless.

"My friend's just had a rough day," Monigan said. "Don't mean any harm."

"Tell him to keep the door shut."

Monigan stuck his head inside and said, "See you at noon, Bill."

Monigan pulled the door closed. The smell of the coat was almost too much for him but it was better than freezing to death. Monigan forced his arms down the sleeves. It was far too small for him so he left it gaping open in front. He smiled and pivoted.

The only sound from Bill's neighbor came from his head hitting the floor. There we go, Monigan thought, six-incher and walk your sister home.

Monigan was soaked halfway up his shins by the time he hit The Workbench. Inside Katlyn had just turned off the chili. About to put it in the fridge, she heard a rap on the side window and set it back on the propane stove. She pushed the door handle, letting in Monigan and a collection of snow dervishes.

"Bad night out there," Katlyn said.

Monigan peeled off Bill's coat and dropped it on the floor. "Best you get me a scotch or something you don't wanna see me die."

Harold was the only other person in the place, still there rehashing the show in his mind and wondering how Dwayne would ever survive the business. He shoved over as Monigan sat down. The old guy had a peculiar reek about him, a smell that seemed of some permanence. Harold nodded.

"Yeah," Monigan said. "Howdy. Hold off on the conversation, will you."

"Okay by me," Harold said. "I'm on my way after this."

"I seen you in here before?" Monigan sounded short of certain.

"Not often. Drop by late some nights, get out of the cold."

"The cold," Monigan said. "Makes you wonder why they ever settled this stupid country. Them Spanish and Portigees had it right: go to Mexico and get a place with beaches and sun and lots of gold to send back home." He drained half his drink. "What do the English and French do? Pick a country you can't barely travel through, that's got miserable weather and Indians you gotta fight forever, then decide to settle down cause there's lots of big, flat-tailed rodents you can make fucking hats outta."

Harold laughed out loud then turned a coaster over and quickly scribbled a summary of the gag on the back of it. He felt warm sliding it into his pocket. A new bit with a new home. It entirely justified the lateness of his being out, the hangover he would have in the morning and the fact that he had introduced Katlyn and Dwayne, the latter causing him the most concern.

"What's got you so upset?" Katlyn asked Monigan.

"Everything," he said. "Saturday's supposed to be my peaceful day. Then I get kicked out early from the wedding, I run into Doyle twice, then I see how Bill lives. And even the dirtylegs — you see them out there? I don't mind hookers, but the crackheads around here these days working the corners, lepers on a off day wouldn't go near them. And all them scumbags over at the burger joint who help keep the broads on the street are worse. Trouble is, a poor guy like Bill gets lumped in with all them types when it comes to handing out the welfare and the support and the respect, even.

"The guy can repair a stove, can't he? And fiddle a pool table without the key, and you should see the stuff he's fixing over at his place, and he gets stuck living in a shithouse and his wife dies and nobody cares."

After a moment Katlyn leaned in. "You okay?"

"Never mind worrying about me. Me is one guy you don't have to worry about. Worry about Bill and the retards on the street that can't get no help, the ones who wander around banging into stuff and screaming at their invisible pet goats. Worry about the ones like my goddamn son, who went loony when he was about three, and his mother who joined him about the same time."

Katlyn relaxed. Now Monigan was coming around to more familiar ground. When he started grousing about his family it meant the true anger was draining away.

"Oh, yes," Katlyn said and grinned.

"You slipped a gear?"

"I met your son," she said. Having badgered Monigan to introduce her to his wife and son, she felt smug at having reached her goal unaided. "He was in earlier tonight, with Harold, here."

"Harold Arens." The comic extended then withdrew his hand. From the look in Monigan's eyes, especially the wonky one, Harold felt thankful for the retention of his limb. Dwayne's dad. Harold didn't know what he had expected. He had never dwelt on it, but from listening to Dwayne's tirades Harold had formed the image of a played-out old street person who had abandoned his family and was now doomed to an eternity of penance. One look at Monigan had turned that idea on its head.

"You know him?" Monigan asked. "Where from?"

"We're both comics," Harold said very politely.

"Funny boys," Monigan said. "Think you can tell a joke, do you? I can tell a joke. You think I can't? I can."

"I bet you can."

"You a Jew?"

"As a matter of fact, I am."

"Good. I like Jew comics the best. Used to watch them on TV all the time." He paused and considered. "Most of them are named Jackie something, ain't they?"

Harold laughed. "Pretty close."

"Well, you want some advice about your comedy career, you stay away from my son. What seems funny to you at first gets tired real quick with that boy."

Harold didn't disagree strongly enough to protest, even were he so foolhardy. It wasn't a subject in which he wanted to become embroiled at the best of times, and this wasn't anything like the best. He had spent enough time in The Workbench to know how quickly a mild spat could turn into a major conflict. Harold thanked Katlyn, nodded to Monigan and lit out for home.

"Good," Monigan said as the door swung shut on Harold's back. "Now I can look you straight in the eye and tell you that if you ever let that son of mine in here again, I'll string you up with your new curtains. You don't know him. He's like some Old Testament guy, the shit just rolls along with him, locusts and plagues and that."

"What happened to you?" Katlyn said. "You can't possibly be set that much against him."

"Well, I am and I'm not," Monigan admitted. "But I know you — too soft and understanding for your own good. So I'm just try-ing to give you fair warning."

"Thanks for the candor, but I just met Dwayne and know full well he's no demon."

"The thing of it is, the only way to keep strong is to know who the enemy is."

"Your problem is you have too much time on your hands. You get bored and then paranoid."

"I ain't bored," Monigan said. "I got lots to do. What, you want me to collect stamps?"

"I'm serious," Katlyn said. "I need more staff."

"Any staff is more than none."

"Leave Josh alone — he tries."

"He tries, but he's never in here."

"Anyhow, what do you think?"

"About what?"

"About working back here instead of drinking out there?"

"What do you get when you cross a bartender and a pit bull?"

"Heard it."

"Either a bartender that kills poodles or a pit bull that steals."

"You wouldn't steal from me, Monigan. Not from me."

"Don't be too sure of nothing these days."

"I almost forgot," Katlyn said. "The chili's still hot. Help yourself."

"Not hungry."

"Great. I only stayed open because you said you were coming back. Now go get some."

"What's got you so pissed off?" Angry most of his waking hours, Monigan couldn't fathom the emotion in others. "You're right, you need some staff, get out from behind the bar and go chasing firemen and sailors and all them."

"Are you going to eat?"

"Yeah, gimme a bowl."

Katlyn ladled the chili, uncomfortable with Monigan's assessment.

There was a tap at the window and she sighed. It was the time of night that people saw the light through the glass and, like frayed moths, came to dash out their last bits of consciousness against its pull.

"What do you want?" Monigan blocked the doorway.

It was a woman. Cold, wasted, with the fatigue of one whose life force has deliquesced with the struggle of survival. She pulled a thin cloth coat tight around herself and stared with watery eyes up at him.

Monigan looked out over her head. "You with anybody? Shouldn't be walking around out there alone, a night like this."

She stared down at her feet.

"Well," he said. "Get in."

He held the door open and the woman skulked into the room,

taking a seat at the table farthest removed from the bar. Monigan leaned over and poured a draft backhanded from the tap.

"Next time I expect a tip," he said, dropping it at the table and going back to the bar. "Katy, best whistle some chili over that way. Tab."

Katlyn studied the woman then smiled at Monigan, making him shift on his stool. While Katlyn delivered the chili Monigan went over to the mail shelf beside the TV at the end of the horseshoe and dipped into the nesting place for welfare and UIC checks, demands and threats and casual letters, all of which sat waiting to be claimed by the eighteen people living above the bar. Three floors: one bathroom and six rooms per floor, one bed and one dresser per room.

Monigan had three pieces of mail which he had neglected to collect Friday. He threw them in the garbage. He was starting to think his name was FINAL NOTICE. He appraised the woman in the thin cloth coat as she spooned into the chili then wandered back toward Katlyn.

"I don't know if I can get through all this," he said, dipping into his own chili. It disappeared in sixty seconds. "Could use a cigarette."

He was relaxing with the smoke when there was another tap on the window. Monigan opened the door as Katlyn craned her neck, satisfied when she saw it was Frodo, the local bookie.

"Draft, Katlyn," Frodo said. He flipped a hundred on the bar.

"I can't change that," she said. "Catch me tomorrow."

Frodo was a pale sort, whose height no less than his morals had been stunted at some early age. He dressed expensively but oddly: one day a full leather suit, the next dress pants and a T-shirt, the day after an outfit to which a Chicago pimp would set fire. This early morning he wore a houndstooth tweed jacket over a beautiful shirt of Egyptian cotton. And a cape.

"You can flash a hundred," Monigan said. "Okay then, you can afford to come through on the fifty you owe me for the Rangers' game Thursday."

Frodo didn't even look at him. "How dumb do you think I am?"

"Okay."

"Besides, that's the last money to my name. I've been getting burned on hockey since Christmas."

"I thought you won large a month ago."

"Aw, you know."

"Yeah, I know. I know you're stupid enough to take book on everything from horses to bingo and never collect half of it. Bookie ain't supposed to be a clearing house for assholes. If I was doing it things'd be different. Guy doesn't come up, he walks home with two broken legs. Cops show up, he can't talk to them, his tongue is bust. Think I wouldn't do it? I'd do it."

"But they're my friends," Frodo said.

"Then don't book with friends. Lay it off."

"Awww . . ."

"Those deadbeats ain't your friends anyhow, if they stiff you."

"It's not so much those guys. Lately I've been dealing with suits. Higher rollers than the stuff I pick up around here."

"Good," Monigan said. "They gotta keep close to even or nobody'll take their bets. They're easier to find than the bums in this place who just go underground."

Frodo said nothing, toying with his glass.

"Jesus. You ain't collecting from those guys, either? Guys you don't even know, guys work on Bay Street who should be put to sleep with the stray dogs?"

"I was collecting Thursday," Frodo said defensively.

"And?"

"A guy promised me half by next week."

"A guy," Monigan said. "One guy. How much is he into you for?"

"About eight."

"Hundred?" Katlyn asked.

"Thousand," Monigan said. "I bet my life on a bucket of fish guts he's into you eight large and you ain't seen a penny."

"He promised me half."

"Who is this guy?"

"That wouldn't be professional."

"Come on."

"You know that comedy club over by Yonge Street? The one where I told you I saw your son?"

"I seen it."

"The Laugh Chance," Frodo said. "Good place. I've taken people there . . . you know, night on the town with a client type of thing."

"I seen those guys on TV. I can tell a joke, you wanna laugh. Think I can't? I can."

"The owner says I get half next week."

"Half."

"You don't understand," Frodo said.

"Don't you ever say that to me."

"Gambling's a disease."

"I heard somewhere cancer is, too — so the doctor don't charge to fix the guy?"

"He has problems," Frodo said. "His wife's taking him apart . . ."

"Don't talk to me about wives."

". . . his club's not drawing like it used to . . ."

"'Cause his comics can't tell jokes."

". . . his rooming house is going under . . ."

"Look around, tell me these days you see a lotta people can afford even one room."

". . . so it's that kind of thing."

"Gotta do something."

"Yeah, well." Frodo pushed his glass across the bar and shook his head. "I have to get going."

"Don't forget your cape, Dracula."

Frodo waved and was out the door. Monigan had had enough, his fill of the day, so he stared at the woman in the thin cloth coat till she was intimidated enough to leave.

"I'm going upstairs," he said.

"See you tomorrow," Katlyn said.

When he was gone Katlyn turned off the last of the lights, secured the door behind her and started the short walk to her apartment on the second floor of a house just up the street. She had read lately of imaginal disks, bits of tissue in lepidopterous larvae that contain the genetic information necessary to transform the caterpillar into a winged beauty. Splendid destiny concealed under the surface of an imperfect beginning. She hoped to change, wished someday to shed the cocoon, to drink in sunshine while her wings grew, a glorious new imago.

Physical attractiveness was a concept she had given up thinking about for herself, something nice of itself but unnecessary. Of course, she felt she had no choice but to do so. She wondered what it would be like to see herself through another's eyes. Monigan thought she was externally homely but with a beauty that grew out of her compassion. Dwayne could think of nothing but her eyes. In the mirror, Katlyn herself saw a skinny bartender with stringy hair and no tits. She thought again of quitting cigarettes, trying to take the lines off her face. She reached home and climbed the stairs.

Back at The Workbench, Monigan was negotiating the stairs in a noisier and less co-ordinated manner all the way up to the fourth floor. He crinkled his nose as he passed the bathroom, glad he had gone downstairs. Sometimes the smell was simply too much. On entering his room he tripped on a loose piece of linoleum he had been too busy to glue down, righted himself, then realized he had left Bill's coat on the floor by the bar. He dropped his tuxedo in a heap beside the bed and looked around the cramped room. Nothing much to indicate it was occupied by anyone in particular. There were no pictures, no personal touches, nothing to call it home. He went to bed.

From Monigan's point of view, it was a busy day coming up. He had to pick up Bill at noon, watch the Leafs and Detroit on the tube and try to lay down some bets. There wasn't much hope of that, as

he had exhausted his credit with everyone. He also had to talk Bill
into playing partners with him so he could raise some money on
the pool table. As well, he'd have to remember to ask Bill where he
had rented his tuxedo. That meant another chore: breaking into
the rental shop after dark to tear up the contract. He figured Bill
should have one good suit of clothes if he didn't want to look like
a bum.

He lay there going through all these appointments then sat up
with a start and scratched himself as he padded across the room to
the light switch. He had forgotten about the mutt. Friday he had
found a stray roaming the alley between the two streets bracketing
the bar, an ill-proportioned little thing that Dr. Seuss couldn't have
invented. It was also a mute as far as Monigan could tell, not having made a sound as he picked it up and sneaked it upstairs. He
flipped the switch and harsh shadows lanced across the room. The
only place it could be was under the bed, and sure enough there it
was, huddling, staring, as Monigan reached under and pulled it
out. A small patch of hair came away in his hand and the scrawny
creature gave a tentative lick at his face. He carried it over to the
small bar fridge and put it down.

Out of the fridge he took a plastic package of mock chicken loaf
and fed the dog one orange-rimmed slice at a time. The animal
gagged once but finished. Monigan looked around, thought some,
then went to the dormer window and opened it a couple of feet.
Holding the dog firmly by its forequarters, he shoved its ass out
into the frigid night air. It took five minutes for the dog to stop trying to scramble back inside but eventually panic succumbed to
urgency and its bowels voided. Hard little turds tumbled their way
down the slate mansard roof and came to rest in the eavestrough.
A sharp burst of urine hit the outside of the sill and cascaded
down, carving a delta into the thin layer of snow. The dog stared at
Monigan the entire time, satisfied with the performance, as if
accepting the ludicrousness of its position as interest to be paid on
the loan of a meal and a warm place to sleep. Monigan drew it back

inside and stroked its head, covering the tiny brain case with one hand. The dog immediately made for the bed and crawled under.

Monigan was ill-suited to taking care of things. His solipsism and generally cantankerous nature had rendered him unfit even to look after his wife and child. He was none too effective in taking care of himself either, measured by the standards of most people in Cabbagetown.

It was an odd mix of citizens in that part of the city. They ran the gamut from millionaires and lawyers and sports executives and chichi artists to the marginalized and the subsidized and the criminalized and the bums. Monigan's family was somewhere between the extremes, though Monigan now had to look up at his wife and son from his position down on the lower rungs. And he was getting lower all the time, he realized that. It had been an eternity since anything solid had come his way, something substantial to grab onto and lever himself out of the mire. Then again, he always felt he would make it through on his feet. He was Monigan, a man who survived on a curious combination of courage and not giving a fiddler's fuck.

He stared at the ceiling, thinking of his family. His son was a comic, a fact Monigan had difficulty reconciling with Dwayne's inability to focus on anything. At times he found it hard to remember what his son looked like. It was as if he truly were alone in the world. Monigan would like to see him some time but it couldn't be face to face. There was still too much guilt coursing through his system to allow that. He'd be happy just to see Dwayne on stage, where Monigan could sit at the back in the dark and see if his son had changed at all. Maybe one of these days he'd get the chance.

It was when he thought about his son in conjunction with his wife that he got scared. Individually they were strange enough, but the two of them together shared a sort of reverse commensalism, intensifying each other's negative traits and combining to make a package that had helped drive Monigan out of the house. The old man spent half the time blaming himself and the other half being proud of his foresight in ending it when he did. But even when wallowing in guilt Monigan cut it short. Wallowing wasn't his style.

He was tired. It had been a long day. He fell asleep trying to think of a name for the dog. If he was going to keep the thing he figured it needed the dignity of a name.

Saturday.

SIX

Dwayne spent the next two days in seclusion. Having performed professionally for the first time Saturday night, and having it followed by a bonding session with Harold Arens that Dwayne hadn't even initiated, with all of it topped off by meeting Katlyn . . . it was simply too much for him. Dwayne believed the world to be far too raucous, too wild and untamable. He needed to get strong. That was a difficult task, even though Dwayne thought he was Steve McQueen. When feeling in the grip of wildness and craving solitude, he cast himself into *The Great Escape*.

He would sit on the floor of his apartment and bounce a baseball off the far wall, catching it in his glove. But the mitt was too stiff to catch more than a perfect rebound and he didn't know how to break one in. Besides, the ball tended to ricochet off the studs behind the drywall, forcing him to crawl around like a child to retrieve it. It was too hard to practice it very often. In his heart, though, he knew he was The Cooler King.

So Sunday and Monday he locked himself in, thinking of his father and of Katlyn until there was barely room for comedy material. But he tried, shaping bits in his head, looking for a humorous angle on anything and everything, waiting for Tuesday Amateur Night, when for the first time he would be one of the regular comics who followed the neophytes to keep the night from falling on its face.

He was happy with the demands on his concentration. His father spent the better portion of his life in The Workbench, so

Dwayne's not seeing him the night before had been close. In the past little while, Dwayne had been bothered by the nostalgia he felt for Monigan, but he figured if they were destined to meet again it would be under his own terms, when he was secure, at the peak of his powers, with something to show for his life.

Dwayne loved the stage for that very reason. The terror and the concentration effaced all else; the stage was his personal isolation chamber.

Tuesday night was finally upon him.

"Dwayne Goldman." He practiced saying it. "And now, ladies and gentlemen, a man who needs no introduction, fresh off a torrid display of wit Saturday night, put your hands together for Dwayne Goldman!" He shivered and put on his new yarmulke.

As Dwayne continued to work himself into a tortured mental state, Sturgis was impatiently waiting for showtime down at the club. On the wall at the back he taped a list of names. He stood back and went down the roster, evaluating, but after the tenth name he gave it up as a bad lot and went to the bar.

"Going to be a good show tonight?" the barman said.

"Shake your head," Sturgis said. "If it wasn't for some of the regulars dropping down to try new material I'd cancel these Amateur Nights altogether. Everybody thinks they can be a comic. Look at them."

Like African hunting dogs darting in for a bite now that the lion's attention was off his grub, the amateur comics swarmed around the list. Sturgis, with the superiority of someone who's forgotten his own beginnings, dismissed them all by giving them the finger then gasped at the pain in his side. He leaned his head on the bar.

"You're lucky it's just your ribs," the bartender said. "I heard you were doing over eighty klicks when you hit that streetcar."

"You heard. Where did you hear?"

"Things get around."

"That's the trouble with this business. Nobody hears good news, but let one thing go wrong and all the apes in the jungle are screaming about it. What is it with comics that they love the blood and the gore?"

After locking up Saturday night, Sturgis had slipped behind the wheel of his Jaguar XJ–6, pulling the wolf fur collar of his coat around his ears as he waited for the engine to warm up. Twenty years he had been in the business, starting back when there were few clubs available, learning his trade at resorts, strip clubs, opening for garage bands, tough rooms all round. Living in a dump, saving money for two beers so he could gorge himself on the free happy hour snacks. He remembered it all, every gig. Then he started his own club, doing it his way. Hosting every show himself, headlining, tending bar, the works. And here he was: the ex-wife was taking half his money in alimony, the lease was up on the building, he was down large with his bookie and the rooming house he owned was losing big time what with rent controls and taxes.

He forced himself to breathe normally and pulled out of his parking stall. He was stretched too thin, something had to give. He was in too deep in every direction, and even if he could pack The Laugh Chance every night it wouldn't cover his nut. He wasn't about to sell the Jag. That was his darling, the only overt sign of success he had left. He turned left onto Queen and headed west, bound for his apartment near High Park. An apartment. He used to have three bathrooms; big house, five bedrooms and three bathrooms. He used to joke that his wife's Mercedes was a loaner, used to tip the newspaper boy five bucks just to see the kid abase himself with gratitude. Then the income tax gouge and the divorce and the bookie . . . everything. His whole life was in a downward spiral.

Two minutes later he cruised into the back of the parked Queen streetcar and totalled the Jag.

He winced again, cast a last sneer at the comics and headed for his bunker. In the office he sat down, but the supporting wings of the backrest pressed into his taped ribs. He unfastened the ties and

dropped it on the floor. He leaned back against the wooden slats of
the desk chair and settled in, ticking off his problems on his fingers. Something had to give.

He sighed and went out into the club and saw the comics sitting
at the back. The amateurs were pacing around working off the jit-
ters, and he considered going over and scaring the shit out of them.

From the side door Dwayne entered, and stood there surveying the place until a number of patrons looked his way. From the
middle of the room his mother turned and waved. She was
ignored along with everyone else. Dwayne believed that attention
was all well and good, but that he'd gain no respect by fraterniz-
ing. It was good enough that the peasants had turned out with
their tithes. He made a show of approaching the bar and ordering a cranberry and Coke, and it was then the comics saw his
yarmulke. Dwayne Goldman.

Ignoring the amateurs, he took a seat beside Harold and put a
large plastic bag on the table. "Good house," he said.

Harold nodded and went back to his conversation with Reba.

Dwayne tore open the package and held up a T-shirt. "Fifteen
dollars apiece," he said. "Fifteen dollars and you are a charter member of our merry band."

Harold leaned closer. "Bashi . . . ?"

"What language is that?" Reba asked. "And what merry band?"

"Our band of house comics," Dwayne said.

"But what does it say?" Reba asked. She had already checked the
list and was bubbling with relief that she didn't have to follow
Dwayne.

"Bashi-Bazouks," Dwayne said.

"Is that supposed to be Yiddish?" Harold said.

Dwayne laughed lightly. That's what he loved about his fellow
comics: the banter, the ribbing that made him feel part of a family,
a cause. "Bashi-Bazouks," he repeated. "The Rotten Heads. A
Turkish irregular cavalry troop in Constantinople during the
Crimean War."

"I don't see the connection," Reba said.

"Like us, they were virtually unpaid. They lived on plunder and were almost impossible to control."

"Right," Harold said. "Very flattering. Where do you come up with this stuff?"

"And why?" Reba asked.

"I've always loved reading," Dwayne said. "Besides, you never know what little bit of information will lead to the breakthrough routine that propels you to stardom."

"The Rotten Heads," Harold said. "A good topic to get the crowd on your side."

Sarcasm. Dwayne knew it. "Bashi-Bazouks. Fifteen dollars."

Harold and Reba went back to their conversation.

"I should have known not to distract you before a show." Dwayne carefully folded the shirt and replaced it in the bag with the others. "I'll wait till after."

Dwayne went over to the list of performers and frowned. His name was not with the regulars near the bottom. He let his eyes creep upward until they came to rest at the top of the list. First: the death spot. He looked closer, convinced there must be something wrong. Dwayne was a professional. And Dwayne *Feller*, at that. He pulled out a pen, crossed out his last name, and had just finished inking in *Goldman*, when a tiny hand shoved his aside and drew a ragged line through the whole name. Whirling around, Dwayne found himself staring at a bar tab, behind which was the owner himself.

"Please?" Dwayne said.

"Why didn't you pay your bar bill Saturday night?" Sturgis said.

"I was distracted."

Sturgis reached a foot over his head and grabbed Dwayne by the collar. "Get out," he said. "You're suspended for a week. And I'm garnisheeing last week's wages to cover the tab."

"The bill's only for two sodas."

"You've become a big tipper."

Harold couldn't let it go any longer. "Hey, boss," he said.

"Shut up, Arens," Sturgis said. "I don't need any of your wise-ass remarks tonight."

"It will never happen again," Dwayne said.

"You still owe me for the tab," Sturgis said. "And the suspension stands."

"Why?"

"Cause you fucked me Saturday night. And every other night, for that matter. Go home and don't come back till you have an act."

The comics flinched as one.

Dwayne stared over the owner's head and ignored his comrades. His eyes moistened. Deliberately buttoning his coat, he left without a word by the back stairs.

It was mild outside compared to the frigid atmosphere in the club. Clear, with only the odd passage of high stratus across the moon's crescent to dip the urban jungle into indigo shades. Dwayne was taking it well. Rather, he was talking himself into taking it well. Someone with his ability had nothing to worry about, he reasoned. Setbacks were part of a performer's life. He'd learn from it, that's all. He slipped off the yarmulke, hesitated, then threw it over a construction fence on Dundas Street. The Jews would have to go it alone.

The usual clot of dacoits were on the corner of Dundas and Sherbourne and Dwayne was already through them and inside the store when he realized he was broke. He wove his way empty-handed back through his tormentors, enduring the taunts, made it home and went inside. He had forgotten to tape wrestling so he sat on his futon and stared at the blank TV. His tongue probed out of his mouth, cleaning the salty residue of the tears from his upper lip.

The phone brought him out of a fitful doze. 2330 hours.

"Hello, Mother."

"What got you on your high horse?"

"If you're going to start right in with the nagging, I'll hang up."

"Why weren't you on the show tonight? You had one of your panic things and stormed out again, didn't you?

"Sometimes it's better to observe."

"Where's my forty dollars?"

"There was a bookkeeping error at the club. They've frozen the payroll."

"I want my money."

Dwayne shook his head. "I'm going to work tomorrow."

That stopped her at the cattle guard. "You have a job? I've been telling you to get one since you started this comedy business."

"It's time," he said. "Of course, it's mainly for the experience. All story-tellers draw on life to flesh out original ideas."

"What kind of job?"

His mother didn't need any details at this stage. "It doesn't matter. As soon as I have a nest egg of new stage material it will be back to the leisure time I need for my act."

"What kind of job?"

"Leave me alone."

"Well, hang on to it."

"Just sit tight and you'll get your money." A sob drifted over the line. 2346 hours — right on time. "Goodnight, Mother. I'm going to bed."

"Take your hat off tomorrow. Employers don't like seeing people in hats."

Dwayne hung up and checked the security of the door leading to the upstairs. He was starving and thought of a submarine or a large bag of chips or a pizza, so after undressing he opened the fridge to poke around.

SNAP!

Dwayne froze. The sound had come from the front door, as if someone were tampering with the mail slot. He quietly closed the fridge and sneaked into the living area. He couldn't believe he was going to be killed in his own home, mutilated beyond recognition. He looked closer and saw a buff envelope on the tile inside the door.

Moving backward into the kitchen, he scuttled over to the breaker box and slammed the handle, plunging the house into darkness.

Phone.

"What?" he whispered. "What?"

"The lights went out."

"Quiet, woman, or you'll bring them down on us in a mass charge." The battle of Rorke's Drift flashed before his eyes.

"Who?"

"There's someone out there."

"I'm looking out the front window right now and there's nobody out there."

"Are you sure?"

"Not a soul."

"Listen to me carefully," Dwayne said. "Hang up the phone and dial 9–1. If you hear me scream, dial the last number and tell the police if they're not here in thirty seconds they'll have my corpse on their hands."

Dwayne leopard-crawled to the door, his big belly scrunching up the area rug until he could barely see over the bulge. He snatched up the envelope, letting out a gust of breath when it failed to explode. On his feet, he peered through the peephole. Nothing. He went back to the kitchen, threw the breaker handle and the place blazed with light.

The envelope had no name or address. He took a knife from the drawer — he would have to hide a few knives and cleavers in accessible spots around the place from now on — and slit open the flap. Inside was a wad of money and a piece of paper that fluttered to the floor. Dwayne picked it up and read: The Bashi-Bazouks.

A great warmth came over him that led directly to a good night's sleep, and he spent the next two days working hard on his act, aglow with the expression of the comics' fraternity.

Then along came Friday and Dwayne was finally off to work, impressing even himself with his energy. His mother had been worried, justifiably, but with one phone call Dwayne had secured an interview. And if that went according to plan he would be thrust onto the job immediately.

Despite his aversion, if not outright psychotic reaction, to work, Dwayne was excited. Most of the comics at The Laugh Chance held day jobs and all of them drew on the experience as a wellspring of new material. He hummed to himself as he set off up Seaton Street. Fifteen minutes later he was reporting for the interview, and twenty minutes after that he was on duty.

Dwayne stood on the corner in the noodle suit.

He couldn't see much through the mesh eye slit and the top was bending in the wind, hurting his neck. He wondered where the owner of the new pasta restaurant had found the thing. Flat down the front and back, the bright yellow outfit had serrated crinkles down each side and was topped with a diagonal slash. Already several passersby had mistaken Dwayne for a french fry.

Dwayne raised one pasta appendage. He couldn't see his watch but knew it must be time for lunch. His neck hurt and his feet were rubbed raw by the yellow gumboots. He was freezing inside the costume, which didn't allow room for a coat, so he turned his back on the gawkers on Jarvis Street and made his way back to the restaurant.

The top of the noodle jammed in the doorway and it took the lone customer and the owner to wrench Dwayne free. He struggled with the headpiece, threw it back and took a seat at the counter.

"What's wrong? Why you back here so soon?" The owner, King Canelli, was an excitable man with dark, earnest features. He was determined to keep his new employee, as he had been going through three or four noodle guys a week since he opened. This Dwayne was perfect. The right size for the suit, an actor, absolutely perfect.

"People think I'm a french fry," Dwayne said. "Don't you have a suit that looks like pasta? Fusili, maybe, or rotini?"

"The suit is good," Canelli said. "Is not the suit, is your acting."

"Pardon me?"

"I see you on the corner, too stiff. No flopping around, no nothing. You got to look like pasta, you know, wiggle and jiggle and stuff."

"I'm *al dente*," Dwayne said. "I don't jiggle."

"Get up and try."

"No."

"Is what advertising is all about — hitting people over the heads with it."

"Advertising is about new ideas," Dwayne said. "There was a Nationalist holdout in the Spanish Civil War that was being supplied by air. To drop medical supplies and other delicates, the air force strapped the equipment to turkeys and shoved them out of the planes. The birds went straight down but their frantic flapping cushioned the fall just the right amount. *That* is thinking."

Canelli stared at him. "What are you talking — serve pasta with turkey?"

"Use original ideas."

"Noodle suit is my idea."

"French fry suit."

"Try it one more time."

"I think not."

"Okay, I make you a deal. You stay on the job and you don't have to jiggle. Walk up and down the street but you don't have to jiggle. Unless it happens by accident, maybe you step off the curb and you jiggle all by yourself but not on purpose."

Dwayne mulled it over. If a performer had to have a day job it was important that it be as mindless as possible. At least this was connected to show business. And the non-jiggling clause was a bonus. "I must have an advance," Dwayne said. "I can't survive on good will."

"Sure, sure." Canelli pulled a twenty from his wallet. "I take it out of your first paycheck."

Dwayne tucked the bill away and refastened the lid of the suit. "No jiggling." He ducked out the door.

Two hours later he was ready to drop, from the boredom if nothing else. He decided to see what was up farther east on Dundas so crossed the street to avoid the punks at the Dundas/Sherbourne idiot fest. Two blocks farther and he was done for. He had to sit down but wouldn't dare to out where he'd be in full view of the drug dealers on the corner. The fatigue he felt was scarcely credible. The wrestling moves he pantomimed every morning didn't seem to be helping his wind. It was all the cigarette smoke down at the Laugh Chance, of that he was certain. They were trying to ban smoking in Toronto and Dwayne thought even that was too lenient. Before his mother quit, Dwayne had told her that smokers should be dealt with in the manner of King Yohannes of Abyssinia in the Chinese Gordon days: cut off the lips of anyone found with a cigarette. It made her cry, and she exacted revenge by boring a hole in his door and blowing through the smoke from a package of unfiltered Camels. Dwayne was dizzy for two days.

Suddenly he remembered the twenty-dollar advance in his pocket and sighed. That would take care of his fluid-replacement needs. He turned and found himself looking at the sign for The Workbench Tavern.

Katlyn was inside. Dwayne had been reasonably successful at keeping her on the back burner in his mind the past few days, but he knew it couldn't last. He lacked the ability to retain an idea in diluted form. Once something was allowed in it grew on its own to enormous proportions. And then he had to deal with it. Except, of course, for his relationship with his mother and his father and anything else that took any effort.

His father. Monigan would be in the bar, Dwayne was sure of it. He shouldn't even be considering this. He should march down the street and avoid it altogether. He sidled up to a window but couldn't see in. His reflection, however, gave him one of his brilliant notions. No one could possibly recognize him in the noodle suit. He would calmly enter, rehydrate himself and safely study his father and the new angel in his life. He muttered to himself, trying various voices, settling on a baritone, while gathering no more than cursory glances from passersby in more serious discussions with themselves.

Monigan was at his usual spot at the bar. It hadn't been a very good week for him. Monday he took Katlyn's laundry over to the coin-op down the street, the favor good for a couple free drafts. He threw his tuxedo in with her dark clothes and the thing finally reached the end of its life, coming apart in his hands as he was transferring the load to the dryer.

The rest of the week had been similarly disjointed, as if an evil wind, a devilish spirit, had fastened upon him. Katlyn had found him two leads in the wedding announcements for tomorrow, but now he had nothing to wear.

It all meant there was a change coming, Monigan knew that much. No period in his life had ever flowed smoothly into the next. Every change was marked by catastrophe, great destruction ripping through to leave him in new circumstances. And yes, the loss of a suit of clothes can be catastrophic.

"I can't handle all this by myself," Katlyn said. She was slinging draft glasses and pitchers down the bar, where patrons could pass them back to the people at the tables. She looked at the press of bodies and pushed back her hair. It wouldn't last long, another twenty minutes at the most and people would start to go home, leaving the place to the regulars. "I'm going to hire another part-time waiter."

"Get your eye off me," Monigan said.

Abruptly the noise level dropped off the scale. Katlyn stopped serving and Monigan reluctantly pivoted on his stool. They stared at the enormous cartoon.

So done in was Dwayne that he lacked the strength to take off the suit, even if he hadn't been using it as a disguise. After the glare of the outdoors the figures he could see through the mesh eye slit were no more than blobs. He bumped into the bar and, after some fumbling, selected a stool and sat down. He couldn't see and his ears were ringing and he felt very bad indeed.

He was worried. This was no plan, no cagey undercover operation. He had to get the headpiece off or die but there was Katlyn, looking right at him. His pupils were starting to dilate, adjusting to the new light conditions. He looked into her eyes.

"Can I help you?" Katlyn asked. "Bit of a hurry, here."

"Water," Dwayne said, the dryness of his throat making the baritone rattle.

"When did french fries start hanging around bars?" Monigan asked.

Dwayne turned, the top of the noodle suit scraping a Grey Cup pennant on the bar's overhang. Dwayne still couldn't see very well but there was no mistaking the brutal physiognomy. He looked closely, evaluating, and felt an unwelcome surge of emotion. "I'm not a french fry, sir," He coughed and dropped his voice. "I'm pasta."

Katlyn saved the moment by dropping the glass of water in front of Dwayne. He looked up. Katlyn was making no effort to attend to business and Monigan wasn't about to take his eyes off him. Dwayne looked at the glass on the bar. "Do you have a straw?"

"Sorry," Katlyn said. "You'll have to take the head off that thing, I guess."

Dwayne thought yearningly of the door then tried to delay things by watching the pool table. Bill was playing by himself, potting balls and releasing them with whatever trick he used on the mechanism. Dwayne's tissues ached for the water.

"You play pool?" Monigan could use a mark.

"A ridiculous game," Dwayne said. "It's such a joy to see professionals on TV wearing tuxedos. Especially considering their miserable origins."

Dwayne froze, wondering if he had blown his cover. His cutting remarks had always placed him in uncomfortable positions with his father.

"Katy," Monigan said in measured tones. "You hold on, you stand right there and don't come no closer."

"What are you up to?" she said.

With one great heave and a ripping of velcro, Monigan reefed the headpiece off the noodle suit. Some of the patrons, anticipating a brawl, gathered together in a ragged mob, trying to get bets down before the whole thing ended.

"Gah!" Dwayne said, then greedily downed the glass of water.

"Dwayne," Katlyn said flatly.

The father and the son looked at each other. "So this is what you've come to," they said at the same time.

Monigan turned to Katlyn. "There you have it," he said. "Katy, you been bugging my ass over a year to tell you about my family. Well, here's half of it. This is my bouncing baby boy — a fucking french fry."

"Pasta," Dwayne said.

"Okay, okay," Monigan said. "I ain't gonna kill you in here." He grabbed his coat off the back of the stool.

"Monigan . . ." Katlyn began.

"I know you too good, Katy. You wouldn't even chuck Nazis outta here, so I'm gonna do you both a favor. Talk, talk, talk your heads off. When you're done I don't wanna see any more of you." He pointed at his son. "And maybe after listening to him, Katy, you won't be so interested in the part of me I left behind."

"You're acting like a child," Katlyn said. "Sit down."

One of his coat sleeves had been turned inside out and it took Monigan a good deal of ludicrous struggling to set it right. "Bill, come on!" he yelled. "Let's get outta here, go over to the Canada Tavern, drink with normal people."

"I think I'll stay," Bill said. "I'm comfortable right now so I think I'll stay and play some pool."

Seething, Monigan banged open the door, still trying to force his arm down the sleeve.

Dwayne sat very still, shocked and feeling foolish, looking down at his hands, unable to make eye-contact with Katlyn.

"Have some more water," she said. "Listen, there's no need to be embarrassed. *He's* the one who was out of line. Your father

and I are good friends but . . . well, I don't take to heart everything he says."

Dwayne peeked up hopefully.

Katlyn smiled. "You might want to take off the costume."

Dwayne carefully stripped off the noodle suit, folded it and
pushed it down between the bar and the rail. "A job," he said. "Just
to gather material for my act."

"Of course," Katlyn said. "Good idea."

That's about all it took to brighten our boy up and his grin of
relief touched Katlyn's heart. He was an odd-looking man and from
what she had seen in their two brief meetings, no less strangely
behaved, but there was warmth inside, she felt it. Katlyn had
always allied herself with the world's rejects, partly through mistaking vulnerability for warmth, but the two characteristics could
coexist. Dwayne was proof of that.

Now that he was thinking more clearly Dwayne wanted to flee,
mortified at his asinine plan. He should never have accepted the
noodle job. Dwayne's place wasn't among working people. He harbored too much fear and anger and resentment to be anything but
a comic. But he couldn't just leave and put the place behind him.
Not with Katlyn there.

For the next three hours Katlyn tried to juggle her job with getting to know Dwayne. It was one of the benefits of bartending,
allowing a controlled stream of conversation, breaking off by pour-
ing beer, returning when she had something to say.

And she needed the flexibility, as she had several shifts of emotion talking to Dwayne. He seemed to have no foundation. Plainly
he was widely read, but the volumes of information at his dispos-
al had never come together into a basic philosophy. She found that
trying to get at the core of what Dwayne thought and felt was like
operating a particle accelerator: larger and larger collisions were
needed for smaller and smaller bits of information. But he made
her laugh, he did that. And he made her feel good about herself,
and he was attractive in his own way — okay, in a skewed way —

and the fact that he was Monigan's son amplified her emotions, and . . . and she didn't know what to think, what was happening.

Monigan was a good man, had certainly been good to her, taking her interests to heart and making her feel part of his life, things with which she had little experience. She had learned a lot about people from managing the bar and was no longer afraid of personal interaction. But it had been a lonely experience, hoeing the row by herself.

Dwayne brought with him butterflies she was glad to feel. Maybe it was good that she had no chance to talk to him much. It gained her time to think, if nothing else. What they would say if they were ever alone together, she didn't know. But somehow it was all right.

2100 hours. Dwayne should have had the noodle suit back four hours ago, but he was feeling too good to move. He kicked at the costume under his feet. Then it dawned on him in a rush that so taken was he with watching Katlyn at work and talking to her in the snippets of time available, that he had allowed his internal security system to be breached. He looked around the room. Any one of these people would do him in without a second thought. He had seen some of them on the street from time to time, slothful, indigent types with scarred faces and flattened snouts. Anxiety had a good firm bite on him.

But again Katlyn smiled shyly at him and Dwayne reached for his water. 2112 hours. Fine.

SEVEN

Monigan spent the evening at the Canada Tavern, feeling sorry for himself while describing in detail the shortcomings of his wife and son to a revolving set of men with larger livers than attention spans.

He was right when he said that at least the wedding itself had been good. And he had tried to make it work. Monigan's trouble was that he believed every disagreement had to lead to a winner and loser. He was able to admit he was wrong but was unable to compromise. Meeting in the middle over anything indicated the weakness of both parties. At first there had been no disagreements, or none that Monigan hadn't bulled through. But as time went on, his wife had used every minor scrape to drive home her opinion of her husband's inadequacy. It turned ugly when Monigan couldn't find work. A man with his overweening pride felt the shame of unemployment enough on his own. His wife had added to the anguish every waking hour.

The house hadn't helped. His wife inherited it when her father died and it never did fit well around Monigan's ears. It was her house, never theirs. It was her guilt at bringing nothing to the marriage that led her to shake the house in Monigan's face, helping to sink the relationship. Put simply, the two of them wanted different things. Her security was in her house and their bank account. Monigan's security was in his wits and his balls. Had the house been in his name, Monigan would have sold it. The choice between long-term security and immediate gratification was no choice at all. The chance to have a fistful of money for once, able to treat some of the neighborhood folks to the first good time they'd had in years, maybe take a plane trip to see the old family farm near Tisdale — anything other than rotting away in a house.

His wife was scared. Of her son, of Monigan, of the world. But then that was one of the things he'd fallen for. He hadn't had much opportunity to play the knight in shining armor in his life, and it had been nice to do some rescuing for a change. She was scared and needed him, needed looking after, something Monigan had done imperfectly for twenty-one years until he didn't have it in him anymore. He was in his natural element now, taking care of Katlyn and an ugly dog. It was not the first time a person has arrived late to the appreciation of their own limitations.

He stopped thinking of everything but ordering another beer. They had just announced last call and he couldn't go back to The Workbench in case Dwayne was still there. As Monigan surveyed the room, trying to find someone who might have something left from his check, Frodo came through the door in a rush, as if blown inside by an unkind gale. Monigan waved him over.

"Don't have much time," the little bookie said.

"Slow down," Monigan said. "Long as you got time to get into that wallet."

"Nothing to worry about inside there. That's what I'm here for. Got a job for you if you want."

"A job," Monigan said. "Right, I'll think about it. Now get me a beer."

"Be serious," Frodo said. "I need help, is all. With one of the guys. A collection thing. I tried yesterday and couldn't get anywhere with him."

Monigan sneered. "What the hell you coming to me for? That ain't my line of things. I don't mind knocking around a bit but leg-breaking's outta my league."

"There's three hundred bucks in it for you," Frodo said.

"Okay."

Frodo blinked at the turn of events, not sure where it left him.

"Who's the guy?"

"The one I told you about last week. You know, runs the comedy club, the place I saw your son at. I met him about six times already and he's always putting me off. Something about cracking up his car this time, having to wait for the insurance. You don't know what a pain this job can be."

"You weren't drafted into it," Monigan said. "Tired of people bitching about the slings they put their own asses into."

"It was the family business," Frodo shrugged.

"You make it sound like it's a funeral parlor."

Frodo was happy. Finally he had someone to help him out. He knew his size and lack of constitution were severe drawbacks in his line of work, but with Monigan along Frodo might actually walk away with what was rightfully his. He chuckled and happily paid for the fresh pitcher of beer.

For his part, Monigan was intrigued. He had never done that type of work before and was looking forward to the experience. Three hundred bucks worth of experience. Furthermore, it was the comedy club at which his son worked. Monigan had known all along that if he kept putting it off the situation would resolve itself. Now he had a chance to watch his son perform and make a buck while he was at it. Monigan took pleasure in small slivers of luck. He needed nothing big to make him feel good.

He wondered what was happening to him. For the past four years he had worked hard at not running into Dwayne. He assumed it was the drink making him think the way he was.

"Better get me a short rye, too," Monigan said to Frodo. "Fuck a duck, I'm going nuts."

It took a while for Monigan to get his eye open. He first had to hold a handful of snow against it and wait for the meltwater to sluice away the dried and frozen blood. He blinked and was rewarded with a webbed view of an alley. He lay still, breathing in torn gasps, sore everywhere. He pushed himself to his knees, the resultant vertigo causing him to heave violently in the slush. Nothing came out but bile. He recognized the Chinese restaurant at the end of the alley and across the street. He had left The Workbench and gone straight to the Canada Tavern, but from that point on he couldn't recall a thing.

Vaguely, tortured images pricked his mind, wedging themselves into the gaps between the blackness. Frodo, he had been there. He'd offered him a job. Monigan would have to track him down and find out what that was all about. Dwayne had been there too, as far as he could remember. Trying to get him to come see his comedy show. Dim recollection of a fight. His eye was almost closed, but it was only the wonky one. He checked out his hands, which bore no more than the usual scratches and scrapes, so it meant he hadn't even gotten in a lick of his own. His coat was gone, but he didn't dwell on that. Price you pay for passing out. He lurched to his feet and felt a frigid blast pass between his legs. He'd pissed himself. He made it to the end of the alley. Over there was the bus station, so he was able to orient himself. It would be a long walk home, and he didn't bother checking for money. As he stood there wondering what to do, a cruiser pulled to the curb, and a female cop got out of the passenger side.

"You're going to freeze to death like that," she said.

The driver poked his head over the top of the car.

"Doyle." Monigan had trouble speaking. His mouth was sore. "When did you get the trim for a partner?"

"What happened to you?" Doyle came around to the sidewalk.

"Stopped a rape," Monigan said. "There was only four of them."

Doyle looked him over and opened the rear door of the cruiser.

"What am I charged with?"

"Get in."

Monigan flopped down on the back seat after cracking his head on the door frame, and Doyle pulled out into the congested flow of traffic. Saturday afternoons drew all the brainless suburbanites downtown to jam the Eaton Centre, as if there were a shortage of malls in their own neighborhoods. Doyle swore, cut off a Volvo and had to stop a full block away from Yonge Street.

"I could walk faster than this," Monigan said.

"Shut it."

"I could *swim* faster than this. Once we're outta this mess let me off at Jarvis."

Doyle pulled over past the corner in front of King Canelli's Pasta Shop. His partner opened the rear door.

"Gimme a cigarette," Monigan said, refusing to budge.

Doyle offered his pack across the seat, over the top of the lowered plexiglass shield. Monigan dug three from the deck and slid out onto the sidewalk, balancing himself with one hand on the car while Doyle's partner impatiently tapped her hand on her leg.

"Get off the street and inside," she said.

Monigan watched the car pull away. Saturday, almost noon. By all rights Monigan should be at a wedding. He bummed a light off a passerby and pulled deeply. Menthols. Jesus.

Inside the noodle shop King Canelli tried mentally to force him away from the front of the restaurant. He had known Monigan for years and had never had one minute of peace around him. The noodle shop was empty, not an unusual situation. Canelli had hoped for more business from the government building across the street but that was closed now. Once the promotional menus were ready he'd go around the neighborhood and spread them around. And he'd have to talk to the cops, as he had a strong feeling his noodle suit was gone for good. The day before he had phoned the Feller residence when his new employee failed to show up after his shift, but all he got was a blast from Dwayne's mother. Plus, he was out the twenty-buck advance.

Canelli could see out, but from the sidewalk the plate glass acted as a mirror, so Monigan stepped up to it and poked and pulled at his eye, trying to clean it up. Canelli grimaced and backed away to the corner of the room. Monigan licked his fingers and ran them through his hair, then was gone.

The King looked around the empty restaurant and went to get the mop and pail. The floor was spotless but he had to do something.

Monigan needed breakfast but the thought of food was revolting. A red-eye is what he could use, and though it wasn't quite opening time Katlyn would let him in. He decided to be extra nice to her that day, Saturday, his peaceful day. He set off, walking a little taller now that he had a plan.

If Monigan had known what lay in store for him at The Workbench he would gladly have returned to the alley and bunked down for good.

Katlyn and Dwayne were behind the bar, going over the float. Katlyn was doing her best to define Dwayne's duties as the new employee, but the comic was so certain of his ability to master the entire world that he brushed off her every attempt as unnecessary dross. Dwayne had learned a great deal from his voracious reading, but possibly it was the wrong knowledge. He was eager to learn, just not from people.

The night before, without any clear intention, Dwayne had found himself alone at the bar an hour past closing time. Katlyn lightly tripped around the place, performing the nightly rituals, thankfully free of the usual mob who passively refused to leave. When she was done she sat on a stool inside the horseshoe and smiled at Dwayne. After taking refuge in talk about the January weather and safely recapping the more bizarre events of the evening, they found themselves in conversation. For both this was odd, on par with going on an afternoon talk show and trumpeting their misery in front of a million TV viewers eager for bad news. But by far the strangest aspect of their conversation was that it didn't *feel* odd.

"It's always been tough to think about the prairies," Katlyn said, responding to a brief tirade of Dwayne's against the region that had produced his father. "Don't get me wrong — most of the memories are good."

"Then why the long face?" Dwayne asked.

"It's where my mother died."

"Sorry for prying."

"Not at all. It was a number of years ago. My father had already left, so it was just me and Mum. I didn't have many friends so we hung around together a lot. Funny, but looking back on it I realize we never really talked about anything, never shared, we simply were there. It was nice."

Dwayne reached for his thirtieth glass of water and sipped it quietly.

"I was in school when it happened," Katlyn said. "They used to tease me about . . . about the way I looked. The principal came to the door and talked to the teacher, and she called my name. The kids started teasing me, but as I got close to the door they stopped and wouldn't even look at me. Somehow they knew, and I knew, that it was bad.

"At the hospital they wouldn't let me see her, and I remember the doctor and a nurse fighting over it. Probably best they wouldn't let me in."

"I'm sorry," Dwayne whispered. He wanted to take her in his arms.

Katlyn raised her face. "It was a number of years ago."

Dwayne was speechless. All stories of death troubled him, but he was beset with astonishment that a woman would relate such a personal experience to him. It had never happened before. People simply didn't confide in him, and frankly he was at a loss for a response. He looked deep into her eyes and took a breath. Then Dwayne began to speak of many things.

When he had talked himself out he didn't want to go. He couldn't go. The rancid old dump had become the site of his conversion, his turnaround. And, fortunately, he didn't have to leave for long. After some self-conscious skirting of the subject, Katlyn offered him a job.

Dwayne could not fall asleep that night, and when the next

morning he reported for duty, he was no more than mildly upset when Monigan came crashing through the door in a shaft of dazzling backlight.

"Jesus H. Christ in a sandbox!" Monigan couldn't believe what he was seeing.

The side door was open, releasing noxious plumes of smoke and particulate matter. The jukebox was on, driving tenpenny nails into Monigan's skull, so he yanked the plug and crept closer for a better look. He pulled at his eye, his wonky one, though not too happy about the information the good one was giving him either.

"What happened now?" Katlyn asked.

"What are you doing back there?" Monigan said.

"You got into a fight."

"What's the french fry doing behind the bar?"

"Or did you have an accident?"

"You want me to throw him outta here for you?"

"Why don't you take care of yourself?"

"Ain't you working for King Canelli, Frenchie?"

"What business is it of yours?" Dwayne said.

"Why do you have to stick your face in here on my peaceful day?"

"Do you want a beer?" Katlyn asked.

"What are you doing in here before opening time?"

"What happened?" Katlyn asked again.

"Answer my question."

"You want tomato juice with the draft?"

"I want answers! Answers!" Monigan's head was splitting, as much from the confusion as from the hangover. He sat at the bar and gulped greedily at the draft.

"Dwayne will be working a couple of shifts a week," Katlyn said, tipping two ounces of tomato juice into Monigan's glass.

Dwayne swabbed the spillage with a rag.

"Get away from me," Monigan said.

"A clean bar is a happy bar," Dwayne said.

This was the most unnerving thing Monigan had had to deal with in some time, and it was weighing heavily on his brain.

"You can't work here."

"Sure I can. With my memory and organizational skills, I'll master the job in a single shift."

Monigan was afraid this was part of some karmic retribution. He had wrecked his son's home, and now the tables were turned. Additional indignity was added when Monigan admitted to himself that he had been creeping up to re-establishing contact with his son. Now it was taken out of his hands. Had he been able to backdoor the situation, he could have patted himself on the back, but now he'd never get any credit for his maturity and wisdom.

"You sure you're okay?" Katlyn asked.

"Katy, I was gonna tell you that I changed my mind. Maybe a couple shifts a week would be good for me. I'm bored, you were right. Gimme some work, couple shifts, you know. You said it. You said it yourself."

"Let's hold off till that eye heals up."

"You think a shiner's gonna stop me? I could lose both eyes right out my skull and still keep up with any man alive."

"I've already filled the position."

"There's a few things in a man's life that you shouldn't mess with and one of them's the place where he drinks. I run you outta the house four years ago, kid, and I can run you outta here."

"You were the one who ran," Dwayne said. "And judging by your lifestyle, it was a wise maneuver. You're sitting tall in the saddle, sir — I'm proud to call you Dad."

Monigan lunged but bashed into the bar and slid to the floor. "What's happening?" he cried. "Too much of everything! Katy, if you gotta brain in your head, you'll get rid of him now. By tomorrow you'll be in a rubber room or they'll be cutting you down from a rafter."

"Get up," Katlyn said softly. "Get up and sit down. If I can live with my decision, so can you."

Monigan managed to right himself and stood shaking his head in complete, absolute, utter disgust.

"Sit down," Katlyn said again.

Monigan took a stool and sulked while Dwayne and Katlyn went back to the float money.

"So you're a working man," Monigan said to his son. "Big bartender. Let's see you mix me up a Margarita."

Katlyn tried unsuccessfully to hide a grin, giggling as Dwayne swung into action. Inside thirty seconds he had the drink on the bar.

Monigan sipped. Perfect. Fuck.

EIGHT

It was Tuesday so Dwayne's suspension from The Laugh Chance was up. It was a new man who was busy preparing for the evening, a man with a job, the backing of his peers and a woman in his life. Well, if not exactly in his life then at least around the periphery. He carefully checked his shirt, nodding with satisfaction at its spotless condition. His wool trousers looked almost new after their night being pressed in plastic beneath his futon mattress, and Katlyn had lent him a tube of gel that accounted for his dramatic thrust-back hair. He felt good.

Dwayne thought of Shaka Zulu's hordes putting to rout their Ngoni enemies. The Mfecane — the crushing!

He walked down to Queen Street to avoid King Canelli's Pasta Shop. In the past he had considered it an unlucky route but felt it was time to hew to a mechanistic approach to life that allowed no room for luck or fate.

Saturday Dwayne had spent learning the craft of bartending, no great accomplishment considering the way business was conducted at The Workbench. Eight hours serving future landholders in a potter's field. It was neither Dwayne's crowd nor his choice of conversation, but he made it through and was feeling better for it. Katlyn had helped. She had a connection with the people who came into the place that Dwayne could in no way begin to explain. Dwayne hoped the connection extended to him. He had never dated, and the mere consideration of it could drive him to the mattress with anxiety. When he had first seen Reba

Stiles at the club he had been unable to think of new material for a week.

But Saturday night had been rough for Dwayne and Katlyn. Their conversation of the night before had been magic. Neither of them had ever expressed themselves to anyone on a level deeper than about the bottom of their necks, so they both felt inadequate. Rather than building on the foundation that was already in place, they reacted poorly to the new dynamic formed when Dwayne became an employee. There was little the two of them said or explained beyond work-oriented enquiries and instructions. Katlyn was as new to the awkward hurdles at the beginning of a relationship as Dwayne and had been unable to crack his defenses.

And Dwayne had formidable defenses.

Crossing Jarvis, he stepped in a large pile of slush, glad to be wearing the yellow gumboots from the noodle suit. He would have to find some way to return the costume. For now it was jammed out of the way behind the furnace in the basement of the bar. He had no intention of returning the twenty-dollar advance; he considered that a donation from a prosperous merchant to the arts.

And now Tuesday was finally here. Dwayne was ready for the crushing. It had warmed up the past three days, but Dwayne was feeling too good to let it bother him. He took his time getting to the club, tripping along, kicking rocks and bits of trash, bending to investigate objects released from the melting snow, identifying species of birds and shrubs, unintentionally scaring children, and all the while lighting candles to Katlyn. He smiled at the world and let his heart rise up into the rarefied air where only the eagles fly.

At Dwayne's destination things were starting to heat up. Sturgis checked his appointment book to ensure he had cancelled all non-essential meetings for the next day. At two in the afternoon he was to meet with his case officer at Revenue Canada. He had to think of a way to impress the woman with his commitment to paying his back taxes while avoiding doing so. He looked at the computer printout and winced at the enormous total of fines and penalties, which were far in excess of the original debt.

He put a hand to his chest and smoothed down the tape that was rolling up at the end and around the edges, hoping he could soon peel it off and still cursing the streetcar that had popped up in front of his Jag. He considered public transport a waste of space and money. If people couldn't afford a car then they should walk. He didn't care if they commuted forty miles on foot with a lunch and their heart pills in a bundle on a stick.

The door opened and the bartender stuck his head in. "Didn't mean to startle you."

"I wasn't startled," Sturgis said. "Startled of what?"

"Okay, you just look jumpy, that's all."

"Why would I be jumpy?"

"Never mind." The staff disliked any conversation with their boss that went past a sentence. "There's a man out here to see you."

"Who is he?"

"Wouldn't give me a name."

"What does he look like?"

The bartender raised his eyebrows.

"Get rid of him."

"And he has a dog."

"Get rid of him, I said. I'm sick to death of people busting in on me in my own club."

Sturgis had no further chance to work himself into a lather; the man and his mutt shoved their way into his office.

This was new to Monigan. He had tried a number of things in his life, many of them on the shady side of the law, shady only in a technical sense, for he wrote his own code, one that had nothing to do with statutes concocted by people in elected office. However, this line of work was new to him. But he didn't mind doing a favor for Frodo. Three hundred dollars worth.

He strolled around the office, poking and prodding at the video cassettes, pulling a calendar from the wall and tossing it aside. His dog stayed at the door, its eyes glued to its master. Sturgis tried to keep him in full view but with a rapid turn of his wrist Monigan tipped the owner out of his chair. Sturgis shrieked as his ribs hit the edge of the desk.

"Careful of the ribs," he gasped, cradling his chest in his arms. "I broke them in an accident."

"Know the feeling," Monigan said. "And you wanna talk to me, don't use that tone."

"You're trespassing. I can have the police here in two minutes."

"Call the ambulance the same time." Monigan pushed the phone over and pulled Sturgis back up into his chair.

"What do you want?"

"The eight grand you owe the book," Monigan said. "Just gimme the eight and I'm outta here. Otherwise, who knows what happens. Never know when it's coming. Bowling, maybe, the old lady comes back with a couple soda pops and finds you with no fingers left, how you gonna bowl? In the market, some broad from Rosedale picking through the lettuce, finds your stupid head in there, she faints, big fucking riot in the market 'cause a guy's head's in the vegetables. Think I won't do it? I'll do it. Maybe ice fishing, find you in the spring at the bottom with a hundred-horse Evinrude tied to your ass, course you wouldn't have a motor ice fishing but you know what I mean."

"I don't have it right now," Sturgis said. "But it's coming. Ask anyone — I totalled my Jag, and as soon as the insurance comes through I'll call your boss and settle up. You have to believe me. The club is the only income I have, and if I'm not here to run it the eight grand never shows up."

"There's something wrong with that logic, I think."

"It won't be more than a week. Two weeks, the most, they'll pay up."

"Lay on the floor," Monigan said.

"What?"

"On the floor!"

Sturgis eased himself into a sitting position then lay on his back. Monigan took the owner's wolf-collar coat from the hook on the back of the door.

"This is the deal," he said. "I'm going out into your club, gonna sit there, have a few drinks. You stay in here for twenty minutes. That way I know if you got the self-control. If you got the self-control to stay in here twenty minutes, then I know you got it not to piss the insurance money away when you get it, got it?"

Sturgis nodded, figuring this was easy enough. It looked as if Monigan were too stupid to do a proper job.

"This is to help with the self-control." Monigan wedged the coat's sleeve into Sturgis' mouth. One large paw swiped the top of the filing cabinet clear and he grunted as he carefully lowered it onto the owner's chest.

Sturgis screamed into the sleeve and the veins in his neck and forehead bulged. Involuntarily, his arms heaved at the filing cabinet, but there was no moving it.

"What you do is like in wrestling," Monigan said. "After twenty minutes you force one arm across your chest between you and the cabinet, then you roll out from under. I'll be checking, so twenty minutes you wait, see if you got the self-control." He patted the top of the cabinet and avoided Sturgis's flailing legs as he left the office.

The room was filling rapidly and Monigan joined the crowd, selecting a table against the far wall. A waitress arrived and he ordered a double cognac, making three things clear: First, his tab was on the owner; Second, Sturgis did not want to be disturbed; Third, the dog stays. The waitress made no fuss. The look in his eyes — especially the wonky one — brooked no argument, and Sturgis himself did nothing to elicit anything like the desire to make independent judgment calls. Let him figure it out.

At the back of the room Harold Arens returned with two drafts from the bar. He gave one to Reba and sat there brooding over the stagnation of his career.

Reba Stiles was hoping for a good set. She had been hot lately.

She thanked Harold for the beer and then paced at the back, unsure if women could gird their loins but feeling she was doing a fair imitation.

Outside, the marquee and the sidewalk sandwich board advertised SHOWCASE NIGHT. The amateurs who showed up were out of a spot. One night a week was all they had, and here it was kicked out from under them. They started to drift off, not wanting to pay the ticket price to get into their own club and fully aware Sturgis did not comp tickets for castrati. He had told them as much on many occasions, that their balls were cut off when they walked through the door, and they didn't get them back until they were regular house comics. And now another showcase night, when the best club comics had a chance to strut their stuff, denying the amateurs stage time. Sulking and swearing, they wandered off to pool their money for a few beers someplace where they could bitch.

So lost in reverie was Dwayne that he didn't see the SHOWCASE NIGHT sign. Not that it mattered, for he was a regular comic now. Climbing the stairs, he could already smell the cigarette smoke in the club, the faintly uremic tang that usually made him gag on arrival. In comparison to the smell in The Workbench, however, which was of toxic waste proportions, this was pure oxygen, so he did nothing more than sneeze and continue his ascent.

Dwayne ordered a cranberry and Coke and leaned against the bar, surveying the room, critically noting that none of the comics were wearing their Bashi-Bazouks shirts. He casually approached the list on the wall and saw right off there were no amateurs in the lineup. Then he put a finger to the list, running it up and down. No Dwayne.

"Where is that tyrant?" he bellowed at the table of comics. "I'll flush him from his lair and . . ."

"Sit down," Harold said. "Just sit."

Dwayne brushed past a comic and whomped down beside Harold, squirting Reba's purse out from under him like a grape seed.

"Sturgis told us yesterday at the meeting," Harold began.

"What meeting?"

"Oh . . . just an impromptu thing. We happened to be around."
Dwayne pushed an ashtray farther from him.

"There's a scout in the audience tonight."

"A scout."

"He's from the Just for Laughs festival in Montreal. Sturgis
replaced amateur night with a showcase so the scout can see some
of the regulars."

"I did twenty minutes just ten days ago," Dwayne said.

"Listen to me." It always fell on Harold to act as the bridge
between Sturgis and the comics, and that was another role he was
tiring of. "You have some good stuff, but we've talked about this
before. Don't you think you're a little harsh on the audience?"

"I wouldn't have to be if they'd respond properly."

"It's not their fault," Harold said. "You have to work with what
you've got."

"Are you saying that all audiences are equal?"

"No, but it's never *all* their fault."

Dwayne felt betrayed. His best friend was turning on him. Comics
were all the same; the second anyone with originality threatened
them they lashed out. Dwayne wished he had the money to start his
own club, then he could ban whomever he wanted. That would be
perfect for him: Dwayne Feller, Club Owner, an alabaster pedestal
from atop which he would dispense justice and Solomonic wisdom.
He tried to calm down. He could feel the heat rising inside and knew
it boded ill. Usually he had to be on stage to have this reaction but
the ugly turn of events and his father and Katlyn and everything else
were coalescing and acting in concert to drive him out of his mind.
There was some sort of conspiracy in place, he knew it.

"What happened to my purse?" Reba had returned. She bent
and began stuffing articles back into her bag. "God, Dwayne —
have some respect."

"Does anyone show me respect? I'm not even allowed to audition for the festival."

"It's not our place to explain," Harold said. "Talk to Sturgis."

"I will." Dwayne dashed off his drink and chewed the ice. "Sorry to break up your little *auto-da-fé*."

"I want my money back for that stupid T-shirt," Reba said. But Dwayne was out of range.

The intro music went up and the house lights went down and Harold headed for the stage.

Dwayne opened the door to the Star Chamber and there was Sturgis lying on the floor beneath the filing cabinet. He had one arm between his chest and a drawer but was still trapped on his side, facing the door. His coat was beside his head and from his mouth kittenish mewlings issued. Large as he was, Dwayne still had trouble with the cabinet, and by the time Sturgis was free he was as scraped and scarred as Holocene tundra. Arms around his chest, heaving for breath, he managed to make it to the chair, swivelling back and forth.

"I'm not on the show," Dwayne said.

Sturgis groaned. "I'm crushed half to death and all you can think about is the show."

"Do you want a glass of water?"

"No. Get out of here."

"Why am I not on the show?"

"I'm dying here."

"How did you get trapped?"

"Never mind — get out."

"I've been performing here three years and . . ."

"Performing shitty. You're gone."

"I know my regular spot fell a little short of perfect, but I've learned from my mistakes."

"You've never learned a thing."

"Simon J. Ortiz said, 'Human beings learn from the pressures that are exerted upon them. One's strength buckling under sometimes, that's the main learning process.'"

"If you're not out of here in ten seconds I'll have you shot."

Sturgis was coming around. He wiped the slobber off his chin and tried to regain an air of authority. "You're never to come in this club again. Why I've put up with you all this time is beyond me. You're banned, exiled, excommunicated."

"I don't see . . ."

"Get the fuck out!" Sturgis screamed.

It came at a quiet moment in Harold's act and was heard by the entire audience. When Dwayne left the office all heads pivoted to follow his passage, including that of his mother. And his father.

Monigan hadn't known Dwayne would be at the club that night. For that matter, he thought his son was supposed to be pulling a shift down at The Workbench. Monigan couldn't grasp the concept of someone having more than one job. That was just asking for a breakdown. He hoped his son had missed his shift, then maybe Katlyn would fire him. Monigan had been avoiding the place the past couple of days and he was getting bored not being able to sit at the bar for ten or twelve hours at a stretch. The other possibility, equally attractive, was that Katlyn had already let Dwayne go.

The mutt under the table got a wild look and rose to its feet. A low approximation of a growl drew Monigan's foot to its ass, squashing it back on the floor. It was the first sound Monigan had heard from the dog and he felt a surge of companionship with it. "You don't trust him neither, eh, boy?" Monigan said under his breath.

Dwayne continued out of the room and the crowd turned back to the stage, except for Monigan, who watched his son's progress, hoping Dwayne hadn't noticed him. The owner had thrown Dwayne out, and Monigan knew the last thing his son needed was to know it was done in front of his old man. Against his better instincts, Monigan felt sorry for the poor bugger.

The office door opened again and Sturgis wobbled out into the room. Monigan made to check his watch but remembered he had sold it at the Canada Tavern for a pitcher and a shot. Sturgis looked awful so Monigan decided to give him the benefit of the doubt and

call it twenty minutes. He had no reason to stay now, except that
the free cognac tasted good.

It was too pleasant outside to assuage Dwayne's misery. Usually
the temperature change at the passage of a warm front was too
gradual to be dramatic, but this one had barged into the area, leaving the snow heavy and sullen. The clouds were down low. Over to
the southwest a flickering array of strobe lights was all that delineated the CN Tower. Dwayne slopped along in the slush.

He had always wanted to be a comic. More precisely, he had
always felt it was his destiny to be a comic. He had wit, so that was
a start. And he felt his grasp of diverse subjects should throw open
the doors of the entertainment world. He was meant to amuse. His
physical appearance alone was a monument to comedy. He had no
idea what else to do with his life. Everything else was scrimshaw,
decorative carvings without substance.

He wandered down Queen Street. He was broke again. He
wished his mother hadn't found and pilfered the T-shirt money.
That was the last time. Tomorrow he'd change all his locks and bar
the window, maybe electrify the place. How would he explain this
latest disgrace to his mother? And Katlyn wasn't the type to be
impressed by a hired hand, he knew that much. It was another reason why he loved show business: it was a perfect lure for women,
a hand-tied fly cast into their midst. Now it was gone. He winced
at the thought of going through life on his own merits.

He cut along the path through the Moss Park apartments. On
reaching Shuter Street he looked up Seaton and saw a cab pulling
away from his house. His mother had witnessed his fall from grace
and was home already. He knew the virago had whipped herself
into an ecstasy of doom and would be waiting for him, so he
turned east on Shuter. He would walk until he died.

Back at the club Monigan had to admit the first two comics were
pretty funny, but then, he *was* on his ninth cognac. It had been a
long time since he had tasted a drink that good. He'd think about
stealing some.

On stage a comic was in deep. It was an educated crowd and his thinly disguised, stolen, stock act was being rejected. Switching tacks, he fastened on first one then another man in the house, playing to whomever he thought might be the festival scout. But he was dying. Then he saw Monigan, sitting there all disheveled and unkempt, looking like one of the fringe artsy types who thinks he's on the Left Bank in Paris waiting for Sylvia Beach to finish up at the bookstore. The comic asked Monigan his name.

Monigan knew he might be slurring his words, but he couldn't help responding. The comic was dredging up all the standard put-down lines he could think of, forgetting in his excitement that he could be talking to the festival scout, casting for a line he could use, hacking on Monigan's fumbled attempts to keep up to him. Monigan had lost all awareness of his surroundings. This was between him and the man with the mike. The crowd was laughing as much at the comic as with him, enjoying his discomfort, flicking their eyes between the two men as Monigan got a handle on the form and started tossing back as good as he was getting. Monigan was fully into it now, the snarling beast raising its head, the heat rising.

The comic's anger also was obvious but he was near the end of his set. All he had to do was finish on a laugh and get off the stage. Not a great show but, as in an aircraft landing, any one you walk away from is a good one. Then he tossed off one last gratuitous insult.

That's when Monigan threw the dog at him.

NINE

Dwayne had been walking in large circles most of the night. All that hiking and he was almost home. North on Parliament Street he went, passing hard, dirty men and women roaming the streets before the city was awake. Dwayne couldn't pin down his feelings for them. Revulsion was present, and so was a certain anger, mixed with fear of what terrific secrets they carried in their shopping carts, duffel bags and hearts. He hated this neighborhood. His mother could have sold the house, something Dwayne badgered her about continually, but she had a regard for tradition and heritage. Once her husband had left it was all she had. But Dwayne felt she should be worrying more about him than dwelling on the few happy years she had spent with Monigan.

There had been happy times, he admitted, recalling a selection of Christmases and holidays when his father was working, rough but authentic displays of love from the old man. Dwayne did not think his father was inherently weak, rather he was a man weakened by circumstances. And Monigan had never given Dwayne even an inkling of the circumstances with which he was trying to cope, so all he saw was the end product and none of the processes. Monigan had a latent power and a sense of responsibility, but Dwayne and his mother had given up waiting for its manifestation. Dwayne missed him.

Across the street was a row of townhouses, no more than five years old and already looking thirty. Another sign of failure. A streetcar rumbled past. Dwayne liked the sound. He was a city boy and supposed the whine of the streetcar had a part in some mystical alliance with foghorns, pounding surf and wailing prairie freight trains. With his fingers Dwayne combed some of the dried gel from his hair then pulled up short.

There was a man sitting propped up against a wrought-iron fence. Dwayne stopped, fascinated against his will with the bum. The old man looked like a child, or someone arrested in his development. A scruff of growth on his face, a long scratch down one cheek. His right eye was closed and there was a wound on his brow. Large ears stuck out from underneath a mat of hair. There was no strength in his face. The skin was puckered and pulled, not so much molded as tacked onto the skull and allowed to drape. Etiolation almost complete. Sickened, Dwayne turned away but immediately looked back. It was hard to tell, what with the injuries, but Dwayne was pretty sure it was the old pool player from The Workbench. He shook his head and continued on his way.

By the time he reached home and stuck his key in the lock Dwayne was ready to scream with relief. Undressing quickly, he checked the security of the small window high on the basement wall — surely his thieving mother's entry point — and stretched out on his futon. 0810 hours. He slept.

Phone.

"Yes, Mother."

"I forgot to tell you the noodle man phoned the other day."

"What noodle man? What are you dreaming up now?"

"Don't lie to me. The noodle man who says you worked for him and took his suit. He says you owe him twenty dollars."

"Send it to him from the money you stole from me."

"Don't make things up. You know I'd never do anything of the kind."

"Denials, empty denials."

"How could I get into your apartment now? You found out all my tricks and turned it into a fortress."

"In any event, I have another job. Working . . . let's say it's social work."

"Speaking of people who need help, I saw your father."

A wave of anxiety surged through Dwayne's body. "It's bad enough I've seen him. You lack the strength to deal with the evil old hobo."

"We didn't speak or anything, and I don't think he saw me."

"So it was just a glimpse of him on the street again."

"No, it was last night at The Laugh Chance."

Dwayne was being stalked, he knew it. Monigan realized his son's reappearance in his life meant some type of retribution was in the air and he wanted to nip it in the bud. Dwayne was being stalked, no doubt about it.

"He caused a disturbance."

Dwayne didn't want to hear it. His father always caused a disturbance; his very existence held such mass that it bent space-time. "I'm hanging up. I don't want to hear anything more about that man till the day he does something to prove he wants me in his life."

"Of course he wants you in his life. Your father, I'm afraid, is a bit of a disaster, but he does love you."

Dwayne slammed down the phone and flopped on the futon, limbs shrieking with fatigue. As soon as he was famous he'd bribe a government official to have his mother imprisoned. 0850 hours. Dwayne pulled up the covers and stared at the ceiling, coming close to tears at the directions in which he was being tugged.

Monigan was in a much better mood and feeling highly pleased with himself. He'd had a thoroughly entertaining evening at The Laugh Chance and his dog had done a bang-up job of chasing the comedian offstage. It was the first time Monigan had caused a public disruption and been applauded for it. In future he'd be wary of cognac, though, as he couldn't remember making it home. He padded nude around his room then took a cold beer out of the fridge and sat down with it at the card table in the middle of the room. He shoved aside two empties, a cribbage board and an ashtray fouled with butts.

Looking for cigarettes, he checked the drawers, the bar fridge, under the bed and in the pockets of all his clothes. He could go over to the store for a pack but didn't want to be gone when Bill arrived for their cribbage game. Monigan wasn't sure what afflicted Bill, but he was no better than his dead wife for wandering off. He knew Bill missed his wife and felt for him. Monigan missed his own wife even though he had deliberately walked away from her.

Monigan headed naked down the hall to the bathroom, wondering what was keeping Bill. Sitting there with his elbows on his knees, drinking his beer, Monigan could hear music and laughter from the room to the right. It was shared by three or four young men from somewhere in northern Ontario. They were skinny guys, kids really, with the greasy hair and bad complexions of a garage band. Jailhouse tattoos, bad teeth, track marks. Except for the noise they never bothered anyone, content to come and go in their search for rock and junk, phlegmatic about the possibility that they'd all be dead in a year.

Monigan finished up and went back to his room, and the sound of the dormer window opening drew the mutt out from under the bed. Perfectly comfortable with their routine, it allowed Monigan to raise it up and stick its rear end out over the sloping mansard roof to do its business. It had even taken to cocking a leg against a phantom tree. Monigan craned his neck out to see where the mess was going, as the eavestrough was plugged and should have filled up days ago.

He put the dog back on the floor and it scurried under the bed. The animal showed the same traits as half the people in the area. Scared, afraid to meet your eyes on the street; shuffle the shoes on the corner, stare at the ground or over your head as they're bumming a smoke or spare change. It wasn't surprising given the abuse that had been flung their way most of their lives.

Monigan sat back down at the card table, waiting for Bill and trying to think of a name for the dog.

But Bill was still sleeping on Parliament Street and wouldn't arrive for a while yet. Doyle and Ogilvie were cruising by when they saw him and pulled over to the curb. They had spent the whole morning checking on people passed out in various locations, in parks and on benches, in doorways and in parkades, on the sidewalk and in the gutter. Ogilvie climbed out of the passenger side and joined her partner.

Bill had been dreaming again. He used to have nightmares and he didn't like those, but nowadays it was just dreams and they were okay. Sometimes the dreams came when he was awake, cooking a little supper or going for a walk. Jean had visited him yesterday when he was in the park at Allan Gardens. He had been looking at the raised flower beds and trying to remember all the colors the flowers were in the summer. He had heard that the gardeners changed plants so there were blooms the whole summer through and felt a little sad, because he liked to think there were plants that just blossomed and blossomed the whole season, sending out flowers of different shapes and colors.

Thinking about the flowers got him thinking about Jean and when he turned to go there she was on the bench by the water fountain, the fountain with the three spouts that the birds came to for a drink. Jean was sitting there like she used to do at the end, sort of looking at him and smiling, but not really looking at him. Not like before, when he had that job at the warehouse. That's when he bought her the dress, the floral print one. She hugged him and kissed him that time. She used to hug and kiss him a lot, but at the end she just wandered away and some kids found her by the pile of snow behind the arena.

He should go home now. Jean might be there, visiting him again like yesterday, and he could make her a little soup — that Habitant pea soup she liked — and some tea, even if she didn't drink it.

Doyle had been roughly shaking him until Ogilvie grabbed her partner's elbow.

"He's hurt," Ogilvie said. She was a good-looking woman, but her anger drew down her mouth. As Doyle stepped away she felt for Bill's pulse and nodded. "Strong and regular. He's okay, just passed out and beat up."

"Maybe not even beat up," Doyle said, angry at himself for his rough treatment of the old man. It wasn't like him, but everything in the neighborhood made him angry these days. "That's a scrape over his eye. Probably fell."

"Mister . . ." Ogilvie flinched as a gust of wind threw a feculent cloud her way. "He's pretty ripe. You're welcome to him, Partner."

"Hey, Sport." Doyle gently shook old Bill, who awoke with such a spasm that the cop jumped upright. "Do you live around here?"

Bill didn't answer. He was comfortable sitting there, not too cold and he didn't have a hangover, hadn't been drinking much at all lately. One eye hurt and he felt a scab or something stuck to the brow, but it was nothing serious. He was hungry and his hands were stiff but that was about all.

"Can you stand?" Ogilvie asked. "Come on — let's get you to your feet."

It was nice of the police to help him stand up, but there was no need for it. Could he stand? — cops could be funny sometimes.

"It's you," Doyle said.

Looking for the source of the voice, Bill had to swivel all the way around to his right, as that eye was almost closed. He staggered, his insect mass betraying him in the mounting breeze.

"Why do I keep running into you?" Doyle asked. "Don't you have a place to stay?"

"Sure," Bill said. "Me and Jean have a place."

"How do I get in touch with Jean?"

"She's dead."

"I see. And now you have nowhere to go."

"Sure," Bill said. "Same place."

"Where?"

But Bill was checking himself out for other injuries. The scratch on his left cheek was nothing, no scalp wounds, and his arms and legs were working fine. He was a little hungry and his hands were stiff, that's about all.

"Let's go," Doyle said to Ogilvie. "Help me get him into the car."

When they stopped in front of The Workbench, Ogilvie got out to open the rear door for Bill just as it swung wide. "How did you do that?" she asked. "There's no handle in the back."

Bill shrugged. He didn't know. He just had a way with stuff.

On the top floor, Monigan was staring out the window wondering where he would get the money to pay his bar tab. Katy had been on him about it since the weekend. When he thought about it, she had only brought it up since the french fry started working. He wouldn't be surprised if his son was trying to run the whole show already, maybe skimming from the till. By leaning out the window Monigan could catch a glimpse of the sidewalk, so when he saw the cruiser disgorge Bill and the cops he bolted for the stairs.

Down in the bar the regulars gave the cops the usual freeze-out. Bill helped himself to a stool, and while Doyle conferred with Katlyn the door flew open.

"We got proof!" Monigan said.

"You," Doyle said.

"I bet we take measurements of this skid mark on Bill's head and it matches that stick you got hanging from your belt."

"Don't be ridiculous," Ogilvie said.

"Hi, darlin'," Monigan replied.

"They're trying to help," Katlyn said. "They found Bill over on Parliament passed out against a fence."

"I don't know, Doyle," Monigan said. "That medal's looking farther away all the time. You gotta have eighty pounds on old Bill. Or did you just hold him so the lady, here, could practice up on her whomping?"

"Shut up, Monigan," Doyle said. "I'm so bloody tired of you."

"How you doing, Bill?" Monigan said. "Cabbagetown Fats, is who you are, the two of us are gonna clean out this town on the table."

"I'm doing pretty good," Bill said. "I'm hungry and my hands are stiff, but pretty good."

"What? Don't let them hands go stiff." Monigan grabbed Bill's hands and massaged them, a vigorous attack on the digits that almost popped them free of their joints.

"Ow," Bill said.

"Katy! Bill needs food. Been sleeping on the street, this town's making me crazy. On the fucking street! Get some chili going."

"I hate to break this up," Doyle said. "I want to make sure your friend's going to be okay. I don't want to find him on the street again."

"You're lucky you can find your car."

Doyle wanted to take him apart, lay right into him.

"What's your partner's name?" Monigan said.

"I can speak for myself," Ogilvie said. "And I remember you from Saturday morning."

"Flattered." Monigan stared at them then said with irritation, "You can go any time."

A wave of laughter curled over their heads and flushed the cops out the door.

"Gimme a rag, Katy," Monigan said as soon as the door had closed. "Gonna fix Bill's peeper up."

Katlyn tossed a clean towel over the bar. "Why do you give him such a hard time?"

"Doyle?"

"Yeah. He seems all right."

"He is."

"Then why don't you leave him alone?"

For once Monigan actually thought before speaking and Katlyn did a double take, not expecting the pause.

"Cops are always either doing stuff to you or for you."

"What's wrong with them doing things *for* you?"

"Shouldn't have to go around doing stuff for people. I mean, sometimes they gotta do it, but they shouldn't have to. It should work that everybody can figure it out by themselves without needing someone around to protect them."

"Like your family," Katlyn said softly.

"Drop it, you."

"You're strange, Monigan."

"Thanks."

TEN

Dwayne had finally fallen asleep, but now a dream was tearing him apart. He was aware of the unreality yet desperate to continue. He was at the club. Harold had introduced him, but he couldn't climb the steps to the stage because he was naked. The house lights had gone up, and all eyes were on him as he rushed around the room, looking for clothes, any clothes. At the door to the Star Chamber, Sturgis and his mother and Monigan and Katlyn and David Letterman were shaking their heads and disgustedly observing his attempts to salvage what was left of his pride. The crowd began clapping for him to start his set. Harold Arens stared at him from the stage, refusing to help.

He awoke face down on his futon, dimly aware that the phone was ringing. It was a blind stumble to the thing. He swallowed hard as he held the receiver to his ear.

"You're late."

"I know, I know, but I have to find some clothes. Tell Harold to stall."

"Your boss phoned."

"Boss?"

"I wish you wouldn't leave these people my number."

"Mother."

"Who did you think?"

Dwayne flicked on the main overhead light, blinking as both his retinas and his consciousness adjusted.

"I said, I wish you wouldn't leave my number with people."

"I can't afford an answering machine so I screen the calls through you." He was fully awake now.

"Your boss phoned."

"Oh, I'll send the noodle suit through the mail if those indolent sods aren't on strike again."

"Not the noodle man. Some woman named Katlyn. She sounded nice enough on the phone. Is that the social worker who hired you?"

"Katlyn." Wednesday. 1830 hours. He had slept the whole day and was half an hour late for his shift. An evil image of the bar's misfits materialized but then was quashed by the shining light of Katlyn's face.

"You have to be punctual when you're working with the unfortunate. They slide into crime the minute they have time on their hands."

Dwayne didn't bother saying goodbye. He raced to the bathroom. A handful of Katlyn's gel slicked back his hair. He squeezed out a mouthful of toothpaste and swirled it around with his tongue as he dry-shaved. The wool trousers were in bad shape but he pulled them on and fastened his belt over the tail of his Bashi-Bazouks T-shirt. Slowing, he withdrew his sports jacket from the closet. Not technically a sports jacket, it was his only impressive garment, a mint condition RCAF officer's tunic that showed only a faint trace of where the rank stripes used to encircle the cuffs. He had left the wings on over the breast pocket. He did up the gold buttons, shone each one with the back of his sleeve then was out the door on the dead waddle.

"This ain't hot enough," Monigan said from his spot at the bar. "Chili should burn the lips right offa you."

"You're not the only one eating," Katlyn said.

"So what's the deal?"

"Deal?"

"You finally talk me into coming around again while the french fry's working, and he ain't even here on time."

"I just talked to your wife," Katlyn said. "She heard the door slam. Dwayne's on his way."

"He's late," Monigan said between shovelsful of chili. His mouth was rimmed with a thin line of orange grease. "Go easy on him and he'll take you to the cleaners, push for all he's worth. Gotta come down hard on him, let him know who's the boss, you don't wanna wake up and find the bar's cleared out, heading down the street in the back of a moving van."

"Don't be an idiot," Katlyn said. "I've never had kids, but there's no way one boy could cause that much trouble. What happened between you two? Or three, for that matter."

Monigan stared down into his bowl. He spoke low and indistinctly. "Don't know all of it, Katy. The wife and me, well, I guess it went bad earlier than I was ready to admit, but it wasn't too tough till the kid started to grow up. Then all she ever cared about was him, and all he ever cared about was her, and all I ever cared about was me, so it didn't exactly make for a tight family. Never had no experience with a family when I was growing up so I had no tools. Something broke and I couldn't fix it and I got so tied up working with no tools that I had to get outta there. Look at them now, even. The kid's gotta be over thirty and he can't move outta the house. Good thing for him he's a shitty comic, 'cause if he ever made it big and had to go to Hollywood he'd be fucked."

"But to cut all ties when they live two blocks away?" Katlyn said.

"Boat was sinking. Wasn't going back for my hat."

Katlyn went to swab the beer fridges. In the past she had considered Monigan to be unassailable, able to stop life's blows instead of recoiling from them. But a shift was going on inside him and she had no idea if that was good or bad.

Outside Dwayne stopped to let his breathing subside. He adjusted his clothing and entered. "Good evening."

"Don't talk till your head's filled out." Monigan grinned and shoved his empty glass at Katlyn. It didn't take much to get him back on his game.

"What's wrong with my head?" Dwayne said.

"Look at it — it's too small for any human being. It's like the head on a match."

"You're hardly one to be talking about well-proportioned heads."

"What?" Monigan yelled. "This is a *man's* head." He took the item in question by both hands, thumbs over his ears. "This is just . . . well, it's just a good honest fucking SKULL!" He demonstrated this truth by slamming it twice on the bar.

"Will you two babies please cut it out?" Katlyn said. She looked with disbelief at Monigan, who sat there weaving on his stool, a lump already forming on his forehead.

"You're late," Katlyn said to Dwayne.

"Sorry, I was working on my act."

"Don't know why," Monigan said, coming around. "I was down at the club by accident last night and I heard it clear as day the owner threw you out."

"An artistic difference."

"What were you doing at a comedy club?" Katlyn asked. The thought of Monigan at large was shocking, never mind his actually intermingling with the public.

"Free drinks. Doubt I'll ever go back. Rather watch erosion than them little buggers try to tell jokes. You wanna hear a joke, I can tell you one. Think I can't? I can."

Dwayne eased inside the horseshoe and Katlyn's perfume buckled his knees. Staring at her, he lost the drift of the conversation till an old man banged a draft glass on the bar. Dwayne poured the drink while Katlyn chipped in by setting up his float.

"You did a good job Saturday," she said. "But I'm not doing anything tonight so I'll stay in case you need a hand. It'll be nice to be a customer for once." She slipped out from behind the bar and sat down beside Monigan.

Dwayne straightened his tunic and squared his narrow shoulders. He was down a pint from shaving cuts but felt good.

"Comedy isn't all I do," he said to Katlyn. "Maybe you caught my acting debut on the cable network."

"The local one?"

"Last year I was in an ad for Krazy Karl's Stereo Shop. My mother said that all Krazy Karl's chatter couldn't take away from my screen presence as I stood by the counter."

"I don't think I saw that one."

"It doesn't matter." Dwayne wondered what was coming over him. He and Katlyn would be stuck at this stage of their relationship forever if he couldn't stop the banalities.

"Commercials are one thing," Katlyn said. "But doing standup must be terrifying."

Dwayne smiled and shot his cuffs, even though he was wearing a T-shirt.

A general lethargy overlay the room, yet as always The Workbench had about it the air of loose trouble. A group of locals were discussing the merits of figure skating, in agreement that it was not so much a sport as fringe theater; the pool table was being abused by two rambunctious customers; a man in the back was threatening someone on the TV, even though it was turned off.

Monigan was stealing glances at Katlyn, who was stealing glances at Dwayne, who was stealing glances at both her and his father. Monigan knew this would be a waste of time, and to top it off he was uncomfortable. With a cold draft beer in his hand Monigan wouldn't feel out of place talking to the Queen, but the combination of Katlyn and his son was driving him mad. And he had to stay clear of mind. One of the local boosters was due in with razor blades, sport socks and steaks, and Monigan had to find a way to raise some cash to restock his supplies. Even thieves were acting like hardened businessmen these days, nothing at the bar being done on credit anymore.

"So you can make a living telling jokes," he said to his son, as much to break the silence as anything else. "Shame you got tossed last night. Me and the dog were looking forward to a few laughs."

"I can make a living doing anything," Dwayne said. "I *choose* to tell jokes."

"What's this about a dog?" Katlyn asked.

"What dog?"

"You mentioned a dog."

"Didn't I tell you before?"

"This is the first I've heard of it."

"Sure, I did. That other day when I was in here."

"You didn't."

"Funny."

"Hilarious."

"Lay off, Katy."

"What about the dog — are you keeping it in your room?"

"It ain't a dog, exactly."

"Then what is it?"

"It ain't a dog so much. More of a doggy-type thing."

"Monigan!"

"It was starving, beat up pretty bad."

"You can't keep it upstairs."

"Goddamn it, Katy, you got crackheads and pukes like that living here."

"There are no pets allowed. I start letting pets in here and before you know it there will be a hundred cats and dogs being left to fend for themselves. You know full well how many half-dead animals the humane society has dragged out of those rooms."

"It ain't really a dog. Dogs take up space, they bark and stuff. This is just sort of doggish."

"This may seem trivial, but I don't want . . ."

"It's deaf and dumb, I figure. Mind you, it ain't stupid. When it got to the guy on stage last night it chased him off like a cut cat and run him straight into a waitress."

"You can't keep animals upstairs. Do you at least take it for walks?"

"It gets partway outside a couple times a day."

"What if the other tenants want a pet?"

"Oh, you gotta draw the line somewhere."

"What about complaints?"

"I wouldn't worry my head about that."

"You're nuts."

"As you ain't scared of telling me only ten times a day."

Meanwhile, Bill had been sitting on the toilet for over forty minutes, in fact, had forgotten why he was there. Jean hadn't visited him since the other day at the park but that was okay. She was probably wandering. He had stocked up on pea soup so any time she came he'd be ready for her. He was jarred into awareness by someone the next stall over, talking to himself as he laid out a line on top of the toilet paper dispenser. Bill did up his pants and flushed. The handle wasn't working so he fixed it and went back out to the bar.

"There's my partner," Monigan said. "Thought we'd lost you. Let's get over to the pool table, take some of these buggers for a wad, whadya say?"

Bill allowed himself to be steered over to the table, where he fiddled with the mechanism till the balls dropped.

"That man with Monigan," Dwayne said to Katlyn.

"Bill."

"I'm amazed he was able to make it this far under his own power."

"What do you know about it?"

"I passed him on the street this morning."

"You walked past him and did nothing?"

"What could I do?"

"Anything!"

"He has free will."

"He was passed out and could have frozen to death."

"It's not that cold out," Dwayne mumbled. Here was Katlyn throwing him into confusion again. He had never met anyone who could so easily demolish his basic precepts. Not that it stopped him.

"Attempts to help people around here worsen the problem. The passion between the sexes ensures maximum productivity of children. Hence, overpopulation, hence the outstripping of the food supply. Social programs unnaturally interfere with poverty, so it follows that the elimination of governmental and philanthropic support will prove best over time, as it eliminates the poor in a natural fashion."

"Are you demented?"

Her tone struck Dwayne flush in the heart. "Thomas Malthus," he said.

"I know, Dwayne. But he wrote that two centuries ago, and he was wrong even then." She lit a cigarette and aggressively pulled on it. "Tell me the truth — do you truly believe what you just said?"

Dwayne looked down at his feet. "I've never really thought about it."

"Exactly."

"But there has to be something to natural population control."

"Through disease and exposure and starvation? We're talking about human beings here."

"Do you favor some sort of redemption program for them? When Tito was gaining control in Yugoslavia in 1944, Hitler sent in the 500th Parachute Battalion, which was made up of men under various army charges who were allowed to clear their names by volunteering for dangerous operations and . . ."

"Stop it," she said. "Stop twisting things with stupid, false analogies. Don't you have any ideas of your own?" Katlyn couldn't remember ever being this angry, this aroused.

"I don't know. I mean, sure."

"The things we talked about Friday night — those were real. You have your own opinions, your own wisdom. Don't rope in quotes from people who may have been right for their time and place but not for you and yours."

Dwayne couldn't help himself. All he wanted to do was hold her hand, hold her and share his passion. But Friday he had spoken of things he had been pondering all his life. To improvise with Katlyn would reveal his weakness. He wondered if she would listen to what he had to say. Nobody else ever had.

Monigan turned from the pool table. He had never seen Katlyn so riled up. But it wasn't his fault; he had warned her about Dwayne. He wished things were back to normal, where he could play some pool, have some drinks, forget that he had a weird comedian for a son. He put his cue down but before he could go to interfere in the conversation Frodo came bouncing through the front door.

"Round for the house!" Frodo threw an arm around Monigan as the customers chugged their beers to clear the way for the free stuff.

"Never thought this would work out," he said. "But thank you very much. The man came through."

Monigan's attention was still on the bar but Katlyn had calmed quickly and was still talking to Dwayne. Monigan forced his anger down.

"I'd like to show my gratitude," Frodo said. He adjusted his button-down tweed cap and hitched at his leather pants.

"Just pay up," Monigan said. "That's enough gratitude."

"Umm . . . I didn't collect it all."

"How much?"

"A grand."

"You let him slip you a thousand?"

"He promised me half by next week."

"Half."

"It's okay. This is the first time I've collected this much in years. Let's celebrate. On me. I really appreciate your help."

"You owe me three yards."

"Can I hold on to some of it till I get the balance?"

"Make you a deal," Monigan said. "You clean up my house account and we're square."

Frodo smiled as they went over to the bar.

"Hi, Frodo," Katlyn said.

"Gimme a cigarette." Monigan probed in her pack, stuck one in his mouth and another behind his ear. "French Fry — what's my tab come to?"

Dwayne fished around for the bar tabs, which were scribbled on scraps of paper, coasters and napkins and were piled underneath the bar, held down by a paperweight replica of Sudbury's Big Nickel.

"Monigan has a separate pile," Katlyn said. "It's over by the pickled-egg jar."

The pocket calculator was astray, but Dwayne found it under a stack of old magazines. As he manipulated the figures, the others stood by with an expectant hush. "Four hundred and eighteen," Dwayne said, looking up with disgust.

"That's more than my rent!" Monigan said. He snatched the calculator from Dwayne and stared at it. "Looks okay to me." He handed it to Frodo.

"Wait a minute," the bookie said. "That's way too much. It's almost half of what I collected."

"No fault of mine," Monigan said. "You slept in your bed, now you gotta pay the fiddler."

"Gee," Frodo said. He wished he had gone into a normal line of business. His father would be ashamed if he were still alive. With enormous reluctance he dug out his wallet and handed the money to Dwayne.

"Tip," Monigan said.

Frodo added two twenties.

"*Tabula rasa*," Dwayne declared, dropping the markers in the garbage can.

Frodo sighed, tucked his bottom lip under his front teeth and left by the side door.

"Draft," Monigan said. "And I'll pay cash for this one." He wandered back to the pool table, where Bill was clearing the table left-handed.

Dwayne pulled out a pad of paper and began transferring the jumble of house accounts onto a single clean sheet. "Need a little organization around here."

"Is that right?" Katlyn said.

"When David Livingstone got to Tete, Mozambique, in 1856, he reported to London that the reason the Portuguese had made nothing of the colony was that they were decadent, lazy, spineless and rotten with VD and drink."

"I know," Katlyn said. She laughed. As angry as Dwayne could make her, she found something hilarious in his ramblings. "You figure that's the problem here?"

"Well," Dwayne admitted. "I wouldn't go that far."

"What's the longest you've ever held a job, Dwayne?"

"I've been a comic for three years."

"A job."

"The exalting nature of labor is a myth."

"Just what I thought."

There was no action at the bar, but rather than sit down and lose another argument with Katlyn, Dwayne paced inside the horseshoe, carefully positioning glasses and rags and all the paraphernalia of the hooch trade. He shined the buttons of his tunic and clasped his hands behind his back, puffing out his chest whenever he passed the manager. Captain on the bridge, that's what he felt like. Sir Francis Drake, a pirate and a gentleman, a rogue and a hero.

Katlyn slid her glass over. She was happy relaxing out front for a change. She felt comfortable and secure in her shabby mansion, no matter the strange beings cavorting on the croquet lawn. "By the way," she said. "When I was talking to your mother she asked me about my case load."

"It's hard to worm sense out of her sometimes," Dwayne said.

"Does she work?"

"My mother's never worked. She lives on money inherited from my grandfather, who never willingly parted with a penny when he was alive. And you can see . . ." He trailed off, looking at Monigan.

"He told me you and your mother are close."

"Well, she leans on me quite heavily." He swallowed and wiped the bar of imaginary grime. "Yes, I suppose we are close."

As casually as possible, Katlyn said, "Nice, seeing you and your dad here together."

"Together," Dwayne said flatly.

"I don't mean to pry."

"That's all right," Dwayne said, feigning indifference. "Natural curiosity."

Katlyn went over to watch the men play pool and Dwayne went back to work now that the bar was filling up. An hour later The Workbench was loose on its hinges, a turbulent sea alternately cresting in euphoria and sinking into the trough of drunken despair. A local artist embodied the mood swings, rising off his stool to salute some artistic triumph then lapsing into tears. At one point Katlyn was accidentally knocked to the floor, but before Dwayne could play the hero Monigan had her up and on her feet, like a retriever proudly depositing an unpunctured duck on the grass. She managed a smile of thanks then fled to safer ground behind the bar, though why she considered such an enfiladed position secure defied comprehension. The night continued apace until closing time.

Another cold front had moved into the area but the warm air being bullied out of the way was dry and stable, so Katlyn and Dwayne were not bothered by falling snow or bitter winds as they locked the side door and stood awkwardly together.

"I should walk you home," Dwayne said.

"I just live up the street."

"Still."

They set off.

Dwayne had hoped to have the chance to talk to her at length that night. They had shared such an intimate beginning and now it was slipping through his fingers. "Did you know the word *bedlam* comes from Bedlem, the old English insane asylum?"

"It *was* a bit rough around the edges in there tonight," she admitted. Katlyn was reassured by Dwayne's presence. His uncoordinated gait complemented her uncertain stride, so they walked nicely together, they fit.

"I admire your poise around those people."

"They're different than you, Dwayne, but there's nothing wrong with them."

"I didn't mean . . ."

"What *did* you mean?"

"It's just . . . it seems to me that a woman . . . around those men, Monigan and them . . . a woman like you who has . . ."

"There's enough misogyny in that place," Katlyn said. "I don't need more of it from you."

"No, no, that's the farthest thing from my mind. If anything I think the male of our species is the weakling. Look at our aggression and misguided priorities. Just think of who represents the male:

"Fundamentalist ministers defrauding millions of people of their life savings; elected public officials sleeping with every woman they can lay their hands on; overpaid athletes battling larcenous owners; lying bureaucrats; anarchic labor leaders.

"We have warmongers, hatemongers and white supremacists; skinheads and pinheads; deadheads and crackheads. We have slimy real-estate magnates. We have child molesters, professional protestors and last-will contesters; losers, boozers and drag queen cruisers. We have dictators and minority haters. We have boxing promoters, Rhino party voters and contraband toters; stockmarket connivers, yuppie strivers and tow truck drivers. We have con men. We have gun runners. We have environment rapers and civic red tapers; street corner fiddlers and Catholic church diddlers; Hell's Angels bikers, post office strikers and loan shark pikers. We have rapists, racists, looters and freebooters.

"And!" Dwayne thundered with an elephant seal bellow. "We have Donald Fucking Trump!"

By this time Katlyn was giggling hysterically. "That's hilarious," she said. "Nuts, but hilarious."

"It doesn't work on stage," Dwayne said sadly.

"That's part of your act?"

"Yes."

"Maybe you should tone it down a little. And give more detail to some of the categories. It's funny here in private, but it comes across more as a diatribe than a joke."

Dwayne was offended. What did Katlyn know about comedy? Tone it down, she had said. Precisely what Sturgis and the other comics told him. Then he caught her eye as she stopped on the sidewalk and his anger melted, just like that.

"This is where I live," Katlyn said. "Thanks so much for seeing me home."

"Not at all." Dwayne stared at the door to the house.

"I have the second floor. It's not very big, but it's fine for one person."

One person. Dwayne wondered if she were sending him a message.

"So," Katlyn said.

"Yes, I have to get going. Sorry again for being late for my shift tonight. Punctuality is the backbone of . . ."

"Of what?"

"I forget. This is strange. I'm not used to talking myself into a dead end."

"It was a hard shift."

"Right. I hope Bill will be comfortable up in Monigan's room for the night."

"Why the sudden concern?"

Dwayne was paralyzed. He figured it must be some sort of cerebral parasite he had picked up in The Workbench. "I don't know. It just seems important."

"Night." Katlyn reached out and took both his hands in hers, squeezed gently, then disengaged herself and went inside.

Ten minutes later Doyle and Ogilvie cruised by, slowing to investigate the large man staring at the house. Dwayne snapped to and headed for Dundas, casting tentative peeks back over his shoulder at Katlyn's home. The voices were chattering inside his head every bit as feverishly as when he was on stage. That's what bothered him about Katlyn. She robbed him of clarity, allowing him no time to formulate answers and keep the conversation in line with his overall campaign.

By the time he wandered down Seaton Street and arrived home, he was convinced of another truth: when a woman takes your hand, both hands, and unprompted, there must be more behind it than mere appreciation. She had not squeezed his hands very tightly but there had been discernable pressure, and Dwayne thought the lightness of her touch was due more to her gentle nature than to romantic reluctance. She was gentle, he saw that plainly.

He entered his basement apartment, carefully hung his RCAF tunic in the closet and dropped everything else on the floor.

"Yes, Mother." 0200 hours.

"Why are you home so late?"

"The derelicts were in a festive mood. What are you doing awake?"

"I couldn't sleep. My foot hurts. I bet I go completely lame one of these days."

"I'm sorry to hear it, but you'll be fine. Soak it in epsom salts and have a good rest. If you need any errands done tomorrow, I'll fit them into my schedule then massage your foot if it's still giving you trouble."

"Are you drunk?"

"On the fruits of my inamorata."

"What kind of booze is that? When did you start drinking?"

"I'm fine, Mother."

"What's wrong with you? You sound so happy." His mother would feel better after a good cry, but Dwayne wasn't co-operating.

"I *am* happy. I'm blessed."

"You're drunk."

"Not at all."

"Did you bang your head? Tall people have to watch out for that."

"Thanks for your concern."

"My foot was so sore earlier that I spilled cranberry juice on my best clothes."

"I'll take them to the cleaners tomorrow."

Dwayne's mother slammed down the phone. This was too much; her son's buoyant mood had her in no end of a dither. Add to that the fact that her ankle was aching and it was easy to see sleep would not be hers tonight.

She reached down and unraveled the tensor bandage from her left ankle, revealing a plump foot imprinted with the faint cross-hatchings of the elastic wrap. She tested her weight on it. Not bad.

She thought with mortification of the moment she went over on it. Dwayne's basement window was right at ground level and only two feet high, so when his mother crouched down to hammer the chisel into the wood frame, her poor positioning and the soft ground caused her to tip sideways and turn her ankle. She was getting old, and waxed nostalgic for the days when she could have had the frame off and been inside his apartment in under two minutes.

And now her son was acting polite toward her and seemed happy beyond reason. She went to check her horoscope — something weird was afoot.

Dwayne threw back the covers on his futon. He felt a surge of love for his mother and all the world. He stretched out and moved to the edge of the bed, estimating how much room there would be for another person. A lascivious image of Katlyn loomed in his mind, a scene that took all his concentration to expunge. He rolled onto his stomach but that made his erection too difficult to endure, so he shifted onto his back and forced himself to think about pro wrestling.

ELEVEN

Two days and two nights passed. Dwayne's next shift at The Workbench was not until Saturday evening so normally the circumstances would have been perfect. The time would allow him to hone his act. He was sure Sturgis had acted out of stress and would come around to inviting him back.

He actually considered changing his act, completely overhauling his material. But Dwayne was having trouble evaluating his career. All along he had been performing for himself, but now there were new elements in the equation.

Katlyn was the most difficult bit of algebra, and Dwayne panicked when he thought of her and his career in conjunction. If he was to win her it wouldn't be as the present Dwayne Feller. No, he had to be a success, a star. But he was unable to concentrate on the essentials. Inspiration is impervious to a bludgeon or crude siege machinery and Dwayne would never find the key till he cleared his mind of chatter. Katlyn would not allow it. He felt powerless, and it was no less terrifying, this need to succeed, to impress her, for the fact that nothing so far had really happened between them. Dwayne heaved a great sigh. He'd have to do something about his father, as well. Another blot on his mind.

So the days passed slowly, restricting Dwayne to lounging and the minimum attendance to bodily functions. By Saturday he was a wreck and he finally admitted that he needed guidance, a steadying hand. He phoned Harold Arens.

By the end of the conversation Dwayne had transferred his

angst onto his friend. Harold had two shows to do that night, but now he was drained, sapped of anything resembling humor. He wandered around his apartment, resentment gaining the upper hand over sympathy for Dwayne. He sat on the couch and reached for his plastic baggie. A small sweet stone was what he needed, but as he was rolling up he came across a two-for-one brochure for a new restaurant.

"Damn," he said. He had phoned Reba and promised to take her out for dinner to celebrate her nailing a spot at the Just for Laughs festival. He jammed the baggie in his pocket, picked up the brochure, went over to the mirror to see if he could pass as a funky Bohemian and thus skip a shower and shave, and left.

Reba was late and they had a show to do that evening, so Harold went ahead and ordered for both of them. They were the only people in the restaurant other than a flea-bitten man at the counter who was having a beer and watching a college basketball game on the portable TV. Spare surroundings: bare tables; red, white and green tile floor; one large poster of the Italian World Cup team. Reba sat down and helped herself to a slice of garlic bread.

"This is nice," she said. "What got into you?"

"Taking care of the team," Harold said. "You ever let me slide inside the sheets with you and you'll never have to work another day in your life."

"Hard to work under quarantine," Reba said.

King Canelli, tickled beyond reason with two customers, arrived with their entrees and made a huge fuss of positioning the plates.

"I ordered for you," Harold said. "Couldn't wait any longer."

"Great." Reba dug in.

Canelli laughed to himself. New customers! He knew this place would work out. Every restaurant he opened had gone under before the paint was dry, but this was his turnaround; he felt it, it was straight up from here. "You like the lasagna? Is good — you try."

"I'm trying," Reba said.

"I like you people," the King said. "Come back any time."

"We've barely started," Harold said.

"Start, then. Start and try and come back. How you find out about my place — advertising or what?"

"*Scientific American* magazine," Harold said. "They gave you a great review."

The King was confused, unable to remember any restaurant critic. He didn't like the idea that they had snuck in a spy. Canelli believed that critics should announce themselves in order for the staff to get their bowing and scraping down pat. Snap inspections violated his code. He eyed the wreck at the counter, trying to see if his fingernails were clean, or if he was wearing socks.

"Another quick carafe," Harold said. "Then we'll have to go. Not long till showtime."

"Showtime?" Canelli lit up. "Entertainers, you are entertainers, how wonderful. All of my family has their hearts on the stage, but my sister was the only one who chased her dream. She had a promising career in the opera until the incident with the pike at rehearsal. They say the man playing the Swiss guard was quite drunk." He crossed himself.

"We're comics," Harold said.

Canelli visibly started to vibrate. "I am looking for a comic. Dwayne Feller."

Reba started laughing and Harold dropped his face in his hands.

"He has my noodle suit and twenty dollars."

"That's Dwayne," Reba said.

"How do I find him?"

"Who knows?" Harold said.

Canelli didn't believe him. In his experience everyone stuck together like family. He went to get the wine.

"That bloody Dwayne," Reba said, keeping her voice down.

"I just finished talking to him for forty minutes," Harold said.

"Anything new under the sun?"

"He ran into his father again. I've seen the old man at The Workbench now and again, and there's no question he's a piece of business. But he's not all bad, not the way Dwayne's always described him." Harold studied the remains of his lasagna. "And Dwayne's sort of seeing someone."

"Now I *know* you're practicing a new bit on me."

"The manager of the pub. I like her a lot, and she's smart enough to know what she's doing."

"But Dwayne . . . ?"

"Now he has more pressure on him than even a sane person could deal with. He's desperate to please both of them, but here he is barred from the club. He doesn't have a lot else to fall back on."

"He told you all this?"

"God, no," Harold laughed. "I've learned to take everything he says, chop out the quotations and hanging analogies, reverse it 180 degrees, downshift out of capitals, then when you have a nicely printed report in front of you, go get drunk till you figure out what it really means."

Reba chuckled. "You have more patience than me."

"Come on," Harold said. "You don't mind him that much."

"Yeah, but I liked Stalin."

Harold looked at his watch and called for the bill. They'd have to rush to make it down to the show in time.

At the club, Sturgis was foaming at the mouth, as much at the missing comics as at the need for action now that he had decided how to reverse his fortunes. He had a plan.

Sturgis had spent half Saturday formulating the decision, roaming alone through the building, drinking bitters, hunching over the computer, calling up numbers that underscored the fragility of his satrapy. He was relieved that he didn't have any kids, though when he thought more about it, children would be handy at a time like this. Having raised and pampered them he could expect them to come through for him now. By then, he was halfway convinced he truly had children, whose ingratitude sent him into a towering rage. The tape was off his ribs but he had been gaining weight and his clothing pressed too tightly on his chest. He pulled out the tail of his shirt and loosened his belt. He fiddled with the computer again but with all the manipulations it failed to poop out anything positive. He had built this place, turned what had been a bad dance club into the best comedy spot around, and he didn't want to walk away.

The way he had it analyzed there was only one choice, and that was the rooming house. When he bought the thing his plans had been for a complete renovation, including the gutting of the first two floors. Comedy had been booming then and Sturgis was eager to expand his empire, so a new club on the ground floor, a wine bar on the second, upscale rooms above it all and he would be set for life. It was located in a predominantly low-scale business area, though casting agencies, film production houses and sound studios were transforming the neighboring blocks into an entertainment industry hub. But then the economy and standup comedy marched lockstep into a hole and construction was delayed. Sturgis might still have made it had his wife not bolted at the same time. But she had, and his financial enemies had multiplied, so the place was the same as when he had bought it. There it sat, gray and offensive, filled with the type of people Sturgis would have thrown out of his club.

So the thing had to burn. A little fluke lightning, insurance money, pay off Revenue Canada, the wife, the lawyers, the bookie, get a new Jag. He smiled at the thought of new wheels so he could stop taking cabs. He hated listening to a new accent every day coming from a driver who couldn't even find Yonge Street. So up in flames it would go. The way he figured, the people in the rooming house didn't know how good they had it anyhow. Let them live on the street till they found a job, was the only sound approach in tough times. The weak go to the wall. Devil take the hindmost.

Sturgis laughed and reached for the phone. Then replaced the receiver. He was short for the last stolen liquor order, so that avenue of help was closed. He punched at the keyboard and the screen told him he hadn't yet paid the booster for the computer itself. He adjusted the backrest and stared at the wall, wondering if there was anyone he could trust and who would trust him. He knew it was an easy thing to torch the rooming house, so there had to be someone out there. Someone with the combined traits of stupidity and desperation, someone who owed him.

There wasn't much sound filtering through the door. He looked over at the clock. Ten minutes! Sturgis raced out of the office and looked wildly around for Harold and Reba. The night before the headliner from New York had passed out on stage and Sturgis had been forced to fall back on his usual standbys. Now they weren't even there. As he got to the door, they sauntered in.

"What are you trying to do?" Sturgis hissed as he barrelled up to them. "Drive me completely out of my mind?"

The intro music blared out of the speakers and the house lights went down. Harold, with his coat still on, strolled to the stage.

"You're all going to pay some day," Sturgis said. "Never forget that." Back in his chair in his office, Sturgis listened to the silence. It was a bad house, but he was beyond caring. He unbuttoned his shirt, freeing up his ribs, and ran a hand across his hairless chest. He could sense the comics turning on him, a recrudescence of their early attitudes, back before he had pummelled them into submission. It made him feel weak. It was strength he was after, the power he felt when dealing with someone like Dwayne.

Dwayne Feller. Sturgis slowly smiled, picturing him in his mind, the odd frame at once fat and bony, the food-encrusted shirt, the flat feet. What had Sturgis said to himself? Stupidity and desperation. Sturgis thought hard on the many benefits of the plan: he wouldn't have to pay anyone; it gave him control over another comic; it would cause Dwayne immense distress. Beautiful.

Both shows that night turned into lifeless affairs, so frustrating that even Harold and Reba at some spot in their routines turned on the crowd. Not in the rabid, visigothic manner of Dwayne, but harshly enough to make the audience feel part of the opposition rather than in the alliance. Their subsequent black mood was being indulged in an all-nighter at Harold's apartment, beer, pizza, joints and cigarettes providing in the wee hours solace and mindless release.

The crowd at The Workbench was equally as surly as the one at The Laugh Chance, though in their case it represented no break in continuity. No, the difficulty there had been between the manager and the bartender. So twisted out of shape was Dwayne by the time his shift started, so psychologically bent, that he was unable even to converse properly and thus found himself in the same position as when he was on stage. Feeling threatened and lacking a firm anchorage, he panicked and lashed out. Everything Katlyn said Dwayne took exception to, everything she did he questioned, with predictable results. Katlyn didn't know what was going on so she sniped at him in return.

For two days and two nights Dwayne had been waiting to walk her home again, anticipating the tenderness, fantasizing about actually holding hands as they walked, a casual glance and bump and hold her elbow and steady her with a hand to the shoulder. But now they were acting like spoiled children, almost deliberately try-ing to get under each other's skin.

By the time Katlyn got home she was close to tears. She didn't know what had happened. She tried to recall if she had ever han-dled anyone as roughly as she had Dwayne that night. As she got older, as she grew stronger, the residual disappointment and shame of her childhood she funneled into understanding and acceptance of the downtrodden in her life. But that night she had taken her anger and directed it at Dwayne. She was none too happy about the world at that moment. And right then, odd as it seemed, Dwayne was a large part of her world. She didn't know what to do about him. Monigan had said it right. No tools.

TWELVE

Katlyn dragged herself out of bed. She had slept only five hours, and at that it was a fitful rest. The radio played in the background as she made toast for breakfast then cleaned the kitchen. She wished she could stay home. One day at The Workbench was too much like the next. Despite her run-in with Dwayne she wanted to see him, but out of that environment if possible. That option she felt was closed for now.

She went to the mirror and pulled her hair up into a bun, then thrust it over her forehead, then pulled it apart into twin ponytails. Then let it hang and lit a cigarette, studying her face. She was tempted to experiment with some makeup but knew it would be a waste of time. Her features didn't take to embellishment, and for that matter she knew less about the nuances of cosmetics than your average thirteen-year-old hanging around the mall. She thought for the umpteenth time about quitting cigarettes.

Dwayne was in worse shape than her. He was on a hunger strike, determined to stay in bed till his internal organs disintegrated and fell out his ass. He wondered if anyone had gone on a hunger strike for a woman before. He reached over the edge of the futon, dug in a bag of potato chips and rammed a fistful in his mouth. The purpose of a hunger strike is to force action and the procedure is to deny the body nourishment. The action part was up to Katlyn, but Dwayne had control over the procedure. By limiting himself to junk food, eliminating from his diet anything with positive nutritional value, he figured to achieve the weakened state necessary to his mission without provoking hunger pangs. The end without the distressing means. He would like an ice-cream sandwich but that would mean going to the fridge, so he licked the salt off his fingers and tried to relax, waiting for the exalted state of being that is concomitant with near-death.

He wondered if Katlyn found him unattractive. He cursed himself for not having worn the tunic. That was the edge, the hook he had needed. His roughness could then be passed off as the hardened edge a man develops from combat. He envisioned himself with a mustache and goatee, a white kepi aslant on his head, marshalling the last of his strength to finish the forced march back into Sidi-bel-Abbès. A French Legionnaire stopping at a little cafe, shaking off the dust of the desert, lifting the chin of the waitress to gaze into her eyes as Katlyn stews in jealousy off to one side. *"Voici la Légion! L'affaire est dans le sac!"*

He didn't know how long the phone had been ringing.

"Yes, Mother." 1125 hours.

"Your boss phoned again."

Dwayne's heart came to the end of the bungee cord. "What did you tell her?"

"She wants you to work today."

Dwayne cried aloud. Stretching the cord to its furthest extent, he reached out with his foot and hooked the bedside table, tipping a submarine sandwich onto the floor. The hunger strike had worked! With his teeth he tore the plastic off the sandwich and assaulted it with great shearing bites. He hung up, already feeling better. He slowly nodded his head with satisfaction, knowing it was time to show everyone who was the boss. Time to stand his ground. Enough! *Basta!*

As Dwayne was reassembling the elements of his self-confidence, his father was getting out of bed. He didn't feel bad, despite his drinking jag of the night before. Monigan drank most days and was pretty sure he could be considered an alcoholic. But it was a functioning alcoholism. He seldom got blind drunk, and as a result his body had adjusted, feeling no more than a general malaise that seemed no worse from one day to the next. He hadn't always been a heavy drinker and, in fact, could still go long periods without need for the stuff. But it was boring. There wasn't much that gave him pleasure in life other than the jagged camaraderie with his friends over a glass of beer.

Monigan had been by the house again yesterday, furtively scouting the place from across the street in the dead of night. He stood staring at the building till he began to ache. Not so much at the thought of his wife. He knew that was over. It was the sense of loss that attends failure. A glorious beginning, the hope and the confidence and the certainty that the rest of your life will consist of an upward spiral of love, luck and at least a meager prosperity. Then nothing.

He was holding a small bunch of daisies he had filched from the Chinese grocer's up the street. Now and again he left her an offering like this, and he wondered what she thought when she found them on the steps in the morning. He knew it did no good, that he should stop it altogether. It was too maudlin, too demeaning, and if he were ever found out he'd die of mortification.

But he was paying homage, if not to the family itself then at least to the idea of one. Monigan didn't want to go back to those days but he needed to feel that period of his life actually once existed, was real and good and tangible and important.

He glanced up and down the street, dashed across and flung the flowers at the front door. Then he went to drink some more.

As he opened his eyes and rolled onto his side he saw Bill sleeping on the floor, a heap of bones and clothing. The dog had crawled out from under the bed in the night and was dozing with its snout stuck under the back of Bill's neck, cushioning his head from the cold linoleum. The mutt stirred, withdrew its nose and Bill's head banged on the floor. Monigan heard the dog click over to the window so he threw back the covers and gave the thing relief. He was too tired to go down the hall so took a leak after the dog and closed the window. Bill got to his feet then sat on the edge of the bed.

Monigan was out of smokes. He looked out the window at the shadows and guessed it was about noon. He remembered inviting Bill upstairs the night before, talking to him, trying to dig deeper into his story, but it hadn't gone very well. It upset him deeply that Bill had no place where he could be taken care of. Monigan yawned. He didn't mind being tired but would have liked it to be the result of a wedding reception. He'd work this week on getting a new tuxedo. He started to dress, preparing himself for the day.

Down the street at the corner store, Dwayne flung down a handful of change he had scrounged from his pockets. He gave the kid behind the counter detailed instructions on how to wrap the flowers. He had found some battered daisies on the front steps that morning but they were too shabby to give to Katlyn. He paid for the flowers and left quickly, before he could be misidentified as the accomplice of the punk stealing merchandise down the aisle.

Seldom have two people been so uncomfortable with each other as Dwayne and Katlyn were when our man walked into The Workbench. Dwayne casually proffered the flowers, and when Katlyn didn't respond he deposited them on the bar.

"Good day," Dwayne said stiffly.

"Hello," Katlyn replied.

Dwayne shuffled behind the bar.

"Thanks for coming in on such short notice," Katlyn said.

"Your concern won out."

"Pardon?"

"The hunger strike."

Katlyn moved away from him.

"I'm not complaining," Dwayne said. "But what came up?"

"I'm expecting a busy day. A hockey tournament over at the Moss Park Arena is ending this afternoon and the organizer will be coming soon to set up the back for the trophy presentations. I thought if you weren't doing anything . . . you don't have to stay if you don't want to. I can handle it myself."

"Those are for the bar." Dwayne gestured at the flowers. "Though they may wilt in here, so if at the end of the night you'd like to take them home . . ."

"They're nice."

They busied themselves with unnecessary puttering behind the bar until the phone rang, mercifully giving them something to do. Their hands reached the receiver at the same time. Dwayne snatched his away while Katlyn answered.

"Hello, The Workbench. Yes, he's right here."

Puzzled, Dwayne took the phone from Katlyn, trembling as their fingers came into contact.

"Feller — is that you?"

Sturgis. Dwayne straightened his back and cleared his throat. "How did you get this number?"

"Your old lady gave it to me."

Dwayne knew he hadn't given his mother the number. All he had done was write it down in his address book beside his phone. His window grate was anchored in concrete, the front door had four deadbolts and the stairs leading to the main floor were sealed off with a barricade a battalion of Gurkhas couldn't penetrate. How did she do it?

"So what is this — the Salvation Army? Your old lady told me you were working with derelicts. What's the deal?"

"I'm treating a case of delirium tremens right now. How can I help you?"

"By getting down here within the hour."

"For what?"

"If you ever want to hold a mike in your hand without calling Bingo for a bunch of rubbies, you'll get in here."

"I'll administer the daily round of thorazine and be there in fifteen minutes."

A shaft of excitement shot through him and all the old feelings cascaded through his mind: Dwayne Feller on stage, terrified but never so much alive; the almost sexual pulse of a show flowing smoothly, Dwayne in control, savagely taking an ungrateful house to task; the promenade down the aisle after a triumphant set. He could actually see the pride in Katlyn's eyes and the reluctant, but very real admiration from his father. "I have to go," he said.

"You're just walking out?"

"This will only take an hour or so."

"At least tell me what's going on."

"That was the owner of The Laugh Chance, a tyrant. My professional life hangs by a thread. Please."

"Oh, go on, but be back as soon as you can."

"Thank you, thank you so much." As he turned for his coat he smacked into Bill, bouncing him off the maroon carpet.

"Where did you come from?" he asked.

"How come everybody's always beating up on old Bill?" Monigan wailed. "That's the last straw, Frenchie, time I tore you a new asshole, coming in here and turning things upside down."

The father and the son stared at each other. Monigan actually looked at him for once, reading in his face the fear and the insecurity and the innocence. "Where you off to?" he asked softly.

"Oh, just some business to take care of," Dwayne said.

"You working later?"

"As soon as I finish with this."

"Okay. Sure. Well, I'll be around when you get back. You might pick me up some smokes on the way."

Katlyn was afraid to break the spell.

"What brand?" Dwayne croaked.

"Oh, whatever. Whatever you come across."

"Okay."

"Right. See ya."

"See ya."

So Dwayne set off for The Laugh Chance, perplexed at large and uncertain of what had just happened. Monigan sat down at the bar with no more idea than Dwayne. And Katlyn set to work, happy and with a leg up on both of them.

At the club, waiting for Dwayne, Sturgis was laughing to himself. Nothing filled him with glee like the opportunity to further his personal agenda while doing serious damage. He heard the front door open and close.

Dwayne was hot and itchy after his walk to the club. He climbed the stairs. He would have to be on his guard around Sturgis, quick on his feet, nimble of mind.

The Laugh Chance was set up as if for a show. Candles in place and lit, house lights down, spots focused on the stage. The owner emerged from his office, smiled and pointed to the head of the room. Dwayne shrugged off his coat and climbed on stage, blinking into the lights as Sturgis pulled up a chair in the front row.

"How does it feel up there?" he asked.

"Odd," Dwayne said. "Very odd." Involuntarily, his hand snaked out for the mike.

"The sound's off."

"Oh." Dwayne was awash with a sense of dislocation, up there staring at an empty room.

"It feels odd cause you haven't been doing enough shows to be comfortable with it. You take too long a break from strutting your stuff and next thing you know you've lost it. I know — twenty years in the business and even I'd be nervous on stage again. Use it or lose it."

"Where's this leading? You know why I'm not performing."

"You tell me."

"Huitzilopochtli."

"Is that some kind of wop curse?"

"The hummingbird god. While initially a beautiful bird who guided the Aztecs to a new homeland, he was transformed into the god of battle and eventually became the sun god, in whose name human sacrifices were made."

"Talk like a human being."

"I've been sacrificed," Dwayne said.

"You were screwing up, Mister."

Dwayne sniffed.

"You show promise," Sturgis said. "Unshaped, but raw talent. I like a guy who doesn't take shit from the crowd."

"I still have it."

Sturgis walked to the bar, allowing Dwayne to absorb the atmosphere of the stage. But Dwayne was absorbing nothing, steeling himself for the owner's judgment.

Returning with a soda and bitters, Sturgis climbed on stage beside Dwayne. "Looks good from here," he said.

"Yes," Dwayne agreed.

"I can guarantee you two regular spots a week," Sturgis said. "Friday, Saturday, whenever you like. More than that if the house comics are on the road, and I'm telling you right now they'll be finding themselves on the road."

"Two regular spots a week," Dwayne said. "I accept. Now I have to go — I've left a woman in a dangerous situation."

Sturgis shoved him back behind the mike. "Hold on," he said. "I'm not just going to fling the shows at your feet."

Dwayne sighed. "To what do I have to agree?"

"How's your cash flow these days?"

"I have simple needs."

"Wouldn't you like to make the big bucks?" Sturgis said. "But hey, what am I saying? You're an artiste, someone who just wants to practice his craft, have people appreciate him, laugh at his jokes, look up to him."

Dwayne reached out and touched the mike.

"What's with the social work?" Sturgis added. "You don't strike me as the type."

"I'm working in a bar," Dwayne confessed.

"So you got your old lady buffaloed."

"That's part of her nature."

"How do you work around those lowlifes? Here we are busting

our asses to get a couple bucks together, giving half of it to the government, and these jokers live on the public tit, never putting in an honest day's work."

"Not all of them," Dwayne said.

"They lie, cheat and steal, and who pays the price? Us, that's who. Paying for housing and free lunches and medical benefits. It's enough to make you sick."

"But Katlyn says . . . never mind."

"Katlyn — who's that? Your girlfriend? You got a girlfriend, Dwayne?"

"No!" Dwayne shouted. "I was thinking out loud. Working up a new bit. It's from standing on the stage."

"You should bring her down to one of your shows. Nothing impresses a skirt like seeing her honey on stage. Chicks love that shit."

"She's neither a skirt nor a chick." Dwayne played with the word in his head. *Girlfriend, girlfriend*. It was exciting, exotic. Katlyn in a colored sari, dancing for him in the court of Siam.

"I have a situation," Sturgis said. "Let's go over to the bar."

After a cranberry and Coke, Dwayne's stomach settled. Sturgis poured him another.

"I like that T-shirt idea," Sturgis said. "Bashi-Bazouks."

"Like any emblem, it helps to bond."

"Comics *should* bond," Sturgis said. "It's us against all of them out there. The house comics are having a party today."

"That's none of my business."

"Just saying it's a shame you can't be considered a house comic if you don't do regular shows."

"I don't want to mill around an apartment full of smoke and narcotics, rehashing old jokes and past triumphs."

"Saying, that's all."

"I have to get back to work."

"Got to talk to you about something," Sturgis said.

"Right. A situation."

"Not much of anything. Little business, nothing more."

Dwayne drank.

"I own a rooming house over on Parliament," Sturgis said. "It's falling down, hardly anything left of it. The people who live there are animals, real animals. They piss in the halls, wreck the furniture, smash the windows. But I can't evict them because of the laws set up to protect people like that, instead of the honest businessmen who keep this country running and maintain our way of life. So you see the situation."

"Not clearly."

"I figure, hey — what's a few more people on the streets? Anyhow, if the government's going to dip into our pockets to subsidise housing, let them build more shelters, keep them all in one place where we can watch them."

"Kitchener's practice of concentrating the Boers in laagers."

"Whatever," Sturgis said. "How's your drink?"

Dwayne pulled his glass away.

"So if you were to help me out we'd both get what we want. It's a very simple, foolproof plan. A little fire happens to spring up and Bob's your uncle."

"What?" Dwayne cried. "Bob may be your uncle, but he's no relation of mine. That's horrible."

"Hear me out," Sturgis said. "Nobody'll get hurt. The exterminator's supposed to fumigate the place, so I'll post a notice saying he's coming and everybody has to get out. That'll give you time to torch it with everybody clear. Let me finish! Those things go up in that area all the time, and there's no way to trace it to you."

"Certainly there is."

"I'm the only one with a motive. And it's in my best interest to shut up about it — that's pretty obvious."

"It's full of holes."

"Go."

"What if the insurance company determines it's a case of arson and refuses to pay up?"

"I've got no choice but to try. Don't think I'd be doing this if I had options."

"What if there are people left in the building?"

"I'll personally check after the exterminator sign's been posted. I guarantee the place will be empty."

"Doesn't the city have a plan for this type of thing? Isn't there a requirement to rebuild the rooming house?"

"Don't worry about it. I'll handle all that."

"Wait!" Dwayne cried. "What am I saying? Arguing the details means I'm considering the whole. No, no, I have to go, please let go of my arm."

Dwayne had too much information to sift through for him rationally to evaluate any of it. The last few weeks had so overloaded his logical apparatus that he was foundering in a stew of unconnected particles. He started to hyperventilate and Sturgis refilled his glass, trying to calm him down.

"It's your only hope of performing," the owner said. "Fame isn't for the weak of heart."

"I want three shows a week!" Dwayne suddenly yelled. "Three!"

"You got it."

"No. Never."

"Enjoy your life as a wino bartender."

"I'll move."

"To where? No city appreciates bad comics."

"You said I have promise."

"You do, you do, but your style . . . let's say it suits Toronto. Besides, your mother's here."

"This is monstrous!" Dwayne shouted.

"It's getting by in the world, giving up something to get something. And this is the only place you're going to get what you want, baby. What you need."

"I've never broken the law in my life."

"The law is made by people trying to protect the losers from those who pick up the checks. I'll throw in a house account."

"With tips?"

"With tips."

"Impossible. Hire a professional."

"I want you."

"Will I be allowed to audition for the Just for Laughs festival?"

"They've already drawn up their list," Sturgis said. "But anything else that comes down the pike you'll be in line for."

"I don't want to go on first."

"Go on whenever you want."

"This is shameful." Dwayne beat his glass on the bar, sloshing his drink all over himself.

"It's practical."

"Well, Gordon Liddy believes there's no shame in doing something illegal as long as it doesn't break your personal moral code."

"Exactly."

"But he wanted to kill a man by driving a pencil into his brain!"

"Don't worry. It's time to rely on yourself. Nobody gives a shit about you, Dwayne. An empty building, wood and bricks. Big deal."

Dwayne was thinking, searching for alternatives, looking for answers. He was terrified but strangely excited. He was used to having few options in his life so decisions up to now had been relatively simple. His father had left, so a normal home life was out of his hands. He was so full of conflict that he had to get on stage and give vent to it all. Showbiz, Katlyn, Monigan, Mum. They went together, independent elements that had a colligative power much stronger than his own feeble beliefs and moral underpinnings. Showbiz, Katlyn, Monigan, Mum.

"There's only one way to the top," Sturgis said. "Kicking and clawing and screaming. You think the big names didn't step on fingers on the way up the ladder?"

"I'd get caught. It's my karma to get caught at everything."

"It's me on the hook. I'm the guy they'll come looking for, and frankly, I don't care. It's my only way out."

"I want complimentary tickets for my girlfriend . . . for my friend."

"Sure."

"I can't. I just can't."

"See you."

"What?"

"Get the fuck out of here. I'm not going to beg. You tell anyone about this and I'll have you maimed. And I'm serious — never doubt the intentions of a desperate man."

"Wait, wait. This isn't how it works. We're supposed to keep dickering back and forth. Haven't you read Kissinger's memoirs?"

"I have nothing more to offer."

"A jacket. One of the leather ones with The Laugh Chance logo on the back."

"No problem."

"I couldn't pull it off." Dwayne hung his head.

"It's a building, not people."

"Is there any other . . . ?"

"Get out. Enjoy your life, whatever life you've got to look forward to."

Dwayne stepped away from the bar. "I need time to decide. There can't be any loopholes."

"Tomorrow," Sturgis said. "Take more time than that and you'll end up talking yourself in circles."

"Twenty-four hours, then." Dwayne had to get out of there. He couldn't think straight. "This time Monday."

Sturgis watched him leave, wondering what he was getting himself into. He kicked the bar, but had a gut feeling that Dwayne would come around. Bad decisions go hand-in-hand with a skewed mind.

Dwayne was suffering a rampage of conflicting emotions as he trod the sidewalk, avoiding the patches of ice and snow insisted upon by the gelid February air. Dwayne did not break the law, and it's difficult to attach a moral imperative to something to which you never give thought. It had little to do with respect or righteousness, it was more that he had never found himself in a position in which being a criminal was an attractive option. He lived a plain, unchallenging existence outside of his odd choice of profession.

He walked for miles, until he could walk no more and think no more, then went home. At two in the morning he bolted upright with the realization that he hadn't returned to work after the meeting with Sturgis. Crying with rage as he raced around trying to find his clothes, he finally burst half-naked into the night, clutching his shirt to his chest.

Katlyn wasn't at the bar, but Dwayne checked at every window to make sure. Without stopping to evaluate the consequences he plunged up the street and was soon pressing her buzzer, tentatively at first, then with greater insistence.

Katlyn padded down the stairs, wondering who it could be at this hour.

"Please," Dwayne said. "I know it's presumptuous of me, but I have to talk to you."

He was already halfway through the door so Katlyn pointed to the stairs and followed him up. Before going to bed she always threw the windows wide open. There was nothing she liked more than bundling up in old clothes and jumping under the comforter, just her eyes peeping out, bulwarked against the freezing air. Had she known it was Dwayne she would have changed out of her flannel work shirt, shapeless blue sweatpants and knee-high socks.

Dwayne could see his breath in the apartment, it was that cold, and he thought it was perfect. He flung himself on the couch.

"Would you like something to drink?" Katlyn asked on her way to the kitchen.

No answer from the living room.

Katlyn turned the front ring to simmer and scooped the scum off the top of a pot of hot chocolate. When she was back she lit a cigarette and waited for Dwayne to begin. He looked pathetic and, for once, too small for the room he was in.

"What do you want to do?" Dwayne asked.

"Go to bed."

"No, no — ultimately. What do you want to do with your life?"

"That's a complicated question for two in the morning. And before I even try to answer it, I think you owe me an explanation. I waited and waited at the bar then finally called your mother. She had no idea where you were, either."

"You were worried?"

"Yes, I was."

"Nothing to worry about. Uneventful day."

"Which is why you're here."

"Have you ever wanted to get to the top of the pile?" Dwayne asked.

"I suppose I have some vague notion of doing something worthwhile one of these days, but I must admit I haven't fastened onto anything specific." She could tell it was to be a one-way conversation, as no sooner did she finish than Dwayne was jumping back in.

"Ambition is cruel," he said.

"Not of itself. Turn it into a competition and it can be."

"Same thing."

"Not on your life. Accomplishment doesn't have to be tied to competition. You don't have to beat anyone to reach your goal. Happiness isn't measured by the number of whipped, unhappy people you leave in your wake."

"I don't know, I really don't."

"Of course you don't," she said. "And you don't have to know. The trouble comes from thinking you do. Seems to me a lot of people these days can't conceive of success if it doesn't come at the expense of the less able."

"What's that I smell?"

"Hot chocolate." She went to the kitchen and filled a mug for Dwayne.

Our man stared at her back. He found her intensely attractive in her casual clothing. It could have been the domesticity of it all. He looked around her apartment, noting with pleasure the tasteful touches, the simplicity. He nodded approval and took the mug from her hand.

"On Pizarro's second expedition into South America he was faced with mutiny on Isla del Gallo. He drew a line in the sand and only thirteen men crossed it to join him in conquest and glory. A decision always has to be made. Do you cross the line or slink away like a dog?"

"Crossing the line, conquest, glory." Katlyn spat the words out. "That kind of crap was eventually translated into social Darwinism. There's no racial or social hierarchy in my mind."

"Society is stratified," Dwayne said.

"Only economically," Katlyn said. "The same standards should apply to a little booster selling stolen razor blades at The Workbench and to a billionaire junk bond salesman. Wrong is wrong anywhere."

"I've wondered why you put up with the thieves in that place."

"Just giving them a small break on this end, the same as the courts and the system give the billionaires on theirs."

Dwayne digested this a moment. When he spoke it was with a dawning sense of relief. "You do tolerate wicked behavior though, don't you?"

"Not wicked," Katlyn said. "But yes, I'm lenient with my judgments."

"If someone was desperate . . . ?"

"Depends on the individual circumstances."

"If the goal was a worthy one . . . ?"

"I'm not saying the end justifies the means."

"But if . . . if there were feelings involved? You know, personal feelings?"

Katlyn blushed. "I could forgive almost anything for love."

"Leave me alone!" Dwayne suddenly wailed in confusion.

"Look around you — you're in my apartment, keeping me from going to sleep. I didn't start this."

"I'm sorry. I had no one to talk to."

"It's okay."

"I have to cross the line in the sand."

"Do what you have to do, but beware of the fallout."

"You've got to make sacrifices."

"Your own," Katlyn said. "Anything else is greed and cruelty. We're all in this together."

"No, it's us against them."

Katlyn got to her feet and thumped her mug down on the coffee table. "I'm going to bed."

Dwayne was lost in reverie, absently picking at a spot of food on his shirt.

"I'm going to bed," Katlyn repeated with emphasis.

Dwayne went to the door, fastening the buttons on his coat. "What days do you need me this week?"

"Wednesday and Saturday, like last week. You've got the hang of things around there, so if you want to put in a third shift let me know."

"Yeah," he said. "Three shows a week."

"Are you going to be all right? Are you okay?"

Dwayne smiled tightly and left.

THIRTEEN

Dwayne had to move quickly. He knew full well that indecision would replace his determination if he didn't attack with dispatch. On the way he had one more piece of business to take care of.

Dwayne's shoulder throbbed and ached. He wasn't used to power tools. He stood back and admired his handiwork. The drop bar rested snugly in its bracket on the inside of the door. Monofilament fishing line led from the bar up the door and through the hole he had drilled. He lifted the bar, opened the door and went outside, gasping as a blast of cold night air bit through his rayon shirt. The streetlight cast Dwayne's shadow over the hole in the door, but he found the fishing line and tied a loop on the end. He slammed the door and heard the iron bar drop into its bracket inside. The fishing line cut into his fingers, but after he attached the metal ring from his house keys to the loop, the contraption worked perfectly. He yanked on the ring — raising the bar — and opened the door. His mother would never figure this out. He closed the door and the bar banged home. Dwayne briefly considered a career as an inventor. Certain women like eccentric types.

On the third test the fishing line snapped.

Dwayne looked wildly around. He inched up to the door and put his eye to the hole. The line had parted somewhere inside. He was trapped out in the elements, a musher abandoned by his dogs.

Dwayne made it to The Workbench in record time and let himself in. A dull cast of phantoms cavorted along the walls, choreographed with his movements, his shadows multiplied by the security lamp and the wash of moonlight penetrating the windows. He was uncomfortable being in the place when it was empty. He went down to the basement, a small room that was home to the beer kegs, discarded chairs and tables and the hulks of crates and boxes. At the back, where Dwayne had hidden it behind some pipes, was a green duffle bag that he dragged out into the circle of light thrown by the lone fly-specked bulb. He opened it and checked the contents: a jerry can of gas, a week's worth of the *Toronto Sun*, a pair of rubber gloves and a balaclava. He fastened the bag.

Now he just needed something to wear. Scrounging around, he found an old overcoat, but the thing was so dense with filth and mold that it took his breath away. He would have to hurry now that he had no protection against the cold. He flicked off the light on the way up the stairs.

The rooming house stood lumpish and unimposing beside an abandoned lot on the corner. The original surface had been slathered with so many coats of paint over the years that it was barely recognizable as brick, pockmarks and bumps and blemishes giving it a look of final agony as it shed swatches of paint and dirt. Most of the windows were painted shut and the front steps were crumbling. The flat roof was home to a collection of chimneys and ducts pointing in all directions, giving it a cartoonish look in the glow of the city lights.

Dwayne skulked around the back, building up his nerve, then let himself in with Sturgis's key. Inside, the muffled nightsounds of wind and wiring and settling wood and brick sent Dwayne's heart into palpitations. No air in the hallway, no air at all, and he leaned against the wall, setting the duffle bag down at his feet. He pulled off the balaclava, not having to hide his features indoors. A couple of minutes had him breathing normally, though still not deeply, and he opened the bag. He put the gloves on. The top of the jerry can was stuck and it took a determined twist to get it free. He stacked the papers on the floor.

There was no hurry, he kept telling himself. Sturgis had told the residents to clear out for the exterminator until tomorrow morning. He couldn't see his watch but his internal clock said it must be after 0300 hours. There was no smell of anything except dirt and urine and a great overlay of misery.

Dwayne splashed half the jerry can's contents onto the pile of papers then stood there wondering what to do with the remainder. Should he trail it along the hall? Throw some on the corners of the building? Carrying the can, he walked down the corridor to the front of the rooming house. There were only two rooms on the main floor, the rest of the space given over to an office at the front and a large, sparsely furnished common area with an old TV and some kind of snack bar along the far end. Dwayne put down the jerry can and looked up the stairs. He wondered if he should check the rooms in case some bum had missed the evacuation notice, or ignored it and sneaked back in.

But he could not mount the stairs. One hand on the bannister, Dwayne let the plan collapse around him. He had known in his heart that he wouldn't be able to go through with it and was amazed he had made it this far. Faced with a line in the sand, he could merely scuff it with his toe.

He felt the press of anger. It was all the others who had forced him into it, of that Dwayne was sure. He had been solitary as a child, mostly ignored, and then abandoned as a young man. The mental calluses he developed had protected him from desperation up to this point in his life. Entertainment became his sole concern, but once he had exposed the hostility and the rage it all acted as a water bath, loosening the horny surface and exposing his need for acceptance and approval. He was not a strong man. He was no Legionnaire. He was Dwayne Feller, and right now he loathed himself.

The light going on up on the second floor took him full in the face. Dwayne staggered under its impact. A thin version of *Farewell to Nova Scotia* spilled down the staircase. Dwayne had no strength to run, to hide. The singing grew more resonant and was joined by the tinkle of water on water, then the toilet flushed and the song's chorus burst upon the building. A door opened, marking the start of a drunken argument between the singer and his neighbor, which in its turn triggered the opening of more doors and more complaints and so on, with the irresistible momentum of such a late-night encounter.

The place was full.

The enormity of the situation finally overcame Dwayne's inertia and he fled for the back exit. A lancet of light from under the rearmost room glistened off the gasoline-soaked pile of papers as Dwayne raced past. He hit the exit and sprawled out into the gravel behind the building. Righting himself, he scrambled along until coming to the frost fence at the edge of the property. All along the back of the rooming house lights were coming on. A couple on the fourth floor, five or six on the second, three on the third. Both rooms on the main floor were lit now, but with a different hue than the others. They pulsed in intensity, an arhythmic throb of incandescence throwing the garbage and the jettisoned scraps of furniture in the yard into stark relief.

The bottom windows blew out in concert with Dwayne's wail of disbelief. The bricks themselves shrieked as the flames licked at the layers of paint. The fire spread, and soon the street in front was serving as bleachers for the spectators that appeared as if by magic, and for the knots of semi-clad people who had emptied out of the rooming house and now stood watching their stake in society, their claim to existence, however mean, be borne aloft on the spears of the flames.

Dwayne was isolated in a pocket of calm. The fire escape was on the side of the building while the front door allowed others access to the street. There was no activity where Dwayne was at the rear of the property. He was in a world of his own except for one old man who stood at his second-floor window looking out at the flickering cityscape. Dwayne staggered to the back of the place and cried out to the tiny figure. The window was open but the man didn't seem too interested in jumping. He leaned out over the sill, looking this way and that, until eventually the smoke invaded his room and curled out around him and up into the sky.

The old fellow held the pose a minute, then dropped straight over the sill and down. Dwayne took a wild stab at the falling bundle and it hit him, driving him to his knees and jamming his face in the gravel. The skinny bum lay in Dwayne's arms, cradled underneath his torso. Dwayne let the man go and shoved his head back. Closing his lips over a mouth sour and slack, he forced air into the smoke-filled lungs over and over again. When the man was breathing normally, though still choking on smoke and saliva, Dwayne carried him to the frost fence and propped him into a sitting position. Then he climbed the fence and ran.

Bill coughed again and looked at the back of the building. Good thing he had fixed the window the day before. That would have been bad news if it was still jammed shut. Jean had been at him about it for a long time. Funny, the way he was so good at fixing stuff, that it took him so long to get around to it. The fire trucks were here and they'd put out the fire. They were good guys, those firemen. He knew some firemen. His hands were getting cold and stiffening up on him.

That was a pretty good catch that big man had made. Bill didn't think he could have done it. He used to be a pretty good ballplayer, but that was a long time ago, even before he had that job at the warehouse. Here come the firemen now. They'd seen him. Maybe they'd help him get up, because his leg was pretty sore and he didn't know if he could stand, what with it twisted up like that. He better call Monigan. His friend Monigan told him always to call if something happened. But this wasn't much. His hands were a little stiff and his leg hurt, but that's about it. He was sure glad that big man had been there.

No sooner were the doors open the next morning than The Workbench was buzzing. The soupline telegraph had done its job, so news of the fire had spread more quickly than the flames themselves and superseded all normal conversation. There was excitement in the air. News of disaster was life-affirming. It was something they had all experienced and so related to with under-standing. No bathos here, rather a great commonality.

Monigan came downstairs, having already contributed to the new social order. "They're going," he said.

"Just like that?" Katlyn said.

"I pointed out to them how they been keeping people awake all night with their partying. Also, I pointed out it was useless to argue, there being only four of them, so eviction it is."

"I haven't seen any rent from them for two months anyhow," Katlyn said.

"You let them slide on their rent?" Monigan was indignant.

"Have you ever been on time with yours?"

"But I'm special," Monigan said.

"What's Bill going to do for clothes?"

"We're having a whip-round, get him some stuff from the Sally Ann," Monigan said. "And let the boosters know that we need all the stuff they got that fits Bill. Maybe fix him up that way, won't have to line the pockets of them Salvation Army types who proba-bly use the money to send missionaries to Africa with." He headed for the door. "Smokes."

Katlyn watched him go then set to work. She was unable to fath-om how it was that once bad luck started it seemed to act of its own accord. How many times can someone take a kicking and not cower when they see footwear? She glanced up and let out a shrill yelp and ran for the door, followed closely by one of the regulars.

Monigan was leaning against the window, slumped but strug-gling to remain upright. Katlyn locked an arm around his waist and the other man supported Monigan by the arm.

"Maybe you should lie down," Katlyn said.

Monigan locked his knees and Katlyn felt the tremor. He blinked and took a deep breath. "Get away from me," he wheezed.

"Are you all right?" the regular asked.

"Course I am. It's this weird warm spell in February, is all. Or maybe something wrong with the chili."

"Come inside," Katlyn said.

By the time they made it through the door and got Monigan back on his stool, Katlyn was shaking. She had seen Monigan drunk, stupid, horny and angry, but always in control, even if only in his own mind. But the look of helplessness on his face when his body betrayed him had transformed him into a child. He had looked scared and small.

"Probably all the racket them kids make, keeping me up all night," Monigan said. He tried a grin that turned Katlyn's stomach floppy. "Good thing we're chucking them out. Bill won't make any noise."

"That's it," Katlyn said. "It's those kids. That and the sudden warm spell."

"Okay, that's enough," Monigan said. "What's that word?"

"Eh?"

"You know. Don't do it to me."

"Patronize."

"That's it."

"Everyone gets dizzy now and again."

"You could dizzy me half to death and I could still walk through fire. They could of used me last night."

Katlyn jumped at the diversion. "I passed there on my morning walk."

"Fire's the worst. Anything else you can butt heads against."

"What are those people going to do?"

"Same thing they probably done only a hundred times before," Monigan said. "Half of them wander around till somebody cracks them in the head while they're sleeping in a alley. Lucky ones'll find another flop where the landlord don't give a shit. I been in that place and it should of been burnt long ago."

"We'll be able to keep an eye on him here," Katlyn said.

"Till he wanders off like his wife, they find him dead by a snowpile."

"Don't lose all your faith in the world."

"In the world? I got all the faith in the world in the world. It's just the fucking things right around me that I can't fix that get my goat."

"I have three gallons of blue paint in the garage at home," someone called. "I suppose you could use it for Bill's room."

"Great," Katlyn said. "That'll brighten things up. And I'll dip into the slush fund and get him a new mattress."

"What about my room?" Monigan said. "I kick them kids out for you and you don't offer to paint my room and gimme a new nothing."

"You're right," Katlyn said. "After we paint we'll get you a canopy bed. Pink curtains, a Louis XIV chair. You can set up a salon Saturday afternoons, have all the boys over for a chat about Oscar Wilde."

"Now you're talking like the french fry. Speaking of which animal, where is he today?"

"His mother's sick. He won't be in till she's better."

"That's a lie," Monigan stated. "I never met a woman with more complaints in my life, but she doesn't get sick. Drives everyone else into the grave, but nothing touches her."

"Dwayne's taking care of her. Why would he lie?"

Monigan stared at her as if she had asked for his fingerprints.

"Never mind," Katlyn said. "How long will Bill be in the hospital?"

"I left this number with them. Turned out his leg ain't bust, just sprained his knee. We'll have him set up in those kids' room by tonight." He thought for a minute then sighed and levered himself off the stool. "Better go see if I can give them a hand with their moving preparations."

FOURTEEN

The community set about adjusting to the disaster and in a short time the new circumstances adopted the same rhythm as the old. Two and a half weeks slid by and Saturday was upon them, the first weekend in March. Bill was ensconced in his room above The Workbench and it was as if he had been living there forever. His mail was delivered and nested with the rest by the TV shelf; everyone called him by name. His room was a glaring, robin's-egg blue and was home to a new collection of gadgets and contraptions that seemed to accumulate by magic, as if they were ambulant and knew this was the place to go when their springs gave out or their cogs slipped or their housings cracked.

It was March, and some of the bulb plants were already splitting the soil. The lamb had broken from the gate a few strides ahead of the lion and was purposefully rousting winter from the city.

"Get over here." Katlyn reached over the bar and straightened Monigan's tie, a savagely flowered thing that stood out in obnoxious repose on his new white shirt. "If you're going to do it, do it right."

Monigan cuffed at her hands. "It don't matter."

"It does matter. In the first place, you're supposed to wear a bowtie with a tuxedo. Second, your jacket's too big."

"I been getting into shape, that's all. Fit fine when I got it. Had a bowtie but the mutt tore it up."

"Comb your hair."

"Check out Bill, you wanna check somebody out."

"Bill looks fine."

The old man was leaning against the pool table. His tuxedo hung flat and shiny, and except for his battered features — or perhaps because of them — he could pass as anyone's grandfather. His knee was still tender but he could walk, and Monigan had assured him the limp would garner the sympathy vote at the wedding they were about to crash.

"Enjoy yourselves," Katlyn called as they left by the front door.

They were back in an hour.

"What happened?" Katlyn asked.

Monigan's tie was missing, and his jacket was torn at both shoulders. A small amount of blood stained the front of his shirt.

"I don't know what it is," he said. "With times being as tough as they are you'd think people'd be more understanding."

"The bride was beautiful," Bill said.

"Ain't been to a wedding for a while," Monigan said. "Forgot one of the rules."

"Jean looked like that when we got married," Bill said. "She was all in white and she had those little baby's flowers in her hair."

"Forgot to wrap up a empty box for the gift table," Monigan said. "It's important to go into the reception carrying something, fools them right off. So I tried to lift one out the back of a car at the church."

"She was big," Bill said.

"Jean?" Katlyn asked.

"I was doing okay," Monigan said. "But I shouldn't of worn a regular tie with the tux. It got caught in the window crank and there I was bent over when the walloping started."

"She had a branch," Bill said.

"Who?"

"The lady that hit him."

"Bride's mother or something," Monigan said. "You know how women get at a wedding — they fly apart and go wonky in the head with the PMS and that. She give me a couple good shots with a tree branch while I was bent over getting my tie out the crank. She was pretty tired by the time I got loose, but hey, you can't hit a mother. Not at a wedding."

"Nice job," Katlyn said.

Monigan sat down and took a cigarette from Katlyn's pack. He felt okay. They had been thrown out of the wedding but Bill had seemed to enjoy himself. Monigan was happy to be able to do something for the old man, and he himself was drinking less and feeling healthy. His main concern was with his son. He was not a stupid man and could sense that Dwayne's absence the past two weeks had nothing to do with illness in the family.

He looked at Katlyn and tried to avoid the conclusion that it had to do with love. He was certain there had been some back-handed attempt at a relationship that had soured along the way. It was just that his son didn't usually react like this. Most of his life Monigan had been abandoned, cheated and beaten on, but he always rode it out. It wasn't as if he saw a silver lining in every cloud as much as he accepted the cloud for what it was, and if he couldn't find or steal a hat he got wet and big deal. His wife hid from the cloud. And Dwayne? He'd look you right in the face and swear the cloud didn't exist.

Behind him someone brought up a newly minted theory about the rooming house fire and Monigan turned to set him straight.

The Workbench wasn't the only place where the arson job was under review. It had been a difficult couple of weeks at the station for Constable Doyle. He and Ogilvie were in trouble, and Doyle felt his superiors were talking down to him and treating Ogilvie as the senior member of the partnership. It had always been like that for him, the beaver at the bottom of the totem pole. He liked his partner, but she was his junior, and too good-looking to be trusted.

The night of the fire Doyle and Ogilvie had been assigned the task of standing there shivering, watching two sergeants go about their business while the firemen mopped up in the blackened shell of the rooming house. Their job was to man the perimeter, taking

down names and essentials of everyone in the vicinity and pre-
venting creeps and gawkers from crossing the police line. Bill,
whom Doyle was getting tired of running into, apparently had
been rescued by someone. The old man had gone on at length
about making a catch playing baseball in a warehouse. He clearly
hadn't jumped and dragged himself to the back fence, and no one
at the scene admitted to the action, so it meant someone had
slipped the cordon.

They sat at the counter in King Canelli's, wondering how serious their slip had been and talking about things in general.

The King refilled their coffee mugs. "There you go," he said. "On
the house for free. Finally the police come in like my last place.
Pasta fresh as homemade."

"No time to eat today," Doyle said.

"Who cares? You come anytime, you welcome. At night we have
entertainment now. I play the guitar myself. Nobody else in my family sings as good as me since the Swiss put the pike in my sister."

Doyle shoved two loonies across the counter and Canelli
grabbed them.

The two cops went out and sat in the cruiser on George Street.
Ogilvie felt bad for her partner. He wasn't an inept man, merely one
of those people who creates tiny fissures for himself, only to see
natural events assume command and widen the cracks till he falls
through. She had caught hell down at Division for letting the man
slip the cordon but their superiors had been much tougher on her
partner. Doyle himself was used to the unfairness of it. He was the
kid in the corner store squirming in the owner's grasp while his
buddies flee laughing with the booty; the infielder in a close game
who has the ball skip on a rock and carom off his gourd into left
field; the pedestrian a falling piano pounds into quarks.

He jumped when he felt her hand on his.

"We should get going," she said.

"Where to?"

"Head over to Parliament."

He turned in his seat and regarded her with suspicion.

"I don't see anything wrong with poking around," she said.

"What's there to see? Besides, they already have men on it. No question it was arson. They found the jerry can and evidence of a stack of papers. It was set off with a cigarette butt. Case closed."

"Not till they find who did it."

"What do I know about detective work?"

"You're a cop," she said. "There's no harm in snooping on our own."

"I don't know."

"What about the old guy?"

"They've gone over it with him a hundred times. All they get is babble."

"He likes you. Why don't you try?"

"Where do guys like him come from?" Doyle said. "I saw him in the park yesterday going through the garbage cans. I was driving home looking forward to a good meal, and there he was bent over a can, elbow deep in shit, picking out bags and bottles. He even took half a sandwich — a fucking sandwich. It makes me sick . . . got nothing, got nobody."

"Let's go talk to him," Ogilvie said softly.

Doyle didn't move until she took her hand away, then he started the car and pulled onto Dundas, bound for The Workbench.

Over at their destination, Monigan skipped away from the river of water as the urinal flushed and overflowed. He went to the mirror and took a look, trying to bluff himself into believing there was nothing the matter. His chest and his head and his guts were treating him roughly these days. Five minutes before he had felt good but now he was shaking. He knew he should cut back on the booze, if only to keep from going over the edge and having to quit entirely. And he didn't want to live out his golden years unable to have a cold beer. This was his home: elbows on the bar watching the ball game, shooting the shit with the lads, picking up work for short periods at a time, getting by.

Monigan had long ago chosen this lifestyle, but a great many people had done no such thing. He knew well that for those who have little to look forward to every day, a cold draft and a cigarette bear no resemblance to anything luxurious. They become necessities, the tiniest bits of pleasure squeezed out of a life that holds no prospect of private boxes at the ballgame or new cars or vacations. The pub was their home, Monigan's home.

Pondering the societal and governmental assaults on his friends' world made his heart hammer. He lowered his head and squeezed the sides of the sink. When he had calmed down he ran his fingers through his hair and went out to the bar, where the sight of the two cops sent his poor heart racing again in headlong flight. He shoved his way between Doyle and Ogilvie and took Bill by the elbow.

"First, let's get you sitting down," he said. "That knee's still wonky and besides, it's a shorter distance to fall when Doyle starts swinging."

"Get out of the way," Doyle growled. "We just want to talk to him."

"Only four hundred cops talked to him so far. He don't know nothing."

"Someone saved his life," Ogilvie said. "We want to find out who it was."

"My guess is the guy saved him is the guy started the fire, elsewise he'd of stepped forward by now. Most people around here ain't had a lotta credit come their way, so if he ain't bragging it's 'cause he's running."

"Shut up and get out of the way," Doyle said. "I'm through messing around with you."

"Just trying to help," Monigan said. "Don't wanna see you deeper in the shit."

"What's that supposed to mean?"

"What are you?"

"Eh?"

"You a detective?"

"No."

"Right. Way I see it is a little constable ain't gonna be investigating no arson. So I figure you and the tomato are trying to save your asses somehow." He paused and dug a thumb in his nose. "So I'm helping."

"Why would you want to help?"

Monigan lowered his voice. "Bill and his wife lived in that place. Shithole as it was, it was all they had. Then she went and died, and Bill's so screwy he ain't quite sure whether she's gone or not. We got him living upstairs but he's lost. He don't know from his hands to his feet which to put his shoes on. Only right to catch the guy." He resumed in his normal voice. "Besides, who knows if you get a promotion from this and they transfer you outta my face every time I turn around."

The cops shrugged at each other.

"Can you talk to him?" Doyle asked. "Do you reach him?"

"Sure," Monigan said. "Me and Bill are like brothers."

"I don't want you prying."

"Prying how?"

"Stay away from the site, and don't go running around getting in our way. Not a word of this to anyone. Just keep your ears open and see what you can pick up."

"Gimme a cigarette," Monigan said. "And I might need a couple of bucks to keep the investigation going."

"You're not part of the investigation." Doyle passed him a smoke. "You come up with information and we'll see about the money."

"You better open that wallet," Monigan said. "Who knows if I remember what Bill tells me and what I hear on the street? And I can't live off these fucking menthols."

Doyle and Ogilvie scanned the room and left.

Monigan immediately helped Bill off his stool and onto his feet. "Come on, better get down to the house, do some detective work."

"Monigan," Katlyn said. "Don't go getting over your head on this."

"Over my head."

It was still warm out and Monigan's mood matched the air's clemency. It had been a long time since he had anything to do, something positive and productive, and he was already walking taller because of it. He scowled at people on the street, treating everyone as a suspect. He felt magnificent now that he had a purpose, as if he had just gained employment. He considered stealing a badge.

There was still ice in the wreckage, odd geometric clumps of it seizing blackened and blasted boards in its jaws. Monigan strained at a two-by-six that was decorated with scarred chunks of drywall. It slipped from his hands and crunched down, sending aloft a cumulus of soot with the particular smell of a house fire, the carboniferous flour that deeply invades the lungs. For days after the fire the building had displayed its own bizarre charm. A wasted hulk, yes, but festooned with gigantic icicles from the hoses, a sparkling collection of icework, ropes of ice along the power lines, skating rinks amid the carnage, sheets of crystal draped on the walls. The subsequent warm weather had melted the display, leaving only insulated, isolated lumps of ice.

Monigan heaved and tossed and kicked his way through the slush and crud, having no idea what he was looking for but hugely enjoying the physical activity. He paused with his hands on his hips, surveying the wreckage with a proprietary sweep of his eyes, then chased off another bunch of kids who had come to snoop. He looked at the mess and decided to quit for the day. There was old Bill, standing on the sidewalk, staring up the street. Bill wasn't very interested in helping, but Monigan figured he'd just get in the way anyhow. Monigan could handle the investigation alone, maybe use Bill for questioning. He tried to remember how they did it on TV, the psychologists and specialists and Quincys.

Monigan was extremely pleased with himself. He pictured the looks on the cops' faces if he managed to march the guilty party into the station. As soon as he thought of the cops he thought of Ogilvie, and realized he had better attend to getting laid soon. He firmly believed that a man can go goofy in the brain when the white count gets too high. Also, the investigation was tougher work than he'd anticipated. He needed a cold beer.

"Bill!" he called, calf-deep in black bilge and hooey. "Figure we better leave everything where it is till we can get back on the case. Let's get us home, gimme time to sort out all the facts in my mind. Lots of facts to work out."

He waded out to join Bill on the sidewalk. A middle-aged couple stopped to gawk, but Monigan growled in his throat and advanced on them until they backed off and crossed the street.

"That's all we need," Monigan said. "Civilians fucking up the clues."

The two men set off and were no sooner through the door of The Workbench than Monigan assaulted Katlyn with about four hundred theories he had cooked up. The sheer weight of them finally caused her to tell him to keep quiet. She had her own problems to deal with. The rest of the night they spent eyeing each other, each ticked off that the other had no appreciation for what was important at the moment.

FIFTEEN

It had been a long time since Dwayne had seen the world outside his apartment. Katlyn had accepted his need to be alongside his mother during her illness. Now if only his mother truly were suffering, Dwayne would not feel so alone and abandoned in his misery.

He had seen the news reports on the fire, and while no one had been seriously injured, the event still had him shaking in recollection. Dwayne also had seen the interview with Sturgis on CITY TV. The owner's years on stage stood him in good stead, allowing him to come off as a grieving landlord whose extended family suddenly had to fend for themselves in a hostile society.

Dwayne could remember the night in loathsome detail, as the gravity of the situation had given him an impersonal, disembodied view of the whole. True, he had run wildly all the way back home, but by mentally retracing his route he confirmed it hadn't been a flight of panic, rather of the understandable need to keep out of sight. Of course, crashing through hedges, climbing fences and upsetting garbage cans had lent little to the furtiveness of his escape. And he had to admit he had filled his pants, but was able to convince himself it was from the laxative effect of all the running.

The morning after, his mother wanted to call the police when she saw Dwayne's splintered door, and he was forced to explain about the drop bar and locking himself out and breaking back in with a crowbar. His hands were still shedding skin from around the burst blisters.

The ensuing days passed with excruciating slowness, seconds ticking by, not even sleep bringing surcease to the hammering in his brain. But eventually Dwayne reached the state where he knew action was imperative, as it could scarcely be more terrifying than the alternative. Mostly it was the door. When once again he began to feel interested in what was beyond the injured slab of wood, he knew the healing had begun. The food supply he had cadged from his mother was running low. He had lost twenty-three pounds and some of his hair, and his nerves were shot.

Dwayne flipped through the Yellow Pages and called a lock-smith. The man was able to temporarily repair the hinges as well, and had no trouble with billing the service to Dwayne's mother who, after all, was the owner of the house. When the locksmith was gone Dwayne practiced slipping home the three new dead-bolts. He was glad to have something solid to turn his hand to while trying to get over the guilt and the horror. Besides, he felt better now that he had reached a decision.

Dwayne had decided to turn himself in. After a seventy-two-hour frenzy of reading the collected works of Kipling, he had come to the conclusion it was his duty to do so.

After all, he reasoned, he hadn't really set the fire. The late news said someone from a back room had tossed a cigarette butt into the hallway. But he knew the intention of the deed was crime enough. He thought of jail. Would they give him a year? Two years? Five? Ten? He might even become a folk hero in prison, a living legend. Bravely sequestered away, refusing parole, writing his magnum opus while protestors raged in seething hordes outside the walls demanding his release, publishers indulging in legal battles over the rights to his life story.

He wondered if Katlyn would wait for him. Candle in the window, ribbon around the oak tree, growing old with grace and dignity as her man sat out his time. But what if she didn't? Dwayne immediately changed his mind. He couldn't turn him-self in. He'd bluff his way through, an outlaw in a savage land.

Besides, he figured, no one had been killed or seriously injured. The entire event could be interpreted as a public service, the rooming house an offense against society, and good riddance to it.

Hell, he didn't know what to do. He started to cry. Big sloppy tears coursed down his cheeks and spread into a delta as they encountered his beard. He let them run as he slipped home the last deadbolt and lay face down on his futon.

"What have I done?" he blubbered into the mattress.

Eventually his mind gave up the fight and Dwayne slept. It was a good sleep that carried right through the night and Dwayne awoke with something of his old vigor. He took a shower then walked around the apartment for twenty minutes, air-drying his carcass. As he was pacing he started rehearsing. He knew he would have to tell Katlyn first, hoping her strength and wisdom would transport him out of his predicament. He felt vile and evil, but that all would be quashed by Katlyn's purity. He stopped and stared at the blank TV. How could he tell Katlyn? She'd hate him for life, he knew it. He'd have to dodge the whole issue.

Dwayne went back and forth in this manner until he was physically exhausted. He staggered and came close to falling. He hadn't thought much about Bill at this point. Vaguely he figured the old man hadn't recognized him, as it had been dark and Bill was only half-conscious. Besides, Kipling's heros wouldn't have let that bother them. They would have marched right up and taken their medicine.

He decided to get dressed, hoping that by then the proper course of action would become clear. As he pulled on his clothes his mind tripped along on its orienteering exercise, along paths, climbing hills, plunging into valleys, dodging obstacles and several times going right off the edge of the map. Through it all he cried and cursed and tried to ignore his conscience, and finally decided to force a resolution in the manner of all helpless people: he'd walk into The Workbench, face Katlyn and his father and old Bill and see what the hell happened from there. Dwayne wiped the last trace of mucus from his nose, squared his narrow shoulders and hurled the door open.

Katlyn was just arriving at work. She had spent that Sunday morning at Kensington Market. The mild, early March air had her walking with a spring, had affected everyone the same way. People were coming out of their winter stoops and actually smiling now and again when they figured they wouldn't be caught at it. It was such a grim, gray presence the city adopted over the winter, that it was no wonder folks took to plunging along subway platforms and down sidewalks in such egocentric isolation, hoarding their reserves of patience and sanity till the time when the sun finally climbed more than three fingers above the horizon. It would be a couple of months yet until the weather allowed them to add to their reserves, but with the end in sight it was acceptable to portion out morsels here and there, everyone comporting themselves with a regard for those around them that was absent in the subarctic hours of deep winter. The supply plane was coming in so the rationing rules could be relaxed.

Kensington Market was feeling the change, the Portuguese flinging their fish around with renewed abandon, the shop keepers lavishing extra care on their vegetable arrangements. The comforting mixture of sights and sounds made it Katlyn's favorite part of the city. She had picked up enough for a single meal. She liked shopping that way, scurrying around, buying things at random, finally spilling her knapsack's contents on the kitchen counter and trying to figure out what to do with it all. She turned down Spadina, the wide thoroughfare calling up images of a different time. She much preferred the older areas of Toronto to the visual indignities of Bay Street, the Harbourfront, or anything with Honest Ed's face on it. She stopped and removed her nylon windbreaker and tucked it into the last space in her pack. Stepping up the pace, she was soon sweating under the straps.

The thought of following a morning like this with another day at The Workbench wasn't pleasant, particularly because Dwayne was going to be absent again. As she waited for the light to change at College, bouncing on her toes and loosening the pack straps, she wondered if there would be any problem in making a phone call. There was no reason why she shouldn't. If Dwayne's mother was better he should be able to pull a shift. She tried to write it off as checking up on an employee but couldn't come close to convincing herself. She missed him. She tried to worm out of it, but she missed him.

There was some odd nexus between her and Dwayne that Katlyn couldn't dissect. Monigan had once told her that whenever he thought he might be falling in love he set down on a piece of paper the pros and cons of getting involved. Inevitably, he explained, this reduced the woman in question to such a level that no choice was required at all. Katlyn had no desire to emulate Monigan's approach to affairs of the heart, or most other affairs for that matter, but even a gloss of Dwayne's strengths and weaknesses made her wonder what she saw in him.

But Katlyn knew that wasn't how it works. You can't reduce love to a list. You might as well try to describe a smell, or the impact of breaking out of the trees on a ridge and gazing down at the valley that spreads from here to . . . well, it never seems to stop, does it? Katlyn smiled. She'd call him. After two weeks of worry and melancholy, she needed his presence.

She dropped her supplies off at home and went to open the pub. She had just attended the arrival of the first barflies, gadflies and houseflies when Dwayne entered. As usual, all eyes snapped to the door as it opened, a trait common to people unaccustomed to good news walking in on them.

Dwayne felt the eyes searing his skin right through his tunic and he almost fled. Katlyn was behind the bar. Dwayne's stomach clenched tight and he doubted if he could keep control of his nerves, but, forcing one foot ahead of the other, he slid into the horseshoe. His eyes were brimming.

"I'm so sorry," he began. "I didn't know what I was doing . . ."

"Your mother was sick," Katlyn said. "Why would I be upset?"

Dwayne swallowed and looked at his feet.

"I hope it's not more serious than you thought." She tried to get a look at his face.

"My mother," Dwayne said. "My mother. I don't know. She stole money from me, my T-shirt money."

"What's wrong with you?" She put a hand on his arm. "Maybe you should sit down."

"No," Dwayne said abruptly. He yanked down his tunic. "Nothing's wrong. Nothing."

"Okay," Katlyn said slowly, unconvinced. "Why don't you grab a tray?"

"I need to work. I have to be busy, tax myself to the fullest extent. A chain gang, penal servitude."

"I'll be here to help."

"Fine," Dwayne said. "That's fine, just fine. And dandy. Fine and dandy. What's there to do? I'll clean the toilets, that's what I'll do. Something dirty, disgraceful. I might not use a brush. That'll be fine. Fine and dandy."

As Dwayne broke for the bathroom, Katlyn looked around the bar for support. No one had found anything unusual about Dwayne's outburst and it halfway convinced her it was in her mind. She had been undergoing a lot of upheaval in the past while, what with her burgeoning discontent with the bar, and then Dwayne showing up to toss her into a spin. She thought she might be reading Dwayne wrong. Her emotions around him were too shaky to allow perfect analysis. It was a strange feeling to her, new and unsettling. Not unwelcome, but she had to admit that attached to it was a certain strain.

She hadn't much time to wonder about Dwayne before Monigan and Bill came through the door.

"Don't even think about sitting down like that!" she yelled.

Monigan, trailing a wandering esker of debris, ignored her and flopped on a stool. He helped Bill up beside him and apologized as he bumped the old man's bad knee on the way up. Bill winced.

"We had it this close to being solved," Monigan said, squinting through the aperture between thumb and forefinger.

"I'm not cleaning up after you," Katlyn said. "And you reek to high heaven."

"Almost had some clues, but the thing of it is that deciphering a crime takes a lotta thinking — on your own, is what I mean. So instead of coming straight here, which is where we were gonna come, but where there's too many people bugging your ass, we stopped off for a beer down the road and what do you think we find except Small Wally's dead. Last Thursday, they found him, there he was in his room and they just found him."

Monigan's voice was flat, no emotion evident. "See, I never much liked him," he continued, plainly speaking to himself as much as to Katlyn. "That was 'cause we were too much alike, which is to say — well, I don't have to explain. But the thing of it is there was nothing wrong with him. Somebody had hung a ass-whipping on him according to the guys that found him, but not enough of one to kill him. Had lots of things wrong with him: his heart, and probably a liver bigger than four cows, but it's only that nothing really got him. It's like stuff caught up to him."

Katlyn had never seen him wearing this child's quizzical expression.

"I seen guys die and I know guys that died and all that, but funny how it is . . . Don't even know why I been thinking about it, but it makes you wonder. How come you can be cruising along and then everything catches up? That's just what it is — you're ahead of the game, ahead and ahead and then all the shit catches up. It's like . . . it's like you're trapped in a alley and it's all shooting in on you. All the bad luck that maybe you deserve 'cause of all the good luck you had, all the stuff you done and all the stuff you didn't get to do, and usually it catches up when you're doing something like Small Wally, just laying down or watching TV or taking a dump. I think that's no way to go at all. You got to go out doing something big, something . . . you know, grand!" He sat back and pointed at the draft tap.

Katlyn drew the beer. She hoped Monigan went out doing something grand.

"Sorry." Monigan was still partly in the hook of his crochet. "I don't like the idea of shit catching up to me, is all. Not like that I don't."

"I know," Katlyn said softly. "But you'll find something big." She could have sworn Monigan blushed, ignoring for the moment the impossibility.

"Best get us a couple more here, investigating being more of a thirsty job than I counted on."

Katlyn decided not to ask him to elaborate on the investigation. It would surely get him going again and she already had Dwayne's odd behavior with which to contend. As she dropped the glasses Monigan's tone shifted into a more familiar register.

"The fact of the matter is, none of that bothers me as much as not having a bowtie and a woman. That's what I need to fix this day up."

"Stick with the bowtie," Katlyn said.

"I know how you women are about matchmaking, it being a religion with you, so I'll let you have your way and set me up."

"All my friends are my age." Liar, she thought. All my friends, indeed.

"Younger the better," Monigan said. "Then you get to teach them the right way. Probably have half a hundred of them crawling starry-eyed up the drainpipe to my room at night, fighting one another for the big lamb flagpole."

An old gaffer across the horseshoe snorted and said, "I was in Delila's place Sunday, and she said you couldn't git it hard enough for a cat to scratch."

"I probably just banged her senseless."

"Maybe you should learn from the praying mantis." Dwayne was back. His exertions in the bathroom had done him a world of good, the physical and mental repugnance he felt while elbow-deep in the fetid pools working as a salve on his conscience. "The favored theory of why the female decapitates the male during the mating ritual is that the head is the seat of inhibitory nerve centers, so sexual performance is improved by biting off his head."

Katlyn grinned. Dwayne appeared to be back to normal. At least, his version of it.

"You could be right, Frenchie," Monigan said, looking at his son with none of the usual disgust. "You're the one to know, reading all them books, you and Katy both. Probably something I should have done when I had the chance."

Dwayne felt a pleasant tickle pass through him. He wondered what was wrong to make his father behave like a human being. He didn't have long to think about it because he then caught sight of Bill. Now he was for it. Carefully, he swung over in front of the old man.

Bill looked up casually.

"Hello, Bill," Dwayne said quietly.

"Hello," Bill said. "How are you today?"

"Oh, I'm doing quite well."

"Not so cold out."

"Not so cold."

Against his will, Dwayne's right leg started vibrating. Sewing-machine knee, rock climbers call it, the involuntary jerking that accompanies steady, unrelieved stress. At the first opportunity he returned to the bathroom, and when he emerged, having soaked his face in cold water, he felt better.

The biggest problem he had that shift was with Katlyn. He was so terrified of her reaction to his crime that he turned into a mute. Dwayne decided to put off his confession. He'd wait until the perfect moment instead of blabbing it out just because that was the right thing to do. All night long he could not keep his eyes off her, nor could she keep her eyes off him, yet the entire time they never looked each other full in the face. Something had to give before both the idiots lost their minds completely.

Next morning Dwayne awoke and stared at the ceiling for an hour. By all appearances, and judging by the rhythmic if faintly asthmatic rise and fall of his chest, he had not been turned into the police and executed the night before. He was at a loss as to the sequence of events. Guilt had turned his shift into a wretched exercise, several times causing him to spill drinks when Bill's shadow fell on him. For Bill's part, he had been his typically vague self. Dwayne alternated between accepting this as proof that Bill did not recognize him and being convinced it was some plot the bum and Monigan had cooked up to drive him insane and send him careering down the street to turn himself in. At least his father had been easy on him, nursing a few beers while mumbling about a smallwally. When Monigan did address him it had been with something approaching respect, or at least patience, and Dwayne hadn't known what to make of it: but he knew it felt good.

Dwayne remembered one curious incident. A man at the bar had been crying in his beer over having missed three days of work that week, a result of a brief but titanic binge, when his employer came in and eventually handed the man his pay envelope. As the conversation developed, it became clear that the man had not been docked for the missed days, in appreciation of which he bought all his pals a round, embarking on what promised to be another three-day blackout.

It wasn't the first incident of its kind Dwayne had seen in The Workbench: loans made to people who could not repay so much as a bummed cigarette; markers accepted on bets; merchandise changing hands on a word or a nod. He supposed that was how the hidden economy operated, at least on a rudimentary level. People with nothing binding to those without, cleaving to men with no luck, fusing to women with no hope, and around and around. No one individual strong enough to break the circle, each dependent on the other. So not a hidden economy, really, more of a hidden society, and as with any society, exclusionary, frightened and fragile.

But now Dwayne had to take care of himself and the logical beginning would be to confront Sturgis. Dwayne suspected that his cocking up the arson job abrogated their agreement, but he had to try. The anguish had already taken years off his life and he was looking to salvage anything from the debacle.

He struggled off the futon. For the first time in many days he felt the craving for solid food, but the fridge was empty. Dwayne had been too broke lately to stock it after the food from his mother petered out. He couldn't face Sturgis without fuel in his belly. Scrambling around in the crisper, he came up with a pinch of celery leaves and a grape stem. He threw them over his shoulder. He opened the freezer compartment, which due to accumulated frost had shrunk to one cubic foot. As he was closing the door a glimpse of something behind a breastwork of ice drew from him a shriek of delight. A Haagen Däzs vanilla ice cream tub!

No sooner did he grab it and hold it lovingly up to his cheek, than it dawned on him what he held. He put the carton down and answered the phone. It was his mother.

"I want to get this straight. You've given up on life and refuse to face your responsibilities as an adult, is that right? I'm afraid you'll end up like that man in Flin Flon who locked himself in his car, ran a hose in from the exhaust pipe, then shot himself."

"If he was going to shoot himself, why bother with the hose?"

"It's what they call a double suicide."

"You should have your cortex dissected."

"So what is it? When you first started working with the unfortunate your mood improved so much. We talked on the phone, you took me to the dry cleaners . . ."

Dwayne fiddled with the ice cream tub, refusing to be drawn out.

"Now you're down in the dumps again."

"Mother, I'm going through a hard time. I'm trying to return to the stage, and . . . well, there are other things. If you called about something specific, please get on with it."

His mother's sobbing gave him time to pry the lid off the ice cream tub and retrieve the wad of bills. The rubber band was frozen and broke when he picked at it. On quick inspection it looked as if all the T-shirt money was there. He wished his mother would stop breaking into his apartment. Then there would be no need to hide his valuables. His mother stopped crying.

"Are you still there?"

"Yes," Dwayne sighed.

"With this warm weather, the gardening center has a sale on bedding plants. Would you like to go with me this afternoon and pick out some nice flowers for the front yard?"

"I'd love to, but I have some purchases of my own to make."

"I've never known you to go shopping. You always leave that to me. That's why your Christmas wish list always has things on it like dish soap and cup hooks."

"Nevertheless."

"I know where all the best prices are. What are you looking for?"

"A car, a hose and a shotgun."

Dwayne hung up. He peeled off a frozen twenty and dropped the rest of the money back into the Haagen Däzs tub. His mother's calls were becoming more and more burdensome.

1112 hours. Sturgis would be in the office by noon and Dwayne felt his shrunken stomach clench. How could the meeting be anything but disaster? How could he keep from breaking down? So far he was experiencing wild emotional swings merely from keeping it to himself. It might be impossible for him to recount the evening out loud, looking right in Sturgis's eyes, being judged and sentenced by the man.

He thought of staying home and laying in a supply of food now that he had money. And he needed to pull another shift at The Workbench as soon as possible. Besides, how could he think of talking to Sturgis before confiding in Katlyn? Yes, he would march over there right now and prostrate himself before her. No, he had to get back on stage. No, love was more important. Monigan, what about him? What would be the repercussions of his finding out? Katlyn would know, best to ask her. Sturgis he could deal with tomorrow, or any time.

He leaned back against the wall and let the ice cream tub drop to the floor. Lost.

SIXTEEN

The investigation had electrified Monigan. For the first time in a long stretch he had something important to do. His friend had been wronged, along with many other people, neighborhood people. Monigan wasn't much of a knight-errant, but this was making up for a lot he had sloughed off over the years.

He also had a couple of other things to set right. The first time he had put the arm on Sturgis it was for the cash, but Frodo hadn't been paid in full and this time Monigan was happy to help out of friendship. While he was at it, he would clean up another piece of business. He grinned. He was on a roll.

"Don't worry about nothing," he said. He lit another cigarette and leaned against the rear fender of the bookie's car.

The driver's door was open and Frodo was sitting sideways in the seat. "I wish you'd let me come with you."

"Tough times these days," Monigan said. "Nothing wrong with asking for help."

"Well."

Monigan flipped the butt and headed for The Laugh Chance. The long climb to the club left him wheezing, but his dog was doing fine, happy to be on an outing for any reason.

"Hidy, hidy," Monigan called as he barged into the office.

Sturgis grabbed for the phone, but Monigan carefully took his hand away and pushed the thing aside. The dog trotted over and curiously sniffed around.

"I explained everything to your boss," Sturgis said.

"Course you did."

Sturgis eyed him with a touch of relief. Monigan was calm and much less aggressive than at their first encounter. Still, this was the capper to a string of incredibly bad luck.

The third time the cops had come by to pester him, Sturgis had come close to losing his cool. He watched out the window as the two detectives drove away. Back in his office he slammed the side of the computer monitor, crashing it to the floor. The cops couldn't pin anything on him as long as Dwayne kept his mouth shut. But then, anyone stupid enough to leave a gas can in the place he'd just torched was liable to do or say anything. Sturgis had called and called the Feller residence but Dwayne's mother hadn't liked the sound of his voice, and furthermore was getting tired of acting as her son's answering service so failed to pass on the messages. Sturgis took it to mean Dwayne was terrified, the right conclusion from the wrong evidence.

The insurance company had made it clear that unless they caught the person responsible and proved no connection to the owner, Sturgis would have to eat the loss. Arson it was, beyond a doubt, and the best Sturgis could hope for was to stay out of jail. It was his own fault, he could see that. So addled had he been by his financial situation and so gleeful at the thought of suborning Dwayne into acting as his instrument, that he hadn't thought the thing through. A professional would have been costly but effective.

Still, he thought the plan should have worked. It would have been too obvious if an empty building had gone up, so of course he hadn't called the exterminators and posted a notice. No, he figured, much better to have the authenticity of screaming confusion as people hurled themselves from windows and crushed one another in stairwells. As it turned out, they all had escaped, so Sturgis wondered what all the bitching was about. Yes, it should have worked. But Dwayne had left the gas can and the papers in the hallway.

So he had all that on his mind, his financial state was worse than ever, and now he had to deal with this large, unsanitary leg-breaker.

"I have insurance money coming," Sturgis said. "As soon as it's in . . ."

"Sorry," Monigan said. "You already used the insurance shtick with me. You told me the money for the Jag would cover the nut and all you come up with was a grand."

"That was the car. I'm talking about the insurance on a building I own. There'll be more than enough to cover what I owe your boss and I'll throw in extra juice 'cause he's had to wait so long."

"Quit shaking, you little wiener," Monigan said. He liked using this approach. Subtlety and diplomacy seemed to have all the efficacy of a direct assault. "All I'm saying is you're gonna have to do better than that."

"It's the truth," Sturgis said. "I own a rooming house that burned down a couple weeks ago, and I'm just waiting for the settlement."

Monigan felt a shiver run through him. He couldn't believe that after all his investigating a clue had fallen into his lap. "Whereabouts is this rooming house?" he asked coolly.

"Who cares," Sturgis said. "Over there in Cabbagetown."

"By Parliament?"

"Yeah, yeah."

In one stride Monigan was up against him and had his paw around Sturgis's neck. "There were people in there, you slimy fuck, good people. My friend!" When he realized the owner couldn't reply he released him and flung him into the chair.

Diplomacy can only take you so far.

"Please," Sturgis said weakly. "Please let me catch my breath."

Monigan edged back to the door, hoping the distance would keep him from killing the little shit.

"Listen." Sturgis was glad to be sitting, his position of strength. "I urge you to look at this logically. The total amount of money I owe your friend is seven thousand dollars. I make that in a good weekend here at the club. As well, I have an extensive investment portfolio and land up in Muskoka. You know yourself that I drove a Jag."

"So you told me."

"Between you and me," Sturgis said. "Between you and me, have you ever made a few bets and then have other expenses come up? What usually gets priority?"

"Okay, sure. Maybe I dodge the book for a while. But I come through. And that ain't what we're talking about."

"That's exactly what we're talking about," Sturgis said.

"Why would I torch my own rooming house for the insurance? Because that's what you're accusing me of, isn't it?"

"Fuckinright."

"Why wouldn't I use the rent to pay off your friend? Why not sell the building? We're only talking seven grand, here. With all the money I have coming in, from all the sources, it's obvious I have no trouble covering the bet. But you know what happens. You're a gambler, a good one if I don't miss my bet . . . heh, heh . . ." He trailed off in a susurrus of wheezing and nervous laughter. Rubbed his throat.

"Then why'd you say you can't pay up till the insurance money comes in?"

"To stall you," Sturgis said. "There — I'm being completely honest with you, all my cards on the table."

"TV says it was arson." Monigan was heating up again. "So do the cops."

"Could be. You know the people who live there, you say. Tell me — and I don't mean to be insulting — but tell me how many of them have a grudge, how many of them are used to criminal activity, how many would do something like that out of malice, how many are soft in the head to begin with, how many are usually too piss drunk to . . ."

"Enough, I get it." Monigan could see his point, but something in his gut told him this wasn't the end of it. Sturgis just looked like the kind of guy to do it.

"So what do you say?" Sturgis asked.

"Let's make it simple," Monigan said. "I can't prove nothing, but I do know you owe seven grand and you got one week to come up with it, this being Friday. If you got all this money then there shouldn't be any problem, all you have to do, like you say, is make it your priority. And I ain't saying no more on the subject 'cause I'm tired of all this talking and I got investigating to do. Only remember Friday, you really should."

Sturgis began to relax. He realized Monigan wasn't a pro, had him figured as some dumb loser the bookie knew. He couldn't help but feel smug about his performance.

"One more thing," Monigan said.

"Sure," Sturgis said. "You want to hang out and catch a show again? That was some trick with the dog the other night, by the way. It's the way the comics around here should be treated."

The mutt figured the compliment was directed his way and responded with a satisfied pee on the carpet. It took a while, unfamiliar as it was with relieving itself on solid footing.

"One of the comics," Monigan said.

"Yeah?"

"Dwayne Feller."

A long, tense pause. "What about him?"

"I been keeping an eye on the comedy thing lately," Monigan said as casually as possible. "And I figure he should be getting more shows."

"Feller? That idiot?"

"Maybe a lot more," Monigan said, barely moving his lips.

"Well, in this business it all has to do with . . . you know, waiting for the right time. And I've been thinking it's probably about time the kid got his shot. I'm making up the schedule today."

"You're a good guy," Monigan said. "Co-operative. We should grab a beer sometime."

"Yeah," Sturgis said. "Call me."

Monigan glared at him. "Yeah, I'll call you." He gave the dog a light hoof in the ass to get it started. On the way down the stairs he was laughing. He wasn't convinced that Sturgis was entirely innocent of the arson job but what the owner had said made sense, he guessed. Monigan could see there was something wrong with the argument but as he couldn't detect the logical flaw, he comforted himself with the knowledge that he had another clue.

Fifteen minutes later Dwayne himself was facing the club owner, babbling out his story, all aquiver. Twenty minutes after that he was out on the street, head in the clouds. A jet of cold air tousled his hair, making him gasp with pleasure. Winter was back. The lion had decided lambs have no business cavorting with impunity in Toronto this time of year so was treating itself to a March souvlaki.

Dwayne's general philosophy was, like everything in his life, bipolar. He was offended by notions of creationism and fundamentalism and other religious vulgarities. And if there was a god then Dwayne was a deist; if a supreme being had cooked up this whole mess, then he obviously was taking no further part in its development, unless he had a warped sense of humor or was on mushrooms. Counter to this, Dwayne thought of life as a spiritual progression, with a teleological sense of purpose that had him frothing to get back on stage.

And here was the paradox in its full glory: clearly there had been no god at his side while Dwayne was committing his crime, yet in spite of it all he found himself with stage time. Dwayne had blubbered and wept as he spilled out his story. When he was done he looked up to see Sturgis staring right through him. The owner growled and grappled for words and whined and went red in the face. Then offered him two shows a week.

Dwayne felt invulnerable. He planned to go home and begin work on his act, tear it to shreds and from an objective viewpoint put it back together in a way that would leave no one doubting his genius. The Mfecane!

He stopped on the sidewalk. He'd have to tell Katlyn first. Dwayne knew he had committed an offense against his morals, against hers. He had to tell her. He would. She would know what to do. A career was nothing when compared to the fate of his soul. So he plunged off down the street, talking to himself at volume, periodically screaming at the heavens, scaring tourists and tomcats. The crushing was on hold.

His father had gone straight from The Laugh Chance to the fire scene. He had two clues, though he wasn't sure how either fit into the picture. Sturgis had been slick but he rubbed Monigan the wrong way, so the new detective figured there must be a clue in it all. He would count Bill as a clue. The old man should be listed as a victim or a witness, but Monigan knew the more clues you had the better the chance of solving the case. So he would put Bill down as a clue. It was his prerogative, being the detective and all.

Digging in his pocket, he came up with the notebook he had stolen from the stationery store, a three-by-six inch, cardboard-covered item with a metal spiral binding at the top. From his other pocket he pulled a small golf pencil, which he licked vigorously while squinting up at the sky, allowing the case free rein in his mind. He flipped back the spiral cover and smoothed down the front page. Finally he made the all-important first entry of his investigation:

CLUES
(1) Bill
(2) That prick at the comedy club

It looked good being down in print that way, organized and important. He studied the clues a moment longer then returned the notebook and the pencil to his pocket. He looked at the scene then pitched into the job at hand, heaving boards and drywall, tearing blackened bricks from their mortar, prying ducts and pipes from the debris. Gradually a congeries of unrelated items accumulated on the sidewalk, a filthy collection of boots, crushed eyeglasses, strips of lath, household appliances. A crutch, a stuffed owl, several paperbacks, a set of teeth. Monigan salvaged it all, the loot of an invading army to be sent back through the lines, a stinking surfeit of clues.

Doyle and Ogilvie could hear him laughing and singing to himself inside the shell of the building. They waited for him to emerge, catching glimpses of his chunky frame as he darted past windows and gaps where the walls had been breached. When Monigan had a complete armload of garbage, he stepped out the side door. He dropped everything on the spot when he saw the cops.

"Them are my clues!" He rushed over and planted himself between the officers and the trash heap. "I know enough about police work that you don't go trespassing on another cop's . . . bailiwick."

"Bailiwick?" Ogilvie grinned in spite of herself.

"Listen, you," Doyle said. "I told you in plain English not to go snooping around."

"How else am I gonna bust this case?"

"You're not going to. Your job is to keep your ears open and to try and get something useful out of the old man."

"Bill."

"Bill, then. But keep out of the way."

"You two ain't even on the case, official. Bet the detectives find out about this and you're back on traffic, chasing speeders on the 401 and trying to spot illegal aliens through tinted windshields."

Ogilvie kicked a protruding drainpipe. "What is this junk?"

"Clues. And don't go disturbing them. Don't you know nothing? You wanna look, put on rubber gloves or lift things up with a pencil. Best is if you wait till I get it all numbered and put in plastic bags."

"This is shit, Monigan," Doyle said. "That's what you got here."

"Gimme one of them menthols."

As Monigan lit up, Doyle turned to his partner.

"He can't do much harm," Ogilvie said. "The police line's down."

"Don't patronize me," Monigan said, dragging heavily on the butt.

"Big words," Doyle said. "Get out of here, go to The Workbench and bury your head in a pitcher of beer."

"You say that like it ain't crossed my mind only every five minutes." Monigan surveyed the wreckage through a haze of cigarette smoke. "But duty calls. Nossir, I got work to do."

"The line is down," Doyle said. "But this is still private property. You're trespassing."

"Best you gimme a badge or ID or something, case I gotta grill a couple witnesses."

"You're this close, Monigan."

"Suppose I should get me a piece, never know when the guy who did this comes around looking to whack me. Late at night, figures I'm a easy mark, POW! Drill him right between the squints at forty yards. Think I can't shoot? I can shoot."

Doyle grabbed Monigan by the front of his coat, trying to hoist him onto his toes, but couldn't budge him.

"Gimme another smoke." The blast of rancid breath sent Doyle reeling and gained Monigan his release.

"Get your own." Doyle was done. He backed off and wiped at the charcoal that had transferred from Monigan's coat to his own, but the state of his hands furthered the grimy effect. With a last look of disgust, he spun and plowed off to the car.

Ogilvie remained with Monigan. "Hold on."

"I ain't moved."

"You can be of help to us. Talk to Bill. I have a feeling he has information germane to the case."

"You figure?" Monigan said.

Ogilvie glanced at the cruiser. "This is important for my partner."

Monigan's eyes lost their flippancy. "It ain't near important to you as it is to me and Bill."

"Yes," Ogilvie said. "That might be true. But keep in mind that there are dozens of ways the case could be thrown out of court if proper procedures aren't followed. You watch and you listen and you stay out of the way . . . please."

Monigan watched the cruiser pull away then reached down and jerked a rubber boot from the pile. "Wonder what makes her think it'll get to court," he said.

The wind had died down but the temperature was still dropping. Monigan pulled his coat tighter. The sweat he had worked up was starting to freeze. He pulled out his notebook, and after a minute of thinking wrote:

(3) German
(4) Boot

He took out the package of cigarettes he had filched from Doyle when the cop had tried to lift him off the ground. Menthols. Shit.

SEVENTEEN

Another day ground by at the The Workbench and Katlyn was exhausted. She stared out her window at the front yard, at the bare sumac tree, always one of the last to bud and fill out in spring. She thought of moving to the west coast, where winter's patter of orographic rainfall at least charged the flora with vitality. Looming cedar hedges, spruce and fir and pine, greenery year-round, cherry blossoms in February. But she knew she wouldn't move. Wishing on a star was the leitmotif of her life.

When the hot chocolate was warm she tipped in a small portion of Tia Maria and lit a cigarette. She was wearing a kimono and felt silly for it. The black silk prompted a tickle of pleasure when she spun or turned, but doing so filled her with a sense of emptiness, posing and strutting, styling and profiling all around the room by herself. She danced nonetheless, slowly wheeling around the living room, eyes closed, one hand on the back of her neck, the other holding the mug of spiked cocoa.

Outside, Dwayne leaned against the wrought-iron fence of the house across the way. Up and down, north and south along the street stood homes of similar placid stolidity. Attached and semi-detached brick spires of three stories, steeply pitched roofs, a collection of dwellings that defined Cabbagetown, many of them renovated but still redolent of the days when immigrants planted spuds and cabbages in their front yards to supplement a diet not yet in step with their new world, happy to be in a land of surplus but not yet sharing in it.

Dwayne spasmed each time Katlyn passed the window in her solitary waltz. Quickly he checked the street to see if anyone else was party to the performance, unable to imagine Katlyn capable of such a lewd display.

It took little time for Dwayne to forget all that and fall under her spell, the enchantment achingly real. He had never seen anyone move like this, smoothly and so . . . innocently. Dwayne had tried dancing once at a wedding, where everyone was so inebriated that they heckled and barked insults at him. Rock and roll songs had him galumphing around the floor with oafish enthusiasm, squashing pieces of wedding cake and slamming matronly aunts into their partners' arms. Waltzes reduced him to a lump that backed the ladies off to the fullest extension of their arms. Finally he settled for parading the parquet with squealing children, sticky fingers grabbing the front of his shirt, feet planted on his, pulverizing the metatarsals.

But Katlyn's dancing astonished him with its beauty. A heavy load of inadequacy glued him to the sidewalk for a time, but desperation overcame the inertia. He marched across the street and rang her buzzer.

Katlyn felt even more foolish in the kimono as she led Dwayne upstairs. His big yellow gumboots, wool trousers and army-surplus jacket were so much more practical than the flimsy bit of foolery she was wearing. Dwayne stared at her back on the way up, wishing he hadn't changed out of his RCAF tunic. She was beautiful.

They faced each other in the middle of the living room. Katlyn retrieved her mug of hot chocolate from the coffee table and held it in both hands.

"I love you," Dwayne said.

Katlyn stepped back and Dwayne wailed, dropping his face in his hands.

"I don't know where that came from," he cried.

"Well put it back."

"I mean . . . I came here to tell you the truth."

"You've told me."

Katlyn was angry, not so much at the words as at the delivery. She had always dreamt that the first time she heard a declaration of love it would be companion to great emotion and revelation. That it had been blurted out by a disheveled giant in the grip of madness who was now self-consciously grabbing his crotch like a kindergartener was a bit much.

"No, you have it all wrong," Dwayne said. "That's not the truth . . . I mean, it's the truth, but it's not what I came here to say."

"Go on."

"You affect me so deeply I have trouble speaking."

Dwayne was in such anguish that Katlyn steered him gently to the couch, where he buckled into a sitting position.

"Would you like something to drink?" she asked.

"Okay. All right. Now, then. Let's start at the beginning."

"I would," Katlyn said. She returned with the bottle of Tia Maria and half-filled a snifter.

"Look at me," Dwayne said suddenly.

"Believe me, I'm not taking my eyes off you."

"No, look at me."

"Dwayne!"

"Okay. All right. Now, then." He reached for Katlyn's glass and dashed down its contents. His head lost its seat. "What is that?" he said. "I don't drink." He coughed and Katlyn fetched him some water.

"That was mine, Dwayne. I wasn't trying to poison you."

Dwayne leaned back on the couch.

Katlyn broke the silence. "Can you get on with it? It's late, and I'm starting to think I'm crazy for sitting here in a kimono at three in the morning listening to someone who refuses to tell me why he's here."

"Sorry. Truly I am. That's a lovely kimono, by the way. Did you know the kimono isn't of Japanese origin as most people think, but comes from the Chinese p'ao-style robe? That short-sleeved kimono of yours was introduced in the Japanese Muromachi period — "

"Stop it!"

"Okay. All right. Now, then. Looking at me, would you say I was born to be a comic?"

"I've never seen your act."

"Physically, I mean. Physically. Teleologically speaking, isn't it clear that I was meant to amuse?"

Katlyn considered throwing him out then decided to join him. Perhaps Dwayne would pick up on the banter and be diverted from his strange mood. "Does the name Cesare Lombroso mean anything to you?" she said.

"Cesare . . . ?"

"Lombroso."

"Lombroso . . . Cesare Lombroso." Dwayne shot to his feet, banging his shins on the coffee table and toppling the bottle of booze to the floor. "Of course! What an idiot I am!" He tore at his hair.

"Look what you've done," Katlyn said. She went to get some paper towels. Everything she said to Dwayne backfired in her face. It scared her. She was falling in love with him, she knew that, and the thought that they had started out so well and now were unable to connect was a crushing disappointment. They had shared more of substance during their first long talk than collectively since. She started to cry and fiercely rubbed the tears away with the paper towels. She returned from the kitchen to find Dwayne wildly pacing the room, muttering to himself.

"Yes, it's clear now. You've saved me."

"If you don't calm down I'll kick you out on the street. I was only fooling around when I mentioned . . ."

"Cesare Lombroso," he said, shaking his head and chortling lowly. He hitched his trousers up a foot over his navel. "The nineteenth-century Italian physician. His theory of *l'uomo dilequente* — the criminal man. His belief in criminal anthropology, that the atavistic behavior of criminals is predictable. Biological determinism. By compiling data we can tell who the criminals will be even before they commit a crime. And look at me: my anatomy combined with the genes passed on to me by my father means it wasn't my fault.

"And there's no problem with combining theories. While I was meant to be a performer, I still carry the genes predisposing me to a life of crime. Do you know what this means?"

Katlyn looked at the bottle of Tia Maria and saw that Dwayne had helped himself after he picked it up from the floor. "Dwayne, you're drunk."

"I am not."

"You are," she said. "Have you ever had a drink in your life?"

"You don't see what this means . . ."

Dwayne was unhinged, but Katlyn couldn't help herself. She approached him in the middle of his raving and, reaching up, locked her hands behind his head and pulled him down to her. She felt the terror in his lips but kissed right through it, then let slip her hands and trailed them along his cheeks as the kiss ended. She had never before kissed a man that way, and she stood back, panting.

A shark had taken Dwayne's leg off at the knee. He didn't feel it. "*La Pasionaria!*" he cried with a swollen tongue.

Katlyn smiled.

"It means it couldn't be helped," Dwayne said.

"Dwayne, I just kissed you. And I still have absolutely no idea what you're talking about."

"You know everything. You're a goddess."

"Is there something I should know about?"

The day had been too much for him. Dwayne was almost at the end of his tether. He swayed to the kitchen and drank a liter of water straight from the tap. He returned to the living room and sat down on the couch. His fingers sought out his lips and he sighed. With the world, all the wonderful world, whirling over his head like a mobile, his brain opted out of its surroundings and in a light glissando slid across the frets as he tipped over sideways and slept.

As he came around in the morning he threw an arm over his face. Thus shielded, he was able to feign sleep while letting one bloodshot eye assess his surroundings, however powerless he was to process the incoming information. It was Katlyn's apartment and all was as still as the morning after winter's first snowfall.

The first thing he remembered was the kiss. He smiled. Then his uncovered eye opened wider. He tried to recall if he had done anything shameful. A horrific scene flashed before him: screaming and sobbing, Katlyn pulls her kimono tighter as Dwayne charges at her, slobbering and insistent, tearing the gown, chasing her into the kitchen where she hammers him insensate with a skillet. Dwayne carefully felt his head for lumps. Nothing.

"Good morning," Katlyn said.

Dwayne sat up and drove himself backward into the cushions of the couch, gaining precious distance.

"Do you drink coffee in the morning?"

"No," Dwayne said.

"Would you like some breakfast?"

"No."

Katlyn's kimono had been replaced by a terrycloth robe with embroidered flowers around the cuffs and hem. She was composed and casual, far more so than Dwayne thought was natural.

"Are you sure?" she said. "Bacon and eggs?"

Dwayne rolled his eyes like an inbred dalmatian.

"Dwayne, talk to me."

"What do you want to discuss?"

"To refresh your memory: you came here in the middle of the night, told me you loved me, babbled something about biological determinism then passed out on the couch. With your boots on."

"You got me drunk," Dwayne said. "And you brought up Lombroso."

"For a comic, you don't understand teasing very well."

Dwayne hid his feet under the table and wiped at the couch.

"I'm entitled to an explanation." Katlyn had never demanded anything in her life. Simple requests were difficult for her, due to her concern with inconveniencing people. She held her own in The Workbench, but that was different, that wasn't the world. She wasn't sure if this was the real world either, but it required resolve.

"My mother's a fragile woman," Dwayne said. "By now she'll be catatonic with worry. I have to go."

Dwayne was halfway to the door when the shock of his behavior hit him. He couldn't remember everything, but he was certain that he had tried to absolve himself of blame. If he could see himself from a distance he would have realized the personal growth that admission represented. Not long ago Dwayne would have seized the bogus Lombroso argument in his teeth and run wildly with it, spitting in the face of common sense. But he was learning, boring a hole in his self-delusions. Finally he was realizing that there were other lives involved here, souls if not kindred then at least deserving of respect and acknowledgment.

Katlyn stood in front of him. Every nerve exposed, Dwayne bent to kiss her. At the last instant she shied away. Mortified, Dwayne spun and plunged down the stairs and out the door.

On reaching home, he went straight to the freezer and peeled a twenty from the roll of bills in the ice cream tub. He felt like embarking on a bender, though he had never been a drinker. The only thing that made Dwayne physically giddy was emerging from his apartment after a few days' seclusion. His lair was sealed so effectively with protective devices, caulking and weather stripping, that when the door opened the rush of oxygen sent him on non-narcotic flights of fancy. No, booze was not the answer to anything. His father illustrated as much.

"Yes, Mother." 0745 hours.

"Where were you?"

"Did you phone the hospital?"

"Of course not. I never worry."

"I have no time for this."

"You had a phone call last night."

"Why didn't you tell me earlier?"

"I didn't know where you were. For all I knew you could have fallen in with a band of appliance thieves. Happens all the time."

"Appliance thieves."

"I'm not sure I liked the sound of his voice. It sounded sort of roly."

"Roly?"

"Yes, it just rolled along like he had thought about what he was going to say before he even said it. I don't trust people like that."

"I know few people who even speak in full sentences." He stuffed the twenty in his pocket.

"He didn't sound very tall."

"What did he want? Do you remember that, at least?"

"He didn't say. And I forgot to ask — I have trouble talking to people on the phone."

"Was there anything at all?"

"Just that he had a roly voice. And that I've heard it before."

"There must be something. It might be important."

"Well, he did leave his name and number."

"You should be dumped in a pasteurizer."

Her sobbing forced Dwayne to tattoo the wall sharply with the receiver. 0752 hours.

"Let's see," his mother said, sniffing. "I have it here somewhere. Harold . . . A-R-E-N-S."

"Arens?" Dwayne said. "Harold Arens? He's possibly the only person you've talked to more than once and you couldn't even remember . . . never mind."

"I know you're going through a difficult time, but it does cheer me up to hear you sound happy. Couldn't you whisper something nice to brighten up my day?"

Dwayne thought about it. Really no harm, he supposed. "Thank you very much for returning the money you stole."

"Oh, son . . ."

Dwayne was worried. He wondered if Harold had heard something from Sturgis. Dwayne still hadn't told Katlyn, couldn't possi-

bly tell his mother or father, and felt his only friend slipping away.
He stalled, rearranging his few possessions, showering and shaving, watching a bit of taped wrestling, then finally called Harold.

"Oh, hi, Dwayne."

"My mother just gave me your message."

"Yeah, right," Harold said. "I have a show for you if you want.
Paying gig."

Dwayne held the receiver away from his head, wondering how
his friend could be so cruel. Harold wasn't known for practical
jokes.

"Dwayne?"

"I'm here. What's the punchline?"

"For chrissake, I've got a one-nighter for you. Club up the north
end of the city. I'm emceeing, Reba's headlining and I was wondering if you'd like to open. It's only twenty bucks, but it's stage time."

"Really?"

"I'll give you the address, showtime's eight, get there a little
early."

Dwayne danced in place, as much as his bulk would allow, then
went frantic trying to find a pen and paper. He took down the
address and began a gushing declaration of thanks which Harold
interrupted.

"Listen up, Dwayne. I know I've told you this before, and you
always get offended. But this is a trial gig and the owner won't keep
booking shows if he doesn't like what he sees. I want you to think
seriously about cleaning up your act. And if things don't go well,
take it like a pro and stick with your material."

"Done. Trust me, leave it in my hands. You require clean and
tasteful yet full of originality? Wait till you feast your eyes on this."

"Don't go overboard."

"Overboard."

"Get there early."

"Surely."

"See you there."

Dwayne hung up and laughed aloud. He'd be ready. He retrieved the money from the ice cream tub and dropped the whole frozen lump in his pocket. Shopping.

Over at The Workbench, Monigan was bending Katlyn's ear, but she couldn't screw up any interest while her thoughts were so fastened on Dwayne. Every time she saw or heard something worthy of comment she wanted to tell him about it, and there were confidences of much greater importance she wished to share. But so far every one of their encounters beyond their initial meeting had been marred by calamity. It was going to be a long day, and if the state Dwayne had been in when he left her apartment that morning was any indicator, there was a good chance he wouldn't even show up for his shift the next day — Dwayne didn't rebound quickly. And if he did turn up, she didn't have a clue what to say to him.

"You listening to me?" Monigan said.

"Yes, yes." She automatically dropped a draft in front of him and marked another slash on Frodo's tab.

The bookie, resplendent in a cashmere sweater and lycra workout pants, was gleefully tearing through the two hundred bucks he had collected from Sturgis, but was being forced to do so over by the back wall. Both times Monigan had gone to the trouble to strong-arm the club owner Frodo had caved in and accepted a token instead of the balance. So Monigan was making him sit with the losers in the back.

"How's the investigation going?" Katlyn asked.

Monigan almost had a conniption fit. "Ssshh! Jesus Christ in a powerboat, Katy, don't blow the thing wide open. I got a cover to protect."

"A cover?"

"The walls got ears."

Katlyn let it drop, but that wasn't what Monigan wanted, being worse than having his cover blown, so he pinched her sleeve and drew her close.

"The clues're piling up," he said. "Plenty of clues, all right, but no smoking gun."

"Who do they point to?" she whispered.

"Someone from the city."

"Really?"

"Yeah, it wasn't an out-of-town job. No Germans involved at all."

"How do you know?"

Monigan pointed to his stomach.

"Gut feel?"

"You know it," he said.

"That's as far as you can narrow it down?"

"It ain't easy." He rooted in her pack for a smoke. Their heads were still together and the match flare singed Monigan's eyebrows. "But I'm checking eyes."

"Eyes."

"The eyes," Monigan said. "Looking for someone's got them eyes on him, the beady kind."

"Well, it's a start," Katlyn said helpfully.

Monigan squinted. "The french fry has them eyes."

"Don't be an ass," Katlyn said. "And by the way, are you two fools ever going to sit down and settle this?"

"What's it to you?"

"What's what to me?" Katlyn had started down a row she didn't want to hoe.

"What's what, she says." Monigan shot twin jets of smoke from his nose. "What's what to me, she says."

Katlyn glared at him, embarrassed and angry.

"Ha!" Monigan screamed, pointing a big scabby finger at her. "I was right, I was right all along. You're gonna kill me, Katy, you're breaking my goddamn heart. You can't do it, girl, not with him, not with the french fry. Awww, fuck a duck!"

Katlyn dropped fresh drinks on the far side of the bar, wondering how she had come to be part of such a dysfunctional trio.

Monigan made to start in again, but Katlyn busied herself as far as possible away from him.

"Frenchie makes my beer taste bad," Monigan grumbled. "That's all."

Katlyn was humming aloud, trying to shut him out.

"What is it — some sort of vegetable magnetism between you two?" Monigan laughed to himself.

Katlyn ignored him, plainly irritated, and for a second Monigan felt bad. Then he felt in his pocket for the notebook, secure in the knowledge that nothing could be too bad so long as he had his clues.

He looked around for Bill, but the old man was still upstairs. Bill didn't come down to the pub much any more. He was sinking deeper into his emotional pit, daydreaming, talking to his wife. Monigan decided to give him another hour before checking up on him, but then spent the whole day sitting exactly where he was in his lucky seat, even after the Jays gave up eight runs in the third en route to a 12–5 exhibition loss. From time to time he felt guilty about not actively pursuing the investigation, but he needed the chance to configure the clues into a recognizable pattern. So he sat and drank and watched TV and waited all day for Bill.

EIGHTEEN

Dwayne was pulling out all the stops for this one. He was prepared and enthusiastic and confident. And terrified. A small animal, likely a rodent, a vole or a marmot, was working its way through his system. He was afraid to burp or yawn or to go to the toilet lest he expel a half-eaten organ. Bad shape, yet with an underlying eagerness to get on with the crushing.

He had spent most of his money that afternoon, holding back just enough for a cab to the show. He didn't want to look like a bum, showing up on a bus. He was a professional comic going to a gig. He couldn't just let himself go.

The stage, an eight-inch riser covered with outdoor carpet, was in three unstable sections. The mike stand was jammed immovably at four feet high, the microphone itself a unidirectional unit of less utility than a cardboard megaphone. There was no spotlight. Tables and chairs were scattered around the room except for on the dance floor, which was bare and stretched to infinity from the stage. The comics would need a cellular phone to converse with the nearest patrons, and those on the fringes were past the horizon of the universe. The bar ran along the wall stage left, in intimate proximity to the customers, ensuring that even had the sound system been identical to that used at Woodstock, the blenders and cash registers and ice machines and cognate gadgets were going to transform the comics' witticisms into mere scratches on the arse of life. The performers were working for a percentage of the door, and as there were eleven people in the place — seven of them staff — the pickings would be slim indeed. The manager was wearing a *Free Charles Manson* T-shirt and hated comics more than he did the bands he usually booked into the bar.

It was the worst of all possible situations and the comics were happy to have the work.

Harold Arens returned from a chat with the manager. Having one comedy night a week had been instituted on a trial basis, and Harold now knew they were facing a hanging judge. Harold was dressed up-scale casual for the evening, trying to balance his look with what a crowd about whom he knew nothing might be expecting. He sat down and looked at Reba and started to laugh, giddy rather than amused.

"We'll have to impress the hell out of him," Harold said. "Or this will be the first and last show."

"Should be easy," Reba said. "We got the crowd outnumbered." Her constitution was wilting from this kind of work. Doing bad one-nighters in bars had been a necessary learning process for the first few years in the business, but now she was operating behind the power curve and knew full well she was developing bad habits from so many hell gigs.

At the bar, the manager nervously toyed with the hem of his Manson shirt. He was going to take a bath tonight. Bad enough with bands and all their bitching and moaning and demands, trying to get free beer, doing lines in the shitter, and generally driving him crazy. Now he had to put up with these geeks. He was working himself into a fine lather, trying to figure out how to job the comics out of even the measly return from the door, when in walked another one of them.

At the table, Harold went rigid.

"What's up?" Reba asked.

"I might have made a tiny mistake inviting Dwayne."

"Don't you think he'll show? No big deal — between us we can cover the time."

Harold inclined his head toward the entrance. "Not exactly what I mean."

"Yes, yes," Dwayne murmured with approval as he took it all in. It was Dwayne's first road gig — though technically it was still within the metro limits — and he was immensely proud to be here this evening, joining his compadres at the lovely show bar. He had spent the entire day writing new material and reconfiguring his act, aside from the time required to buy a new stage outfit. He was well aware that many successful comics draw on their upbringing as a wellspring of material, and as his father was from the prairies Dwayne was sanguine that the investment in a new wardrobe to reflect his roots would pay off in audience appreciation.

He teared up when he thought of Harold calling to offer him the gig. A paying gig. Fine man, Harold. Fine race, the Jews. Spying the comics at their table, he headed their way.

Already the new cowboy boots were chafing his feet, and he was sure his heels were bloody. The stiff, shiny blue-jeans tucked into the boots were too short so kept popping out. The glare from the sequins on his square-dancing shirt was blinding, as were the flashes his toy six-shooters threw off as they reflected the rotating disco lights. He stopped in front of Harold and Reba, rammed his thumbs behind his gunbelt and nodded howdy. He was cavalierly aware of his name embroidered over the left pocket of the rayon shirt: *Dwayne*. The sequins around the collar were biting into his neck, but that was fine for now.

Reba stared and waited for Harold to speak. It had been his idea to call Dwayne.

"Have a seat," Harold said.

"Hay for my horses and whisky for my men!" Dwayne screamed at a passing waitress, who ignored him.

"For Dwayne's benefit," Harold said after they had arranged themselves at the table, "I'll recap our strategy."

"Strategy," Dwayne nodded. "Strategy and tactics. They could have used more of that at — "

"It's time we bent Sturgis over the barrel," Harold continued. "From here on in I'll be booking our own shows, for every comic I can convince to come with us. Considering the way Sturgis has gouged us on commissions for outside gigs over the years, I'm going to do everything I can to take his one-nighters away from him. It means accepting less money for some of the shows because I'll have to undercut him, but I bet a lot of clubs go with us simply out of relief at not having to deal with that scumbag. As well, I'll be actively pursuing rooms in new towns, and I plan to hit the college and university markets hard. It will take time, but if we're patient we'll be better off in the end."

"Excuse me . . ." Dwayne began.

"Most of this Reba and I have gone over ourselves, Dwayne." He looked at his partner. "You have anything to add?"

"I've been thinking," Reba said. "Is there any way to do this under the table without Sturgis finding out? I mean, one-nighters are all right, but it will be tough not having an actual comedy club to work out of."

"I beg your pardon?" Dwayne said.

"That's part of the deal," Harold said. "We boycott The Laugh Chance."

Dwayne shifted his gunbelt and his mouth quivered.

"Although I can see your side," Reba said. "If Sturgis finds out we're dealing directly with the bars, he'll ban us anyhow."

"Once it's done," Harold added, "he'll have no choice but to accept us back on our terms, so long as we get enough comics behind us."

This was too much for Dwayne to deal with all at once. Out of the clear blue Sturgis had offered him regular spots at the club, even though Dwayne had made a mess of the job he was supposed to do in return. Of course, Dwayne had known it would happen eventually. To stand in triumph on The Laugh Chance stage, awash in cheers and applause, was his destiny. Harold's calling him had merely added to the roll Dwayne was on. Now to hear that the deal involved boycotting the club! He played with it while Harold and Reba discussed details, glancing at them, fiddling with his six-shooters.

They were his friends. Dwayne had had no friends growing up. Certainly there were children with whom he spent time, but they were the types other kids shunned, at least until it came time to have fun at their expense. Dwayne spent a lot of time with the odd-balls: a boy who at twelve found Fourier Analysis a snap but spent most of his time dismembering amphibians and trying to stitch them back together; a kid who wet himself when he heard *God Save the Queen*; a girl who faked epilepsy for six years, getting up a fit every couple of days, to the amusement of much of the class, who would pelt her with school supplies until the teacher arrived. And, of course, the usual array of those who ate glue and paint chips, swallowed coins and pen tops and anything that came out of their ears.

And then there was Harold Arens. Dwayne studied him. Harold was a good-natured, kind, intelligent man who seemed to like Dwayne a lot. And Reba wasn't Dwayne's close friend but she tolerated him. And Katlyn, his own Katlyn thought he was a good man. His mother loved him, the clot-headed old thing. And even his father seemed to be coming around. He was pretty bloody lucky, when he thought of it in those terms.

"Reba," Dwayne said. "Do you agree with Harold? That Sturgis will take us back?"

"He's hurting," Reba said. "After a meeting last week I sort of borrowed his disks. He's up to his neck in debt, trouble all round. He won't make a dime off the club without us, so eventually he'll have to cave in."

"I'm certainly aware of his financial difficulties," Dwayne said.

"How's that?" Reba was committed to the plan but welcomed any corroborating evidence of Sturgis's weakness.

"Uh . . . instinct," Dwayne said. "Mere instinct and nothing more, and I'm not interested in elaborating so leave me be."

The comics looked at him strangely.

"Hey!"

Heads swivelled to behold the manager.

"It's showtime," he said. "You got one minute to get on the stage or you don't get paid. Should of stayed with bands. Comics. Fuck."

"This will be a pleasant evening," Reba said.

Harold leaned in and turned up his palms. "Well, Dwayne, what do you think — are you with us?"

It was taking a chance, Dwayne knew that much. The silence lengthened.

"We're waiting," Reba said.

And just like that Dwayne had it. Loyalty, that's what it was all about. Loyalty to his friends, his family, his values. He simply had to stick with these people. He had never felt companionship like this before. It was beautiful.

"*Hijra*," Dwayne said.

"Eh?"

"*Hijra!*" the lumpy cowboy yelled. "The traditional first stage of removal from the place of the infidels before declaring *jihad*. Yes, it's a holy war against that tyrant."

"Keep it down," Harold said. People already were staring.

"I'm with you, brothers and sisters; *Citoyen* Dwayne Feller declares for the revolution! We'll besiege the despot and tear him to pieces. Mao had it right: 'When the enemy advances, we retreat. When he escapes, we harass. When he retreats, we pursue. When he is tired, we attack. When he burns, we put out the fire. When he loots, we attack. When he pursues, we hide. When he retreats, we return.'"

"Dwayne," Reba said. "This is getting embarrassing even for us . . . and we're comics!"

"Harold, you'll save us. You indeed live by the words of the Torah: 'For the poor shall never cease out of the land; therefore I command you to open your hand to the poor and needy brother that lives in the land.'

"Sturgis will pay, oh yes. We're the Mamluks and will leave a similar legacy: a caste of warrior slaves who take control and rule their own empire. Thank you for allowing me to be one of you, one of the brave *sans culottes* valuing freedom above all. Thank you."

Dwayne leaped to his feet. With a great whoop and a roar, he tore free his six-shooters and blasted the cap guns at the ceiling. SNAP! SNAP! SNAPSNAPSNAP!

Harold and Reba edged away as the manager raced over to the table. He was livid, and specks of spittle jetted from his mouth.

"You!" he snarled. "Out of here now! Out the door — out the fucking door!"

Dwayne looked down at the man and perused the *Free Charles Manson* shirt. He smiled at his co-revolutionaries and aimed the guns at the manager's feet. "Dance! he screamed. SNAP! SNAP! SNAPSNAPSNAP! "Dance, ya sonofabitch!"

Outside the low stratus was releasing its moisture, a miserable drizzle chilling Toronto to the marrow of its office buildings. The opening move of the *jihad* and Dwayne had already been court martialled and discharged from the ranks. He checked his watch: 2245 hours. The show would just be wrapping up. Harold and Reba had been sympathetic, but Dwayne was too ashamed to wait for a ride home. And he had invested the last of his money in the cowboy suit and the cab ride.

He was truly puzzled at his behavior whenever he was practicing, or even within sniffing distance, of his chosen profession. All he wanted to be was a working funnyman, and now he was having second thoughts about being able to survive the process.

He wondered if he had covered as many miles as the time he walked all night. He fell again, the cowboy boots unable to cope with the slick freezing rain. He would have removed them and proceeded along stocking-footed, penitently, but that was precluded by his swollen feet, and it looked as if he would have to cut the boots off when he got home. They were ruined anyhow, a long gash along both insteps where the leather was pulling away from the welt. He had wanted a good pair, Tony Lamas or Dan Post, but he had spent too much on the jeans and shirt. He wondered if a hat would have made a difference, a big white ten-gallon special.

With the drizzle and all the falling down, most of the sequins had come off the square-dancing shirt, and the ones remaining hung in rows on their threads. Somehow he had torn the "y" and the "e" off his name over the pocket. *Dwan*, it read now. It made him angry. Had it only been the "D" that had ripped off, at least he would be left with *wayne*, a real name. *Dwan* just looked stupid, which is how Dwayne felt. He got up again, still with a good four miles to go.

The lights were out when Dwayne arrived at The Workbench. He squashed his nose against the window, hoping to find Katlyn still there cashing out, but the place was empty. Dwayne sighed, twice changed his mind, then set off up the sidewalk to her house. The second floor was blacked out and he didn't have the nerve to press her buzzer, not after the night before. If he woke her now he could be sure of a wallop with the skillet. He gazed up at her window a while, and when he finally started for home found himself staring down the barrel of a gun.

"Freeze!" Doyle's weapon was shaking in his grasp. "You hold it right there, Mister."

Ogilvie was off to one side. Our man was calm. Or beyond caring.

"Face down on the ground, hands behind your head. Move!"

"Officer, I've spent the last few hours trying to keep myself *off* the ground."

Doyle squinted. "Don't I know you?"

"I'm the new employee at The Workbench. Maybe you were served by me during some drunken binge."

"Doyle!" Ogilvie yelled. "The guns!"

"Oh, yeah. Right — get on your face, I said!"

"They're toys," Dwayne said. "Props. I'm a performer and the guns are part of my new act."

"You said you worked at the bar."

"Temporarily. You must know Katlyn, the manager. She lives in the house behind me and can verify everything I've told you."

Katlyn came groggily out of her dream, aware it could only be one person leaning on her buzzer at this hour. She felt not the slightest annoyance. She went to the closet and slipped on her housecoat, then took it off and pulled on the kimono. Her tummy was doing backflips. She turned on the stairwell light and started down, determined for once to relate to the man under normal circumstances.

She opened the door to two cops and Cowboy *Dwan*.

That was it, now she wouldn't sleep for the rest of the night. After verifying Dwayne's identity she watched him walk with the cops and get in the back seat for a ride home. She felt that she should have taken him in, but she couldn't, she just couldn't. Katlyn sat up on the couch all night. Occasionally her chin would drop to her chest, but as soon as she lay down she was wide awake again. She had to do something about Dwayne. Resolution of any kind had become imperative. She checked the wall clock: six-fifteen.

She decided to start with the father and work her way to the son, clearing up as much trash along the way and around the perimeter as she could. She'd get no sense out of Monigan until about ten in the morning but didn't know if she could wait that long. She sat on the couch, alone and feeling it.

NINETEEN

Much too early that morning Monigan rushed around his room, stuffing clothes and garbage into available holes and niches. Empty bottles, cigarette butts, soda crackers — all disappeared out of sight. The linoleum was filthy but there was no time to clean it, even if Monigan had possessed a mop or a broom.

Katlyn had phoned at seven in the morning and despite the hour Monigan had dealt with the call with poise, if not a little pride at having a phone of his own again. Trouble was, after she hung up Monigan went back to bed. Quickly he went through his mental checklist: clothes away, ashtray and dog emptied out the window, card table set up. Right.

As she climbed the stairs, Katlyn cringed. She knew that major renovations would necessitate raising the rent; she knew the tenants in many cases could not even afford the pittance charged at present; she knew the place was as clean as possible, and that any vandalism was not due to her negligence. Still, the narrow staircases and corridors, the nicotined walls and ceilings, the agglutination of beer and smoke and dust that permeated her lungs and, over all, the air of failure, never ceased to raise both the hair on the back of her neck and a feeling of sorrow in her heart. She paused at the top of the stairs and took in the sounds: soft moaning coming from a room down by the bathroom, a clunk and a curse as a bottle fell from palsied fingers.

She hurried to Monigan's room. The door sprang open before she could knock.

"Hey, Katy," Monigan said. "Get on in here and sit down. Right back, gotta take a squirt."

When he returned Katlyn was sitting at the folding card table.

"You comfortable there? I could put a pillow under you, you want."

"This is fine."

Katlyn was having trouble expunging the sight of Dwayne and the police on her front steps. Miraculously, bedecked and bedraggled as he was, Dwayne had managed to retain an air of indifference, even superiority, which fractured just the slightest when Katlyn sent him on his way. He hadn't the self-esteem to actually claim title to such poise — he clearly had the same extraordinary reserve of bullshit as his father.

Monigan circled the room, looking for something to offer her by way of hospitality. "Wish you'd let me know you were coming." He opened the fridge and peered inside. "Could've stocked up. All's I got is some mock-chicken loaf for the mutt."

"I called."

"Oh yeah. But I needed a nap. This investigation's been keeping me up all night. Them cops got it easy, what with their computers and that."

"By the way — where is this famous pet?"

Monigan picked a slipper off the top of the dresser and skinned it under the bed.

"Rrrf."

"He's talking good these days."

Katlyn laughed.

Monigan sat down on the tiny metal folding chair opposite Katlyn. "I know if you bother coming up here it's getting serious," he said. "But it's only a couple months on the rent, and sure my bar tab's climbing up there again, but I had to get a phone — never know when somebody might call with a clue."

"This isn't about money."

"Oh." Monigan blinked. "What are you doing scaring me like that?"

A scratching sound filtered out from under the bed. Katlyn dipped her head and peered into the dark recess.

"Does it always hide like that?"

"See, it's like I told you. It don't even wanna come out. No harm being under there."

"You can't keep an animal penned up under the bed."

"It ain't penned, just it's scared of climbing past the underwear. And it even sits there when the shorts are where they belong, over in the corner."

"It needs room to run around."

"Times I take it out it does too much running, what with the neighborhood cats chasing it everywhere."

Katlyn required no elaboration; the local felines were a savage crew.

"Never mind about the mutt," Monigan said. "Why'd you go to all this bother? I know you don't like coming up here."

"That's not true."

"Don't try to tell me different. It makes sense, I told you only eleven hundred times you got too much class for this place."

Katlyn toyed with the crib board, spinning it in slow circles. "How's the investigation going?"

"What you really wanna know?"

Katlyn tried to start in but after two failed attempts gave up. She had been able to talk to Monigan from the very beginning, but this time was different. She looked at him, begging for help.

Monigan sat with his fingers laced together over his stomach. "All right," he said. "Maybe I should give up and stick my head in a blender, you wanna see me dead. It's the french fry, ain't it?"

"I don't know why," Katlyn said. "I can't help it. I know he's strange, and he has a lot of warped, preconceived ideas about people. But I don't think he believes all he says, and he's . . . there's a kindness there trying to get out, a fragile thing inside." She spun the cribbage board, unable to look Monigan in the face.

"You picked yourself a good one," he said. "Frenchie's got a good job — everybody knows starting-off comics make millions. Nice giant yellow suit, so you can't say nothing about the way he dresses. Cute, too — only looks like about a foot locker full of smashed assholes."

Katlyn started to cry, which brought Monigan around.

"Hey," he said, raising her chin. "I was only joking. You know me, just a idiot is all."

"I'm sorry." She wiped at her face.

Monigan's pulse was racing. He grabbed his only clean shirt from the bureau and dabbed Katlyn's eyes. "Don't be sorry," he said. "Honey, you shouldn't be sorry, only ready to kill me, coming here for help and I make you cry. Now listen good. You know you could pick anybody and I'd hack on him. It's because I don't think anybody's good enough for you. Now take the french fry. Maybe he ain't tops in the looks or success departments — no, don't cry again — but what I mean is that's just crap you wade through to get to the real guy. So what I'm saying is I seen the spark between you two the first time I seen him walk through the door, so if your heart knows this is the guy for you then you got my blessing. And I'll fight any man says different, only don't get too mad if in the rolling around Frenchie catches himself a six-incher by accident."

Katlyn laughed lightly and squeezed his hand. "Call him Dwayne."

"Come on, Katy."

"Come on yourself." She was laughing now.

"He uses the old lady's maiden name. That one won't get past my teeth."

"Tell me about him," Katlyn said. "Tell me anything."

He looked over Katlyn's head and gradually let his eyes settle on her own. He smiled weakly. "I guess I don't know much. Guess that's been the problem all along, with him and the old lady both."

"He's a difficult man to get to know," she said.

Normally when drowning, Monigan seized any lifeline, but this time he left it to dangle. "Wasn't always a man," he said. "Should be able to figure out a kid, and if you can't, it's probably 'cause you helped screw him up."

"Don't be so hard on yourself."

"Why not?"

She had no answer, but reached across the table and took Monigan's scabby old hand in hers.

"That's why him and the old lady always been so close — it's like them two together was fighting me and I was fighting them."

"Talk to them, for God's sake."

Monigan wasn't listening, off in his own world. "He bought me a hammer."

"Dwayne?" Katlyn was aware she was prying deeper than Monigan might want to go, but she had to learn something, anything. Who the hell were these two men in her life?

"Shitty hammer," he said. "One of them cheap ones where the head ain't wedged onto the handle right so it don't last at all. I was using it once and the head come off and stuck itself into Jimmy Duggan's leg." He laughed.

"That's funny?"

"Jimmy thought it was."

Katlyn waited patiently.

"The kid was about nine, maybe. He was interested in everything already, getting kicked out of school all the time for screwing up the class but then getting back in 'cause his marks were so good. Look at this here . . ."

Monigan pulled out his wallet, a battered trucker's wallet with a chain attached to his belt. He handed across a plastic bankbook protector. Katlyn slid out a filthy blue square of heavy cardboard and when she tried to unfold it found herself holding eight separate pieces. She spread them out and fit them together on the card table, and with Monigan's help eventually deciphered the faded script that detailed Dwayne's Grade 3 report card.

Down the left side were listed the various subjects with the pupil's grades. All straight As. On the right were the teacher's comments enclosed in lined rectangles:

> ATTENDANCE: Perfect when not under suspension.
> HYGIENE: Improvement required.
> PARTICIPATION IN CLASS: Teachers are meant to teach their pupils, not to receive instruction from them.
> DISCIPLINE: Dwayne's intelligence indicates he should know better than to badger others in class. It has caused several of the students to physically assault him during recess periods, an unhealthy trend for eight-year-old girls.

Katlyn had to laugh. She replaced the fragments in the plastic sleeve. Monigan took them out and rearranged them properly before putting the whole thing back in his wallet.

"So it ain't that he's stupid," he said. "And it was the next year that he bought me the hammer, so I guess at nine he shouldn't know about tools."

"I don't know anything about them now."

"I had a job," Monigan said. "I was delivering stuff for a auto parts place, back when I had a driver's license. But somehow boxes and that went missing now and again, and 'cause the boss didn't like me I got the blame for it and he gimme the boot."

Katlyn took out a cigarette and stuck it in the vee his fingers made as he rested his elbow on the table.

"Thanks," he said, then took her matches. "Then I seen this ad on a book of matches, like this one but not advertising a thousand free stamps. This one had careers you could get by writing away. I wouldn't even have to go to a school 'cause they send all the stuff you need right to your house. That was when the old lady's dad died and left her that house she's still in over on Seaton. Anyhow,

I took all the money we had left over from the move, and I mean all of it, which wasn't much but it was every penny, and sent it off to the address on the matches.

"Well, pretty soon I get this course on how to be a mechanic. A diesel mechanic. I'll tell you right now that I worked harder than I ever did in my life on that shit. I'd get down in the basement on a old table we had and go at it like you wouldn't believe. The old lady'd send the kid down with sandwiches and stuff. But I couldn't do it. Nossir, not a bit of it.

"Mind you, let me under the hood of a truck and stick some tools in my hands and you better get outta the way, 'cause stuff's gonna fly. I ain't as good as old Bill at fixing stuff, course it's unnatural what he does, but I know what I'm doing under there is what I'm saying.

"Books, though, and diagrams and all that? They don't have nothing to do with a actual engine, you know? There's no connection there between a book and a truck. So finally, after the old lady asking me and asking me when I'm gonna be done and get a real job again, and all the time warning me that when I do get a job as a mechanic I'll probably break my neck when the hood falls on my head like some guy she heard about in Calgary, finally I couldn't do it. I'd still go down to the basement every day and most nights, and the kid would bring down sandwiches and see all these books and papers spread out everywhere on the table, but I wasn't doing anything. Every day the books got harder and pretty soon even the stuff at the beginning that I did know about, suddenly I didn't even know that any more."

Katlyn hadn't taken her eyes off him. He sat there with his lips moving but with the rest of him frozen into a bas-relief.

"So I burned the whole works in the fireplace," Monigan said. "Burned it all, with the old lady screaming at me and the kid not understanding nothing. Then I tore up the house a bit, if I don't forget."

He lowered his head and stared at his hands, worrying a piece of skin on the back of one knuckle. "The next day the kid bought me a hammer. I don't know where he got the money, 'cause I spent it all on the match people. But he bought me a hammer, a red one, and give it to me. I was sitting at the kitchen table drinking a beer with the old lady still crying and talking about the soup line and the Sally Ann, and the kid walked in and give me the hammer.

"'Here you go, Dad,' he says. 'It's for fixing trucks. An artisan can't ply his craft without the proper tools.' I remember exactly what he said, talking like that already."

After a long silence he continued. "Shitty hammer, but then Jimmy Duggan found that out."

Katlyn knew that the very worst thing she could do would be to cry.

"Hey," Monigan's head came up. "You wanna beer?"

"It's a little early," Katlyn said. "But yeah, I'd take a beer."

Monigan got to his feet. "Then we better go open early downstairs."

"Not right away," she said. "I have to run home for something. Dwayne's supposed to open today, but I'll just go home and do . . . get something. I'll be right back." Katlyn rushed out.

Monigan went to the window and looked down at the street. He wondered if a fall would kill a guy, jumping from that height, or only give him a headache. Saturday. Jesus.

Katlyn was trying to fit her key in the lock, shaking and crying and wondering how a father and son can go so wrong for no visible reason. She got the door open and went up to her apartment and lay on the bed.

Dwayne, oblivious to all the effort being expended with him in mind, was on his way to work, a decided spring in his step. He was convinced his beloved bore him no ill will. Certainly she hadn't invited him in the night before but he attributed that to fear of authority; the police have that effect on many people, and therefore she could not be held responsible. The way he figured, it was yet another area where her weakness and his strength came together in symbiotic perfection.

So Dwayne opened the bar and hit the job with flair, slinging beer and mixing drinks and trading banter with the locals. He ignored customers' jibes and complaints; he smiled when the Sock Guy came in to offload a dufflebag full of purloined merchandise; he shrugged when a man returned from the bathroom looking like he'd taken a cocaine snowball in the face. He was happy. Katlyn had phoned and said she would be there shortly, and the only possible motivation for her urgency was the need to be by her man. He checked his watch for the third time in five minutes, expecting her any second, as she couldn't possibly keep herself away for very long and surely was forgoing her usual preparations to be by his side all the sooner.

Dwayne's overall confidence took a brief dip at the recollection of being thrown out of the club by Charles Manson the night before, but that was fine. He wouldn't abandon the revolution, but would return like Castro aboard the *Granma* and strike the dictator Sturgis to his knees.

In any case, Dwayne was starting to think that nothing else mattered. A man selected a career, practiced or exercised a talent, but was not defined by what he did. It was only in front of Katlyn that Dwayne must either maintain a flawless aspect or adhere to the code of ancient African kings and kill himself. Dwayne may have thought he was getting his life together, but it was astonishing that he could convince himself there was nothing to worry about in his relationship with Katlyn, given his disgrace of the night before. To say nothing of the monstrous secret in his heart.

But he was Dwayne.

Glancing repeatedly at the door, he sang to himself as he raised the carving knife and slashed the limes and lemons into slivers. He wished he had a *shofar* to blow.

TWENTY

Monigan, with Bill in tow, was trying to cadge a free meal from King Canelli. He was smoking, flicking his ashes on the counter. As each gray cylinder hit the formica Canelli attacked it with a sponge and pushed the ashtray in a new direction, trying to anticipate Monigan's next move and head him off at the pass.

"That's okay, but that's no matter." The King didn't know how far to press it. "I got bills to pay, what do you think?"

"I known you for how long?" Monigan asked. "Forever, that's how long. Since I come to Toronto we been friends and now you won't even spot me two lousy plates of spaghetti."

"Pasta," Canelli corrected.

"It ain't even spotting me, really. Start me up a house account and it works out good all round: I eat here all the time plus bring in my pals, up goes your business, fill the joint."

"For that, should have been me stick with the pike instead of my sister. No sir — pay as you go or out you go."

"We been friends since school."

"I never go to school with you, I never even go to school in Canada."

"You still got that dopey accent, Canelli. How long you been in this country?"

"Yes, an accent. How many languages you know, Monigan?"

"None. Just more ways to get in shit."

"None, you bet. Not even English."

Old Bill, unsteady on his stool, feet barely reaching the floor, was enjoying himself. He was comfortable these days, liked his place above The Workbench. It was nice having a mattress off the floor and his bureau was good for storing stuff he planned to fix. He tried to picture his old place, the place him and Jean had, but time had made even Jean's face elusive. It was only when she visited him that he could remember what she looked like. He liked her visits. Yesterday she had walked with him all the way to Yonge and Dundas, but then she disappeared. Probably afraid of all the kids coming out of Ryerson College at lunchtime. She always had been afraid of crowds. Funny, but she had never seemed to mind the rough sections of the neighborhood, was never bothered by the men loitering along Dundas or up Parliament. Sometimes she would get in trouble for spitting on the posters of half-naked women outside Filmore's strip club, or when she barged into the hairdressing school on Dundas demanding a free permanent. She was always doing that kind of thing.

It would be nice if she would talk to him when she visited, but just her being there was okay. She never used to talk much anyhow.

Last week, or yesterday, Bill had a dream. There were a lot of people, a big crowd, and all of them were watching him on a stage in front of City Hall. On the stage was a huge machine. It didn't seem to have a purpose but it was impressive. All arms and pistons and gears and very shiny, so shiny it hurt his eyes. He was on the stage with it, and a man with a beard and a fancy suit was handing him a piece of paper and putting a ribbon around his neck. Bill had fixed the machine and everyone was very happy about it. Jean was at the back of the crowd, way at the back, and she was clapping. But when he called to her and waved for her to come up on the stage, she disappeared again. But she didn't like crowds, he knew that, so it was okay.

Bill figured maybe that's why he had lived so long. Little things like that, fixing things and playing pool real well, and it was pretty good when he found something he could use in a garbage can or in an alley. So maybe that's why he had lived so long, maybe that kind of stuff was why he was put on earth. Even if he didn't look very hard there were lots of things that made sense and made him happy. Jean didn't like very many things and maybe that's why she disappeared. His friend Monigan fought back at everything even if he liked them, so maybe that's what Monigan was supposed to be doing. Other people did things that Bill couldn't do, and Bill did things they couldn't, so it was pretty good when you added it all up. He knew that not a lot of people liked living the way him and Jean used to, and he had to admit fixing things didn't bring him very much money over the years, even if he was good at it. But he liked it.

Canelli suddenly shrieked and raced out from behind the counter. Monigan was on his way to the kitchen.

"You can't go in there," Canelli said.

"Wanna taste your wares. You wanna get paid, you better dish up solid food. I'll just get my laughing gear around a spoonful of sauce and see if it's worthwhile staying."

Canelli fidgeted helplessly. Then the cops walked in.

"Officers — arrest that man."

Doyle's shoulders visibly sagged as the door swung shut behind him and Ogilvie. All he had wanted was a bit of peace and quiet and a bite to eat with his partner. They were in civilian clothes, off duty, and still the neighborhood wouldn't grant them a few hours of normalcy.

"Arrest him," Canelli insisted. "He was trying to extort food from me. Threats, you bet, the whole works."

Monigan smiled and walked toward the cops.

"I'll run you outta here," Doyle warned.

"No way to talk to a fellow detective. I might decide to hold back a important clue and you guys'd be running in circles forever."

"Let's go," Ogilvie said.

"Don't you guys look cute," Monigan said. "Two fresh-faced young kids out on a date. Don't tell me — you're gonna share a pizza and lick the sauce off each other's fingers."

Doyle leaped, but Monigan, with surprising agility, sidestepped him.

"Hey!" Canelli yelled.

In the commotion, Bill had left his stool and gone 'round back of the counter. Canelli arrived just as Bill was lifting the milkshake machine back upright.

"Officers, do your duty and arrest both these men. You see with your own eyes this one try to steal my equipment."

Bill inserted an empty metal container into the apparatus and the machine whirred furiously.

"How you do that?" Canelli asked. "That thing no work for four years."

Bill looked up from the milkshake machine. He had fixed it but now the owner was mad. It was easy for Bill to fix things so he usually just went ahead and did it. He didn't need any thanks, but the man shouldn't be mad at him. It seemed that whenever his friend Monigan was around, people got mad. Well, not always mad, but all excited and noisy, too noisy. He was glad Monigan was his friend, but sometimes he even made Bill excited and sort of nervous. He wished Monigan would be quiet sometimes.

"Get over here, Bill," Monigan said. "You and me and the rest of the posse got some investigating to do." He dug in his pocket for his notebook of clues.

"You have nothing to do," Doyle said. "You're done. I don't care what you learn, I don't want to know about it."

"Gimme a menthol."

Doyle had the pack out and open when he realized what he was doing. "Piss off," he said and replaced the pack.

Ogilvie didn't know what to say. The evening had been a blur. She and Doyle had been talking, that's all. It was a slow night and they had grabbed a coffee and driven out to Cherry Beach to dog it a bit and then the arson case came up and then Doyle was talking about his family and she was talking about hers and the next thing she knew their shift ended and Doyle asked her out and she surprised herself by saying yes and here they were and she still didn't know what to think about it all.

"Can't you hear me?" Doyle had her by the elbow. "What's wrong?"

"Nothing," she muttered. Monigan was staring at her with that smug, infuriating grin of his. She pointed a finger at him. "That's right, buddy."

"Buddy."

"You're off the case."

"Thought you said I was never on her."

"You weren't," Ogilvie said.

"Then I can hardly get my bag in a knot being off it. I think you can see my point."

"Stay clear or I'll have you up on obstruction of justice charges."

"Only you better watch your step too. I like you guys too much to read inna paper one day you're up on six counts of humping on duty."

The cops left, their date hardly off to an auspicious start.

Canelli had his head in his hands, elbows propped on the countertop.

"Cheer up," Monigan said.

Canelli sulked as Monigan went into the kitchen and emerged with two heaping platters of spaghetti. A basket of garlic bread was jammed in the tomato sauce of the lefthand serving and a glass shaker of mozzarella was screwed into the pile on the right.

"You worry too much," Monigan said to the King. He put down a plate in front of Bill. "Always was your problem."

"You don't know problems," Canelli said, sad and sombre. "No business, I get. People cheating me, my one staff he quit because of no tips."

"Gotta advertise," Monigan said. He slurped a ten-inch strand into his mouth, strafing the espresso machine with tomato-sauce tracers. "That's what gets business. You think I don't know business? I know."

"Even that," Canelli moaned. "I get best idea ever to advertise. Big giant suit looks like pasta. Get a guy to walk around handing out advertising, pretty soon everybody knows the pasta guy, they come to King Canelli's. What do you think — the guy runs away with my suit, stolen you bet. No pasta man and twenty dollars he gets off me too."

Monigan put down his fork and luxuriated in the feeling of flat-out good luck. "Tell you what," he said. "Gotta deal for you."

"I'm too tired for deals."

"This is gonna save your business. I figure that suit run you a couple hundred bucks. So I get it back for you, and you spring for dinner for me and Bill once a week till we're even. You ain't selling any of this shit as it is, and this way you get your suit back, do some advertising, next thing you know you own Sicily."

Canelli couldn't be bothered to think about it. "Sure, Monigan," he said. "Go ahead, you want."

With great vigor, Monigan drove his fork into the coiled mound in front of him. He had a good feeling about this. It was almost as if he and his son were going into business together. He realized that was a stretch, but it was nice. Monigan would have to come up with some way to reciprocate, something he could do for the kid for giving up the suit.

"Dig in partner," Monigan said to Bill. "You and me got business over The Workbench before last call."

Had Monigan known it, he could have been doing important detective work over at The Laugh Chance.

The display terminal was beyond salvaging but the keyboard and laser printer were in good shape, at least for the time it took Sturgis to pitch them on the floor and kick them around a bit. Open on its hinges, the safe door allowed access to nothing but useless records and trash. The cash bag was already in a backpack that felt pitifully light on Sturgis's shoulders.

The Saturday second show had been cancelled for lack of turnout. The house comics were still boycotting the place and Sturgis had been forced to pack the last three shows with amateurs, fools, material thieves, ventriloquists and circus geeks of similar ilk. The fat kid headlining the Saturday first show, which had ended two hours ago, did twenty minutes of stock gags and bad puns, bolted the stage before his time was up, then paraded around with a twenty-year veteran's authority. When he barged into the Star Chamber and asked Sturgis for a raise the owner barred him from the club for life, then kicked him so hard in the ass on the way out that he snapped the tip off the kid's coccyx.

That had been the last straw. Sturgis would leave everything he couldn't carry. He had the cash and two cases of booze waiting downstairs by the front door. Any important records had been destroyed. Actually, he wasn't turning his back on much, as he had wrecked everything that could possibly be put to good use. He had gone on a tear, venting years of frustration on the furniture, the mirrors, even the pictures on the walls. Gleefully he ripped the innards from the comics' demo tapes, joyfully he shredded promo shots and résumés.

The day before he had clearcut his apartment, forwarding everything easily portable by bus express to a mailing address in Vancouver. Once there he would turn whatever he could into cash and vanish. Anywhere, till things cooled off. Hawaii maybe, or Mexico, or Paraguay for all he cared. Canada had done nothing but bankrupt him, so he felt that it wasn't like leaving home. A one-way ticket to the west coast was crumpled in the breast pocket of his sharkskin suit jacket.

He winced as he straightened from one last check of the safe. He had strained his still-tender ribs tearing the cash register free and hurling it over the bar. He had to admit he was excited at the prospect of travel, even of the enforced variety. Starting over, new life and all that. He wondered if the people in Paraguay liked standup comedy.

He loaded the booze into the trunk of the cab but held onto the backpack, climbing into the rear seat and setting the cash on his lap. Next day was Sunday. He'd have a good meal somewhere then hole up till the flight Monday morning. The driver pulled away as Sturgis lapsed into a daydream of a Paraguayan llama crushing Dwayne Feller beneath its hooves.

TWENTY-ONE

With his left hand Monigan was clutching a styrofoam box of take-out lasagna, with his right steering Bill along the sidewalk. By the time they made it to The Workbench it was past closing time. Dwayne cautiously pushed the handle on the side door and was thrown aside as the two men hurried inside. Dwayne made to protest but Monigan dismissed him with a wave and settled Bill into a chair in the corner, where the old guy folded in on himself like an origami sculpture.

"It's late," Dwayne said.

"Where's Katy?" Monigan ignored him and helped himself to a draft.

"She didn't show up."

"The whole day?"

"No sign of her at all. I'm not really sure how to cash out, so maybe I should leave it. I have a set of keys. I was going to lock up and go check her apartment, see if she's okay. I should have —"

"Settle down, now. Easy, boy. You're rambling."

The bulbs dozed off as Dwayne put each one to bed, leaving only the grimy filterings of the horseshoe's lights to illuminate Monigan.

"I'm worried," Dwayne admitted.

"Didn't she call? No word at all?"

"Oh, yes. She called around noon. But she sounded strange somehow."

Monigan crooked a finger at him.

"What do you want?" Dwayne would have been happy to whine in solitude.

Monigan fixed him with a look, the wonky eye slipping off to one side. "First," he said.

"First," Dwayne repeated.

"Gimme another beer."

Dwayne complied. "Second?"

"Second?"

"First, the beer," Dwayne said. "Second?"

"No, no — I ain't done with First yet."

"I thought . . ."

"First," Monigan said.

"First." Dwayne was jumpy. His father didn't seem out of control or angry, but he was acting strangely and Dwayne couldn't put a finger on it. He half-remembered the look from the old days, a certain way his father had of carrying himself when trying to muster enough bluff to quash his confusion.

"Before I forget, me and Bill got a few free meals coming if I get the suit back."

Dwayne stared.

"Canelli," Monigan said. "That bum said I get his suit back, I'm his free customer."

The noodle suit. "I don't have it."

"What did you do with it?"

"Threw it out."

"Guess I can't blame you for that. You did look sick in the head when you had it on. Only now of course you owe me and Bill a few suppers."

"I'm not interested in any type of food-sharing scheme. Trophallaxis is all well and good between insects, in fact it's a key ingredient of the social behavior displayed by the *hymenoptera*, but that —"

"Don't get into it," Monigan said. "No need to be so scared."

"Scared?"

"You think I'm stupid? You think I don't know why you drag out all this stuff nobody cares about?" Monigan looked sadly at him. "You don't have to impress me. Not me, you don't."

Dwayne swallowed hard and poured himself a cranberry and Coke.

"Second," Monigan said.

"Second," Dwayne said, glad to be back on the list.

"Second is we gotta have rules."

"Rules."

"Rules. First of which is no running around. Ever. Never. Got that?"

"No running around."

"Right, or down you go. Never know when. Anytime, riding the roller coaster at the CNE, a woman down below goes crazy cause a little peanut head comes flying out of one of the cars, lands in her stroller. Think I won't do it? I'll do it."

"Running around where?" If Dwayne were going to have his head cut off, then he'd prefer to die wiser.

"Anywhere, with anyone. You got yourself Katy. You run around on her with anyone else and you'll have me after your ass till the day you drop, being pretty quick."

"What does Katlyn have to do with all this?"

"Don't mess with me," Monigan said. "I'm like a street — you gotta look both ways before you cross me."

"Dammit, what do you know?" Dwayne had his father by the front of the coat. It was hard to tell which of them was the most surprised. Very likely it was Dwayne, if such things can be judged by the shaking of hands and knocking of knees. "I'm not letting go."

Very slowly, Monigan said, "Good for you. That's good, showing some balls. Maybe Katy ain't entirely out of her head falling in love with you."

In love with him? Dwayne had been trying to convince himself that was the case, wishing for it so mightily, and through repetition achieving a kind of certitude, that it didn't register at first. Love. She loved him. Dwayne let go of his father and stood back.

"Third," Monigan said.

"Second."

Monigan tossed it around. "Nope," he said with conviction. "Third."

"You stated one rule: no running around. Now for the second rule."

"No second rule. First one is all. The other stuff you two figure out on your own. I can't be telling you all the secrets. Nobody ever wants advice anyhow, particular on their love life. People ask you for advice, it ain't what they want, only they want somebody to agree with what they decided on theirselves. That's how come I don't give advice, except if somebody needs it and don't want it, or sometimes a six-incher, which is more of a reminder than anything."

"I agree," Dwayne said. "A thinking man shouldn't be bound by rules. Where's the room for creativity when we're trapped by regulations? Our government is addicted to legislation protecting us from ourselves, as if John Calvin's Geneva Consistory was the model for —"

"Quiet!" Monigan yelled. "That's something else you gotta learn, the shutting up stuff. You get people all mad and excited and noisy and confused."

"I was just trying —"

"You weren't trying to do nothing. You were scared again 'cause I told you how Katy feels. Fear's good only if you use it right. Otherwise you'll cock up the works."

"In any event . . ."

"What?"

"You were working your way down a list of some kind."

"A list?"

This had to end quickly. Dwayne was almost uncontrollable in his need to see Katlyn. His heart was palpitating, his breathing ragged. He wondered if he should march up the street and declare himself. He had already said the words, with rather less than the desired result, so maybe the best course would be to wait and let her come to him. Then again, Dwayne considered, she had broken her word by not showing up that day, so maybe Monigan was mistaken. Suddenly Dwayne felt no good at all.

"I don't remember no list," Monigan said.

"You said First, you wanted a beer. No, wait — you said First, you wanted the noodle suit. Second was the list of rules, which turned out to be one rule, and so no list at all."

"Right. No list."

"No list of rules, but the rule itself was part of a greater list comprising the list of rules, of which there was only one."

"Frenchie, I think maybe your head ain't working too good, what with all the backed-up love in you and such, so to make you happy I'll order another beer and we'll leave off with the list that ain't there, though what Katy sees in you has got me going in circles trying to sniff my own ass."

"Listen," Dwayne said patiently. "Your concern at this late date is touching, but whatever happens between Katlyn and myself is our business."

This was hard to swallow for a man who believed everything in existence was his business. "All I'm trying to do is help." Monigan looked sad and tired. "You and the old lady don't think much about me, I know that, and you're probably right when I look back on things, but I do know one thing and that's I at least got more experience than you in fucking up. I guess you didn't learn very much from me when you were growing up but I can pass that one thing on at least." His voice snagged as he looked hard at his son. "You gotta listen to somebody sometime, as disgusting as it is."

It may have been going on for some time but it wasn't till Dwayne and Monigan took a break from their exchange that they heard the tapping at the window. Monigan pushed the handle and stood blocking the doorway.

"What you want?"

After a moment he stepped aside and let her enter. She squinted at Dwayne then pulled her thin cloth coat closer together in
front and shuffled to a corner of the room, her insubstantial form
casting shadows across the pool table and along the worn maroon
carpeting. Monigan dropped a cup of hot coffee at her table. The
woman warmed her hands on the mug.

"I know, I know," he said when he returned to the bar. "It's past
closing time."

"Doesn't she have any place to go?" Dwayne asked. "Look at her:
Stinking Lizaveta."

"How you know her name?"

"It was a literary reference."

"Oh. Then shut up again."

"There are so many people like her around here."

"Finally starting to learn something. You and your books and
stuff and you ain't learned one thing outta them, not one thing. You
think it's all about choice, like them dumb bastards on TV saying
it's all personal power and making a change in your life and positive thinking and how to apply yourself and how to choose — how
to choose! Don't you know most of them people you see on the
streets can't make a choice? Look over there — you think old Bill
can make a choice, grab himself by the ass with both hands and lift
himself up? We're talking a little wrong in the head, here. I don't
know, maybe some of them are born goofy, some of them go goofy
along the way, some of them take too many licks in the head, some
of them just catch too much shit for too long and it turns them
goofy. I ain't a doctor, but I know most of the folks out there ain't
in any kind of shape to make a choice.

"And let's say according to the doctors a guy ain't technical
mental, who's to say he's gonna make the *right* choices? Everybody
ain't the same, so if a guy tries as hard as he can but makes about
forty hundred wrong choices, what's left of him to get up in the
morning and try again? You're judging people out there by the
wrong rules."

"Katlyn feels the way you do," Dwayne said.

"Because she's people."

"So you're saying they can't do anything to change their lives?"

"You ever done it?"

"Done what?"

Monigan paused. "Some shitty thing that afterwards you can't believe you done. At the time there was so much pressure and crap coming at you that you had to take action, any action, and so you did. Then when you realized it was the wrong thing, or at least the wrong way, you added to the stupidity by shutting up and doing your best to pretend it never happened."

"Yes," he said measuredly. "I certainly have."

"Yeah," Monigan said, not quite ready to give his son the whole story. "Well . . . me, too."

After a long silence, unusual in that it wasn't strained, Dwayne said, "Same as people like her?"

Monigan shot eight ounces of draft down his throat and put both hands on the bar, glad to be off the topic of himself. "You're supposed to be a comedian, so how come you don't know nothing about timing?"

"I have an impeccable sense of timing."

"Not the way I'm talking about," Monigan said. "Don't you remember in high school there was always a few guys and a few broads who were the best looking and the best jocks and popular and all that? Now most of them ain't worth shit on a pizza box. Cause they had their peak, that's how come. They hit the big time when they were too young and too stupid to make the best of it, and it was all downhill from the glory years."

"So that woman over there peaked out early? I can't buy that."

"I ain't talking about her," Monigan said. "Or anyone specific."

"Yes, you are," Dwayne said.

"I had a peak and don't forget it. And leave me out of it. I'm talking about lots of people." He looked over at Bill, asleep. "Maybe I just ain't had the chance to do something big, that's all. Or important, anyhow. But it's timing — you gotta be ready for stuff like that." He broke off in a fit of coughing and hawked on the floor, squeezing the sides of his chest together and lowering his head.

Dwayne rushed around the bar.

Monigan raised his head and shook off his son's hand. "Get offa me."

Dwayne returned to the horseshoe. His father didn't look well but he was determined to make his point.

"Awhile back a guy says to me," Monigan said. "Guy gets outta the joint, says to me that he's ready. I ask him ready for what, and he says he's ready now for a life. Forty, forty-five, this guy, spent most of his life in jail, and he says now he's ready to live. Took him that long, now he's ready. I don't know — maybe some guys don't get ready till they run outta time.

"But anyhow, if they already had their peaks or if they're still waiting for them, you might not ever know. Keep in mind that what seems like a peak to them people, you might not even recognize as a bump. So don't go putting the badmouth on Bill or Stinking Velveeta. Me, I like things simple, and I pissed in the pickles enough along the way I figure I live with what I done and what I got and how everything turns out. Them over there and all them like that, you shut up about. Way I see it, everybody deserves a little dignity. Somebody ain't strong enough to have it and keep it themselves, then what the fuck — how about the rest of us giving it to them free of charge."

Dwayne made to refill Monigan's glass but the big man waved his hand and turned to the woman in the thin cloth coat. "Get home," he said. "Get home now and take care of your brat."

The two men watched her slide out the side door. Monigan hoisted Bill and tossed him casually over his shoulder.

"Next time you see Katy tell her you know the rules and you're ready to play by them. Then you two sit down and make up your own rules and tell me to go to hell."

"Hey," Dwayne said as Monigan headed with his human cargo for the stairs.

"What?"

"Just . . . good night. And thanks."

"Yeah."

When Monigan and Bill were gone Dwayne sat still for a moment. He reached for the phone but withdrew his hand. Incredible as it was to him, he couldn't think of Katlyn right then, not in the proper way he couldn't.

Dwayne was preoccupied with thoughts of his father, who had fled hearth and home for reasons of his own, reasons that were unfathomable to his son but certainly no more inadequate than the reasons Dwayne used to justify the arson. Dwayne had come to see his own motivations must seem pretty bloody abstruse to a lot of people, so while unable to untangle much of his father's reasoning, he could at least empathize in a general way with his urgency, his drive, his fears. And he had learned at least one thing tonight: his father cared. Dwayne wasn't sure how much concern Monigan harbored, but he wasn't the total egocentric bastard Dwayne had believed him to be these last four years.

He locked up the bar and went home, and while drifting off to sleep seriously considered the possibility that his father was running out of time.

Up the street from the bar, in her second floor apartment, late as it was, Katlyn was still awake, staring out the window. She was waiting to see if Dwayne would come by to press her buzzer after he locked up the bar. If he did, in what bizarre costume would he be? What troubled mental state? And what would be her role this time: lover, counsellor, employer, adversary? She wished Dwayne had never walked in that day, forcing her to fall in love with an aberrant slab of pasta. Stabbing her cigarette out in the ashtray, she pulled the kimono tighter and lay down to sleep on the couch, the better to hear the buzzer.

When it went she would rush to answer it. Or ignore it.

TWENTY-TWO

Dwayne wanted to phone Katlyn immediately upon awakening, but he decided to perform his ablutions first, hoping to build up the requisite nerve by putting the matter off.

The hot water tank was empty by the time he stepped out of the shower so he had to wait twenty minutes to shave. In the interval he stood facing the mirror, meticulously grooming himself with a pair of manicure scissors. He snipped the hair from his nostrils, nicked a lobe trying to depilate his ears, brushed his hair forward and evened his bangs, then thrust the hair back into the dramatic look Katlyn seemed to favor. He combed the hair on his arms and legs to give himself a sleek, otter-like appearance. After shaving twice he ironed a pair of khaki army-surplus boxer shorts and drew them on. For a time he paraded around thus, flexing his pectorals, chin held high, extending his arm to a phantom date and bowing from the waist, making grand gestures. He sat on the futon and pulled on a brand new pair of work socks. Next, wool trousers and a beautiful Hawaiian shirt from the consignment store on Queen Street. He stripped the dry cleaner's plastic from his RCAF tunic and hung the uniform on the closet doorknob.

By the time he phoned Katlyn she had left for work. Dwayne knew that you don't call a woman at work to ask her out on a date — though the dating guidebooks he read hadn't specifically ruled it out — but he was too anxious to wait. As it developed, all his worrying was for nothing. Katlyn readily agreed to a late-night bite to eat after she closed the bar. It was Sunday, the one day of the week she felt free to treat herself and close early.

Dwayne hung up. He was stunned at how smoothly it had gone. Had he known it was going to be this easy he would have asked her out long ago. He slapped his belly, which was rounding nicely into shape again. Tonight was the night to do his duty, look Katlyn right in the eye and tell her everything, let it all come out. He'd put it off no longer. He sat on the bed and looked at his watch: 1210 hours. About eleven hours to kill. That would give him time to write out his confession and memorize it. He got a pad of yellow paper, stuck a pen in his mouth, crossed his arms and began composing.

He needed all eleven hours. By the time he met Katlyn out front of Fran's Restaurant he was still running lines in his head. As she approached from up the sidewalk Dwayne gave a small bow and they entered the restaurant. To an outsider they made an odd couple, but with love comes confidence, a cocky certitude, and it bore them along like royalty.

Fran's was crowded. A group of rowdy hockey fans, reeling from the contents of their hip flasks, were rehashing that night's game at their table, in their animation and hollering obviously unaware they were no longer down the street at Maple Leaf Gardens. The waitress led Dwayne and Katlyn past the mob's blueline and seated them at the back. Dwayne shook his head at the boisterous fans.

"Maybe we should find some place quieter," he said.

"This is fine," Katlyn said. "Honestly."

"I have no respect for people who can't hold their liquor."

Katlyn turned around as something — a wrist shot, maybe — went awry, shattering a bottle on the hockey fans' table. "Death of a thousand cups," she said.

Dwayne laughed too loudly and trickled to a stop. "You have a wonderful sense of humor."

"I could never get on stage and do what you do. I'd love to see you sometime."

Dwayne almost swallowed his tongue.

"Why don't you like talking about what you do? You're not exactly hesitant when it comes to any other topic."

"The thing is," Dwayne said. "Well, it's just . . ."

"What?" Katlyn said kindly.

"It's the only thing I've ever done on my own. The fear on stage represents all the fears I've ever had. So if I can conquer that one thing then . . ."

"Go on. This is the first time I've heard you speak of something close to you without roping in someone else's opinion. You can't live on quotes and examples and motivational speakers. You can't let others set your guidelines, no matter their wisdom. It's you alone. You embrace that concept in your work, so try applying it to your life."

"'The first of earthly blessings, independence,'" Dwayne said. "Edward Gibbon."

"*You* figure it out. From inside *yourself*."

"Is that what you do?"

Katlyn looked down at her place setting and the shiny cover of the menu. "I have to, I guess. Not much choice. I don't get around much, Dwayne. I don't see people so I'm forced inward."

"No need to be forced into anything." Dwayne blushed.

On her way to take their orders, the waitress was immobilized by one of the hockey fans who was imitating a defenceman. He hipchecked a table, pinning her to the wall. She dropped her pad and tray and got his sweater over his head, but a linesman got between them and stopped it before she could land a right hand. When she finally reached the back of the room, Katlyn and Dwayne were holding hands across the table.

"Hey," the waitress said.

"Sorry," Katlyn said. She stood up and donned her jacket. "We lost track of the time. We have to go."

The waitress shrugged. Turning, she lowered her head and dug in her imaginary blades, skating hard to make it out of her own end.

Dwayne looked around wildly, thinking himself a fool. Initially he had wanted to take Katlyn to a restaurant with class, a lovely setting for a lovely lady, but had concluded the casual atmosphere at Fran's would stifle some of the embarrassment attendant on a first date. True, he had never been out on a date, but he had memorized three dating guidebooks, all of which stressed the importance of both parties being comfortable while getting to know each other. Now Katlyn was leaving. Dwayne's insecurities welled up, convincing him Katlyn was repelled not only by the hockey fans, the decor and the waitress, but mostly by himself. He was being abandoned.

"Come on," Katlyn said. "We're going back to my place."

Her place, back to her place. Dwayne wondered if Katlyn was humoring him. If so, all the offer had done was increase his apprehension. The guidebooks had said nothing about this happening on a first date. He thought about saying no, of not following, of sitting there all night in his puddle of shame. Then she looked at him and smiled.

Dwayne followed along out the door, where Katlyn hailed a cab. The short ride aroused Dwayne to a heightened reality that was rife with naked terror. On arriving at Katlyn's apartment Dwayne wouldn't get out of the cab. Katlyn slid out on the street side but Dwayne remained in place, sweating heavily under his tunic. Katlyn had to drag him out of the taxi and up the sidewalk.

Upstairs, she poured herself a glass of Tia Maria and Dwayne a Coke. She turned the radio on to an oldies station. When she returned from the bedroom she was wearing her silk kimono.

Dwayne began to shake. A sense of impending failure was strong and metallic in his mouth. He didn't know what to do, for the love of mud! When faced with it, he sensed the absurdity of sexual congress. It was all too complicated and he was foundering in confusion.

Katlyn came closer and Dwayne cleared out of the way with a crustaceous skitter that placed him against the wall in a crouch behind a large ficus tree. Katlyn hesitated, then swallowed the last of her drink and made for her man, who was trying to blend into the foliage. She plucked Dwayne's glass from his hand and dropped it on the floor. He slid sideways until he was lost in greenery. On the left, he was being scratched by the ficus; on the right, a hanging plant's secretions were mingling with his sweat and running into the collar of his tunic; and from dead ahead advanced the carnivore his beloved had become. Dwayne searched for words, straining for something to say to delay the moment.

"*Bombyx mori*," he blurted out.

Katlyn screwed up her eyes.

"The larva of the silkworm moth. Just imagine how many it must have taken to make your kimono."

"I know," Katlyn said.

She opened the front of the robe and Dwayne found himself looking at her small pink-tipped breasts. A soft sound issued from him. He told himself he shouldn't stare.

"Historically, on certain Pueblo Indian hunting parties, a couple caught in carnal embrace instead of tending to business was forced to complete the act in front of everyone at the end of the day."

Katlyn's tongue found his mouth. Both fighting and submitting, Dwayne allowed himself to be pulled down, and as he returned the kiss his hands sought out Katlyn's pale skin. As his fingers roamed her body, Katlyn let loose two tiny tears and it was this last display of emotion that caused Dwayne to squeal and come in his pants.

The mortification was overwhelming and Dwayne fought to be free. But Katlyn was having none of it. She was as inexperienced as Dwayne in these matters but held a far greater reserve of determination. Not since the night she tracked down her father and demanded control of The Workbench had she been so determined.

Dwayne bellowed and surged upright but little Katlyn clung to him, encircling his chest with her arms and clamping her thighs tightly around one leg. He pushed at her and wailed aloud while subconsciously allowing himself to be pulled to the floor. Now that

Dwayne was down, Katlyn darted in like a small scavenger and began removing his clothes.

He looked down at her and felt all his worries fly in the face of his love. He heaved up his hips, the trousers came off and she was on top of him. And by God, if he wasn't already in the running for comeback player of the year! Sure enough, his little knob of a cock was pressing insistently into Katlyn's thigh. But he figured he'd better position it properly in case it again chose to fire on automatic, so he wiggled and bum-walked over a few inches. Katlyn shifted and straddled him and poked him inside her and the two of them drew enormous sighs of satisfaction at a job well done, or if not well done, at least nicely inaugurated.

As they rocked together there on the floor, Dwayne thought of the criminal depicted by old Cesare Lombroso who had tattooed on his penis, *entra tutto* — it enters all. He was about to relate this piece of information to Katlyn, but she gave a certain twist of her hips and Dwayne lost the train of thought.

"I love you," he satisfied himself with saying.

"I love *you*," Katlyn said.

TWENTY-THREE

The next morning, unable to remain still, charged with a vitality he had never known, Dwayne kissed Katlyn goodbye and flew out into the world. He wondered if he looked different, if people he passed could tell. He knew they couldn't compete with him in the arena of eros. After the second time — okay, technically the first — Dwayne and Katlyn talked for hours, and still Dwayne mustered the strength for another round. Now he promenaded down the street with his chest stuck out like the mountain dwellers of Peru.

He pulled out his wallet and realized skipping dinner at Fran's the night before had been doubly providential. Now he had enough money to buy Katlyn flowers.

He continued down Dundas to Yonge Street. Dwayne felt so sure on his feet, so smooth and athletic, that he chanced the revolving door at the Eaton Centre and became wedged inside for no more than a few minutes. He shot into the foyer, smiled broadly at the people who had stopped to stare at him and forced a handful of spare change on a doctor who was waiting for his wife. He cut through Eaton's and emerged in the mall on the far side, certain that the women in the cosmetics section had mentally ravished him as he passed by. Damn, he was some kind of satyr!

He checked the plastic map and located a florist shop. Near it was a bank of pay phones and Dwayne decided to make a quick call.

"Hello?"

"Hello, Mother."

"Who is this?"

"Me, of course."

"Why are you phoning me? I'm supposed to phone you, not the other way around. Turn things around like this and I'll get all addle-minded and the next thing you know I'll walk into an airplane propeller."

"An airplane propeller."

"Happens all the time. Now what is it, dear? You must be in trouble to call. Your voice sounds funny, and what's that noise in the background?"

"Just people," Dwayne said. "A crowd of beautiful people."

"At the police station?"

Dwayne had better nip this in the bud. When in a good mood he couldn't help cracking jokes, and then his mother would cry. She had the sense of humor of an Empire Club luncheon. "I'm not at the police station."

"What division are they holding you at?"

"I'm at the Eaton Centre. I just phoned to see if there was anything I could pick up for you while I'm here."

"Now you're teasing me."

"Wait! No! Don't start —" Dwayne held the receiver away from his ear while his mother dehydrated herself.

"Son?"

"I'm still here."

"Come home."

"I have errands to run."

"I really think you should come home. I really do. It's time we had a talk."

"That's fine for you to say, but I can't have my life governed by the dictates of others. I must reach inside myself and . . . whatever she said."

"Who said what?"

"The Exalted One."

"I don't understand."

"I'm certain you don't."

"You get home this instant, sonny."

"That's quite the demand, mother. If I didn't know better I'd read a threat into it."

"There is a threat in it."

"And with what could you possibly threaten me?"

"For starters, a power saw to cut my way into your apartment."

"That no longer scares me. I've been touched from on high. Be patient and I'll be home soon."

"Do as you like. You're just like your father."

For some reason that didn't cut with its old strength. Over the top of the phone booth Dwayne could see the sign for the florist shop. He smiled and hung up.

As Dwayne was making his run for the roses, Bill was sitting on his bed in a state of exhaustion. Slipping in and out of daydreams and nightdreams and hallucinations and the real world as he did was putting a strain on his very existence. He got off the bed at the sound of the banging and opened the door. Monigan entered and quickly scanned the room.

"What gives?" he said. "I heard a whole lotta yelling going on. You okay?"

Bill's cheeks were wet. He wondered how that had happened. Maybe his friend would like some tea, but Bill didn't have any so he sat down on the bed again.

"Jesus, Bill — talk to me."

"Had a dream."

"That's all you been doing lately," Monigan said. "When was the last time you even played pool? I tell you, you can't lay in bed or sit inna corner all day and think up these things. What is it you dream about all the time?"

"When I had a job at the warehouse Jean would wait for me," Bill said.

"Yeah, so?"

"I'd drive my forklift out the big doors and right up to her and I'd park and then we'd walk home."

"I guess you miss her, all right," Monigan said. "Is that all you dream about?"

"Some other things. I used to play baseball. Sometimes I dream about playing baseball, but I have skates on when I dream about it, so maybe I used to play hockey too. My dad used to watch me play till he died. Then it was just me."

Monigan looked him over. He was physically deteriorating. "We'll talk to the Sock Guy. Usually some pharmaceuticals follow him home, get you something for a good night's sleep. Gonna kill you through sheer wearing out if you keep dreaming all the time."

"I like the dreams," Bill said. "I'm tired after, but I like them."

"Only dreams I like are the ones gimme nocturnal commissions."

"It's sure nice when Jean visits," Bill said. "And last night the big yellow man was here."

"Who's that?" Monigan asked. "You dream about that ugly bird from Sesame Street?"

"Not a bird," Bill said. "The big yellow man. When he first came to this place he was big and yellow. When he came last night I thought he was an angel, except he wasn't very pretty. He can sure catch, though, he could do that. I used to be able to catch a baseball pretty good but I don't think I could catch a whole man." He stretched out his arms and turned his hands over, doubting their capability.

"Bill, pay attention to me," Monigan said. "Pay attention, now. This guy, this big yellow guy — what do you mean about catching a whole man?"

"Me," Bill said. "He caught me. I jumped from the fire and the big yellow man caught me. Then I woke up and he put me by the fence and then climbed over it and ran away. He must have been my friend 'cause that's a nice thing to do."

"What did he look like? What the hell did he look like?"

"You know," Bill said. "Just big. He wasn't yellow that night, he usually isn't yellow. Pretty funny-looking for an angel. He works downstairs with Katlyn. Katlyn's nice, too."

Monigan dove for the pile of clothes on the floor and began flipping items at Bill. "Get these on," he said.

Downstairs, Monigan plopped Bill at a corner table. "Katy, where's the french fry at?"

Katlyn looked up from inside the bar, still lightheaded from last night's lack of sleep and lovemaking and the tingle you get when the world slips up beside you and grins till you laugh. "Come here," she said, lowering her voice so the pack of mongrels at the bar couldn't hear. "Thanks so much for everything, Monigan. I mean . . . well, I'm very happy, that's all."

"Fuck a duck," Monigan said.

"What's wrong?"

But Monigan had out his notebook and was feverishly scribbling in the final clue. Now what was he supposed to do? He had a mission to complete, a job to do, an important investigation, and old Bill had just thrown the last piece of the puzzle right in his lap.

It was Dwayne, his own goddamn son. He had hoped to find out who did it and send him to the Crowbar Hotel but now he'd have to use all his smarts to save his kid. If Dwayne actually was the one, Monigan had to get to him first. If there was one thing Monigan knew about it was skipping lightly around the law and the collective moral conscience.

All the parental need to nurture and protect, all the responsibility he had shirked, came flooding back to him. He was a little upset that he wouldn't come out of it as a hero, but that was small potatoes when measured against the good he could finally do for his son. Of course, if it was his son who started the fire, Monigan might have to give him a little questioning of the six-inch variety, but he couldn't think about that now.

"Where's he at?"

"He'll be in shortly," Katlyn said.

"Shortly won't cut her." He reached past her and snatched the phone book off the shelf. "I been gone awhile so the old lady's probably changed the number about forty-nine times."

Monigan was far too worked up for Katlyn to be at ease. She recognized the loop of anger the man was locked into and didn't like it at all. It came as a surprise. Dwayne had told her about the lecture his father had given him, and Katlyn took it as acceptance of the situation, if a little shy of outright support. So Monigan's agitation had her worried.

"I'll call," she said. "You have to go through your wife and I don't think it's the best time for you to be talking to her." She picked up the phone. "But I'm not dialing until you tell me what this is all about."

"I can't."

"You had your notebook out."

"Just remembered something."

"Monigan."

"The brat's in trouble," Monigan said after an internal struggle.

"What kind of trouble?"

"Just trouble, that's all. Probably nothing much but I gotta get to him before . . . well, before the trouble gets worse."

Katlyn held the phone.

"Come on, Katy — for shitsake this is important. I'll tell you all about it soon's I track him down."

Katlyn would have to take it on trust. When she finally phoned, it took her five minutes of convoluted babble to worm anything out of Dwayne's mother, who initially led her to believe Dwayne was at the police station.

"He's at the Eaton Centre," she said as she hung up. "But I told you — he's due in here any time. What's so urgent that you can't wait?"

"Don't wanna talk to him in here."

Bill had dozed off in the corner so Monigan left him there and bulled out the front door. His son was a criminal, and new to it at that, so there was no telling what he'd do. Monigan had a vision of the cops getting to Dwayne first and throwing him in the can. Some people can ride out their time inside but Monigan was under no illusions that his son was one of them.

Dwayne, his son. Monigan planned to track him down at the mall, wring the confession out of him, then drag his ass back to The Workbench to come clean with Katlyn. It was the only way to make sure nobody else found out about it. Monigan couldn't begin to guess why Dwayne had done it. He considered his son to be weak and dopey but not felonious. He wondered what possible motive Dwayne could have had. Katlyn would be hurt but hopefully not damaged in the long run. Monigan wanted them to be happy, to have a wonderful life together and to grow old with grace alongside each other. If Dwayne had cocked that up, Monigan would kill him.

He shook his head at the sheer mess life had become in such a short time span: his son showing up and Katlyn and old Bill and Bill's wife dying and Monigan's own wife preying on his conscience . . . he wished things were back to being simple, where a man could sit at the bar and not worry about a rooming house burning down and people in love and his own failures, just sit there hoping the price of draft doesn't go up and wondering who's starting for the Jays and planning which wedding to attend Saturday.

The streetcar pulled up and Monigan thrust all such thoughts aside. He had to hurry. His son was in trouble.

Dwayne had Katlyn's flowers. He stood on the sidewalk and looked at the pitiful state the roses were in. He had been caught in a swarm of youths on the corner of Yonge and Dundas. Mostly they were just having fun with him, but they had reduced the flowers to a cluster of thorny sticks. He dropped them in a litter bin and searched his pockets, coming up with a loonie and two dimes. The fifth passerby gave him change for the dollar and Dwayne dropped a quarter in the pay phone outside a donut shop.

"The Workbench — may I help you?"

"My darling," Dwayne sighed.

"Dwayne. Where are you?"

"I got trapped in an ambush and barely escaped with my life."

"You'd better come straight here."

Dwayne was disappointed with her tone. He would have liked a little passion, whispered endearments, even baby talk. Something to reassure him the night before had actually happened.

"You father's looking for you," Katlyn continued.

"Monigan? For me?"

"Something's going on. He looked like he was having a break-down and ran out of here desperate to find you. He wouldn't say, but I know it has something to do with the stupid investigation he thinks he's conducting. I wish the police had never talked to him."

"The police?" Dwayne's colon rumbled.

"Doyle and Ogilvie," she said. "They have Monigan sniffing around for clues about the fire in Bill's old place."

Three thoughts materialized simultaneously in Dwayne's mind. The first was that the resurgence in conservative and fundamental-ist zeal in the land could lead to the re-introduction of the death penalty. The second was that his father's support for Dwayne and Katlyn's love was a ruse, that the fatherly advice had been part of a plan to draw information out of him. And the third was that this could rip apart the love itself. If Katlyn turned on him he'd take a header off the CN Tower.

Of one thing he was certain: it was time to face them all. He rammed the receiver into its cradle and broke into a run. He had never moved so quickly. With all his troubles, all of life's nagging, disturbing vicissitudes bearing upon his shoulders, he instinc-tively knew he was doing the right thing. For the first time in his lonely crusade through the world Dwayne was running in the right direction.

Outside The Workbench, Monigan climbed on the streetcar. He stood at the front by the driver, patting his pockets, searching for a ticket or token he didn't have. The operator, a good-natured type who had seen the act before, let him ride a couple of blocks before starting in on him. That's when Monigan saw Dwayne in headlong flight along the far sidewalk, passing the streetcar in the opposite direction.

"Stop!" he screamed. "Stop, for chrissake!"

Fortunately the driver's foot was on the brake when Monigan jammed down on his leg, for in his frenzy the big man may have torn off the entire limb if the streetcar had increased speed. Rather, it slammed to a halt, and Monigan didn't even hear the explosion of sound, the horns and the curses and the rending of metal-on-metal. He had already dashed out the door and set out in pursuit.

Eastbound along Dundas galloped Dwayne Feller. Had he turned his head he could have seen the accident, the seven cars and the UPS truck that disgorged their passengers, who set about assessing damage, threatening one another and dodging the vehicles determined to bypass the line of wrecks. But he didn't, nor could he hear anything, so overwhelming was the pounding of his heart. His feet slapped the sidewalk, his arms churned the air. His wool trousers were defecting south of his belly and he reefed them up. His armpits burned and his knees hurt and his eyes watered and his mouth tasted full of pennies.

Up ahead were two young girls more intent on their conversation than on making good time, yet Dwayne wasn't gaining on them. His quick start out of the blocks had tapered off into the staggering gait of an exhausted marathoner. He had the terrifying notion that he might collapse, not make it at all, and the irony of the situation was agonizing. Sir Francis Drake and Kipling and all his heroes would be happy in their resting places that Dwayne was finally trying to come clean, but now his efforts were dying. He set his sights on the two girls up ahead. If he could reach them he could at least gasp out his tale and die in the knowledge that he was cleansed.

On the sidewalk across the street, Monigan had caught up with his son. But the years of abuse, the bales of tobacco and the hogsheads of beer had reduced Monigan to the same stumbling wreck as Dwayne. Father and son continued along parallel tracks until Monigan ran blindly into a hot dog vendor. Leaping to the defense of his wares, the vendor poked at Monigan with the short length of broken hockey stick he kept handy for such purposes, keeping the wild man at bay. Monigan wrestled the weapon out of his hands, and the hot dog man fetched up face-down over the relish jars while our crazed hobo lashed him on the ass with the stick.

On the south side of the street, Dwayne stopped and hung his head over the curb. There was not much in his stomach to get rid of, and when he was empty Dwayne stood up and wiped the traces of vomit from his lips. Through the water in his eyes he saw an apparition pointing at him from the opposite sidewalk. Gradually the moisture evaporated and his father's form became clear. As if in an agreement like that between two fighters allowing themselves respite in the late rounds of a bout, Dwayne and Monigan stood measuring each other and forcing air into their lungs.

They remained in place until Monigan shook the stick over his head and croaked, "Fire! French fry!"

And the chase was on.

Back at the scene of the accident, Doyle and Ogilvie relinquished control to the backup patrolmen and set off in search of the man was was the cause of the whole thing. Armed with the streetcar operator's description, they blended it with reports of various passengers and concluded the man they were looking for was a tall, thin, short, fat man with long, curly blond hair cut in a black-and-gray crewcut.

"I don't know why we bothered asking," Doyle said.

"He couldn't have gotten far," Ogilvie said. "We'll go with the operator's description. Keep your eyes open left and I'll scan right."

Doyle pulled over when the two young girls hailed the car. They were Queen Street West specimens done over in black, with jackboots and stylish corpse-like complexions, and both were tying to act nonchalant, without much success.

"Gross!" the first said.

"He was puking," said the second.

"Who was?" Ogilvie said. "Calm down."

"He was puking and he was eight feet tall."

"And he had a uniform on."

"Yeah, and the other one had a sick eye, like that actor on the Late Great Movie."

"That wasn't Late Great."

"It was so. The one the other night with the guy at the commercial break from Scarborough who said stay tuned — the cute one."

"Oh, yeah. So anyway, the other one, the weird one, had this little head and there was still puke on him and the other one was calling him, like, a french fry."

"And the weird one was crying."

"And the guy with the screwed-up eye had a gun."

"Hold on," Doyle said. "Just hold on, you girls. Are you sure about the gun?"

"It was a gun."

"Or a stick."

"No, a gun for sure."

"They were both ugly and I think they were kidnappers."

"How could you tell that?" Ogilvie asked.

"I can tell."

"Me, too. They were kidnappers and probably killers."

"Killers, yeah."

"Do we get a reward?"

"Do we get to go on Speaker's Corner?"

"That'd be the best."

"Calm down and listen to me," Doyle said.

"We're calm."

"Yeah, we're calm. You think we're scared of killers?"

"Or kidnappers?"

"Or guns? We know three guys with guns."

"Four. Four guys."

"Who?"

"Brent has a gun. He told me."

"Brent's a shit artist."

"Just because he dumped you."

"He didn't dump me — I dumped him."

"Right."

"Okay, then — we know four guys with guns. And one of them's a kidnapper."

"He went on Speaker's Corner once."

"So what? So did I."

"So did I. And I showed my tits."

"No way."

"I did! I showed my tits to Moses Znaimer on Speaker's Corner."

"You probably had your bra on."

"I don't wear a bra." She was in the process of demonstrating this truth when Doyle blew.

"Just give me a straight answer!" he barked. "Did either of you see where they went?"

"Oh, yeah."

"Sure — down Jarvis."

Doyle and Ogilvie jumped back in the cruiser and turned right at the corner, southbound on Jarvis Street.

"Fucking cops," the first girl said.

"Killers," said the second.

Dwayne hadn't made it far. He was sprawled against the back of a house, plangent sounds coming from his mouth. He didn't have the strength to undo the buttons on his tunic so was deprived of even that modicum of relief. Off to his right, Monigan was calling his name and saying something about the fire. Dwayne couldn't believe his own father was fated to be the cause of his downfall. Dwayne could hear him creeping along the side of the house, could hear Monigan's feet squashing litter and squeaking through the last traces of snow surviving in the shadows.

Why hadn't he told Katlyn? Even now, if she could hear his confession there remained the hope of forgiveness. But Dwayne knew what was in store for him and didn't want Katlyn to find out about his crime like this. Not like this, beaten to a pulp, arrested, cuffed, propelled into the police station, photographed and printed and very likely sodomized before the sun went down. With the last measure of endurance at his command, he heaved himself upright and lurched for the far side of the house.

Out on the street, Doyle drew his weapon while Ogilvie called for backup. It didn't feel right to either of them. Someone was coming up the gap between the two buildings.

Looking out into the sunlight Dwayne, smothered in darkness, saw the policeman. He tried to call out but lacked the strength. It was all over. He burst out into the light.

"You," Doyle said. He lowered the gun.

Dwayne collapsed in a heap.

"It's okay," Doyle said, turning back to Ogilvie. "It's only the cowboy from The Workbench."

"That's it, Frenchie!" Monigan screamed as he hurled himself into the sunshine. He pointed the length of hockey stick he had taken off the hot dog vendor. "Now I fucking have you!"

Doyle whirled. Monigan didn't hear the explosion. The bullet ripped into the brow ridge above his wonky eye and drove him back into the shadows.

Dwayne whimpered and covered his ears.

TWENTY-FOUR

Dwayne came around in stages. Constable Ogilvie gently pried his hands away from his ears and leaned in close. She was saying something to him but Dwayne's ears were still ringing, so he cocked his head like a puppy and tried to read her lips. What an odd state of affairs, he thought. He wondered how he had fetched up where he was, sitting on the grass, his lungs heaving. Gradually his memory reasserted itself, replaying the events of the past half hour. When it reached the present Dwayne jerked back from the policewoman.

"Gah!" he said.

"Calm down," Ogilvie said. "You're all right. Breathe easily and evenly — you're hyperventilating."

The area was aswarm with the faceless spectators who multiply at the scene of a disturbance, and Dwayne equated them with those at the fire site. Ogilvie looked up the street to where Doyle was talking to three plainclothesmen, the men who were at the leading edge of the proceedings to end her partner's career. Of that she was certain. The subject of police shootings was so volatile these days that Doyle would surely be thrown off the force, if not subjected to criminal charges. One of the cops was holding the length of hockey stick Monigan had been brandishing when he sprang out from the shadows. She returned her attention to Dwayne.

"Citizen's arrest," Ogilvie said. "That's what he kept repeating as they loaded him onto the gurney. Citizen's arrest, then something about not pressing charges."

But Dwayne was checking himself out, poking with his finger all over his torso, trying to find the entry wound before he bled to death. At least he was dying in battle.

"Monigan was shot," Ogilvie said. "Not you. Now what was he talking about — what's this about a citizen's arrest?"

"Me."

"You?"

"I've been tracked down," Dwayne wailed. "Cornered like a fox, treed like a coon."

"Make sense."

Dwayne thrust his hands, wrists together, under her nose. "Arrest me," he said. "I deserve no less."

"Get up," Ogilvie said. "Get up and come with me."

Praise the Lord and pass the ammunition. When the slug hit Monigan it smashed the brow ridge above his eye. Redirected by the bone, it followed the surface of the skull up, tearing through the skin and exiting near the hairline.

It was three days later and Monigan was mighty fed up with all the attention. He sported an enormous padded bandage on his head, adding bulk to a skull already too thick and square. With only his right eye uncovered, he had to turn completely to the left to see Katlyn as she walked into the hospital room.

"Don't move your head." The nurse, a young woman with an attractive Jamaican accent, was tired of giving Monigan instructions.

"Having trouble with him?" Katlyn said.

"Please see if you can get him to behave. Otherwise we'll have to clamp him into a head restraint."

Katlyn waited until the nurse left then took Monigan's hand. "Cleanest bed you've been in for twenty years," she said.

Monigan grinned. "What did you bring me?"

"I couldn't think of anything," Katlyn said. "What would I bring? Candy? Flowers? Books?"

Monigan waited.

"You don't need anything to drink."

"Just asking."

Katlyn went to the far side of the bed. "Now you can keep your head still."

"I hate it here. This place stinks."

"It's called sanitation. Get used to it — the doctor says you'll be here awhile."

"He told you?"

"Yes."

"See how lucky I am? How many times I told you I got a charmed life? That dope Doyle don't shoot me, I don't go to the hospital. I don't go to the hospital, they don't find out my chest is hurting me more than my head. They don't check me out, they don't find the growth. Ugly word, eh? Growth."

"The doctor has high hopes they found it in time."

"Timing," Monigan said.

Katlyn laid her head on his chest and he wrapped his arms around her. When she raised up she was crying.

"Hey," Monigan said.

"I'm sorry."

Monigan regarded her a long time with his good eye. "I'm the one who's sorry. What's gonna happen to him? What do the cops have to say?"

"Officially it doesn't sound too bad. It's his reaction I'm worried about. He's out on bail at home and won't take my calls. He won't even talk to his mother. Won't answer the phone, his door, nothing."

"Way I hear it he should come off okay," Monigan said. "He changed his mind, after all. Didn't actually start the fire, even though he's in the shit for going as far as he did."

Katlyn nodded.

"And they got that greaseball at the airport, didn't they?"

"Sturgis. No, they missed him. He disappeared in Vancouver somewhere but they figure it's only a matter of time. Dwayne has already given the police all the information they need to nail him but then again, it may be only his word against Dwayne's."

"*That* I'd pay to see: the french fry giving evidence on the stand."

Katlyn laughed.

"Why didn't I figure it out?" Monigan said. "Twice I made that turd cough up money for Frodo, and the second time he did everything except tell me the fire was a put-up job."

"It's not your fault."

"That ain't true, Katy. I thought for once; what I thought was just once I could do something that counted for something."

"You do a lot for people."

"I do squat. I'm selfish, face it. But this time I coulda been a hero. I never wanted to be a hero, never wanted to be anything, really, but then when I had the chance I acted like all them I put the badmouth on all the time. Trying to be somebody, be important. And now I screwed it up for you."

"Dwayne did it without any help from you."

"That's been the point all along — no help from me."

"He's an adult."

"What was he thinking?"

"Same as you." She pulled a chair alongside the bed and sat down, keeping hold of Monigan's hand. "Trying to accomplish something."

"By burning a house down."

"Things accumulate," she said. "Each little step doesn't seem so difficult or even repulsive. Sometimes you look at the end result and wonder how you ever got there."

"Yeah, well," Monigan said. "Looking for a shortcut, that's the way I see it. Not that the kid's any different from everyone else. I mean, you try to get something for nothing and you deserve whatever you end up with. Whole country's like that these days, people trying to get themselves to the top by counting on lotteries or gutless lawsuits. Back when I was working regular we didn't have every asshole with a grudge making money from wrongful dismissal claims."

"Didn't you ever have a boss you wanted to sue?"

Monigan looked at her as if she had a brain lesion. "No," he said plainly. "Asskick but not sue."

"Some people prefer the courts."

"Some people have no shame."

"Dwayne has that sense but I don't think he's built to survive the process," Katlyn said. "The goal, the end, was all he could address."

"I wanted to talk to him, that's all. Catch up to him and figure out how to keep his ass out of jail. Do something like . . . aw, shit . . . like a dad would do, I guess."

"You still have time," Katlyn said.

"Don't go nuts on me," Monigan said. "I ain't gonna clear up all the years of screwing up by a big deathbed chat with the kid."

"You're not on your deathbed."

"Too bad, really," Monigan mused. "It might of got me a mercy fuck from the nurse."

Katlyn laughed only because the nurse chose that moment to reappear. The young lady looked at Monigan and shook her head, chuckling against her will. "I'll have to ask you to leave soon," she said to Katlyn.

"She just got here," Monigan said.

"Come early tomorrow," the nurse said. "Stay as long as you like."

"Just a few minutes?" Katlyn said.

"Sure," the nurse said. "Do you know the way out?"

"I'll find it."

The nurse nodded and left.

Monigan turned his good eye back to Katlyn. "Now why can't I find a woman like that? Understanding, one who don't take a compliment like a insult."

"Because most women can tell the difference."

"How about you?" Monigan said. "Are you understanding?"

"What do you mean?"

"Come on," Monigan said. "Is the french fry history?"

Katlyn lowered her head.

"Been my experience that if you find somebody that fits the bill but don't measure up on all counts, you start teaching them. And I think you'd make a pretty good teacher. Sounds like you and Frenchie got some talking to do."

"If you know so much —"

"Yeah, yeah," Monigan said, waving his hand. "But just 'cause I got the experience don't mean I know how to apply any of it. I mean, what am I gonna say to the kid, my own son, when I get outta here? I'm trying to protect him and that, yet at the same time what he did's driving me crazy. I always believed one main thing: you fuck up, you pay the price. That covers it. You take the responsibility for what you do. Case closed, end of story, hang up the phone, walk your sister home. Would've been easy if he hadn't been caught — that's another matter. But now that he's nabbed he's gotta act like a man. Yet here I am trying to find some way for him to dodge the whole thing. I end up having to ask myself too many questions when it comes to that boy."

"You already said it," Katlyn said. "You have some teaching to do. And some learning."

They shared some quiet time. Katlyn had never seen Monigan so little disposed to fidget or talk or needle.

"I guess I should go," she eventually said. "Will you be okay?"

"Eh? Me?"

"I mean with the other."

"The operation?" Monigan said. "Sure, sure. Tell you, I can't wait to get my hands on a cold beer."

"Don't go drowning your sorrows when you get out of here."

"I never do that. I wanna *find* a reason to drink, not *have* one."

"When is the surgery scheduled?"

"Couple days, I think."

"Don't be afraid," Katlyn said softly. "I couldn't stand seeing you afraid."

"Not much chance of that."

Katlyn squeezed his hand.

"Besides," he said. "Least I'd go with my guts on the table. Better than going like Small Wally."

Katlyn bent and kissed him.

"Thanks, sweetie."

"Take care of yourself in here."

"Of course," Monigan said. "Gotta be in good shape for when I kick off one of these days. That old guy up there's got a lot to answer for, and the fucker might bring friends to the meeting."

When Katlyn had gone Monigan stared with his good eye up at the ceiling. Scared.

The next day was the Blue Jays' home opener and Harold Arens had tickets. Despite his authentic passion for the game, he had passed the ducats on to his cousin and now stood with Reba Stiles in front of Dwayne's door. Dwayne's mother was yelling down instructions from her front window.

"Be careful!" she hollered. "It might be wired to explode. Happens all the time. Practically epidemic."

Harold had tried phoning Dwayne since he heard the news but couldn't get past his friend's mother, who was determined to be the first one to talk to Dwayne. He was her son and it was her right. But Dwayne was talking to no one. His mother had caught a glimpse of him one night, a lumpy shadow skirting the bushes on its way to the corner store. Frustrated, his mother hauled out all the old tricks to break into Dwayne's apartment, but every attempt was rebuffed. She even tried when Dwayne was back inside and was answered by banging as Dwayne nailed up another board and attached another chain.

One day Harold and Dwayne's mother had a long talk and eventually Harold won her trust. He was asked to get Dwayne out of the apartment by whatever means necessary. Harold was deeply concerned. Not only was Dwayne a friend but Harold had a large dose of empathy for anyone who had knuckled under to Sturgis, however misguided Dwayne had been. It's hard to retain your dignity when you're constantly riding the line between asking and begging for work; Harold knew all about that kind of pressure.

Of course, as much as those reasons were true, Harold knew he was here for the same reason as Reba: it might be funny. There could be five minutes of new material from the escapade. And Dwayne would understand, so long as they changed his name in the act.

"This is weird," Harold said.

"What if he's dead?" Reba asked.

"Don't be ridiculous."

Dwayne's mother had given them a hammer and chisel. They examined the door. The hinges were on the inside, as with every exterior door. Harold threw the tools on the grass. By the time they located a large pinchbar at a lumber yard on Queen Street and made their way back to Seaton, Dwayne's mother was apoplectic, screaming down from the window.

"Don't hit him with that!" she yelled. "He's very fragile — just try to coax him out or something."

"Get back," Harold said to Reba. He jammed the pinchbar under the molding and wrenched. It took twenty minutes to gnaw the wood away and work the door open. As it sprang free, a feculent cloud backed them off.

"What's going on down there?" Dwayne's mother screamed.

Dwayne was sitting on his futon, tapping his foot and chewing the thumbnail on his right hand. Harold flicked on the light and Dwayne shrieked, covering his eyes then rapidly blinking as his retinas adjusted. Dwayne had eaten nothing but potato chips and Polski Ogorki pickles for the eleven days he had been barricaded in his apartment. He was ashen and the skin of his belly hung in folds. He scratched his bare chest and drew up his knees.

Harold propped the pinchbar against the wall and Reba shuffled in behind him. "You heard us forcing our way in," Harold said. "You could have opened up."

Dwayne looked at his watch. "Twenty minutes," he said. "I did it in seventeen."

Harold and Reba heard Dwayne's mother open the front door so they retreated, happy to let the situation resolve itself. They hailed a cab.

"Sorry," the cabbie said. "Radio's broken."

"So I miss the home opener and don't even get a good laugh out of the whole thing," Harold said.

"I've always wondered," Reba said, "if Dwayne really was a laughing matter."

Now that the outside world had access to him, Dwayne figured there was no harm in going out there and laying his life on the line. Katlyn was shocked at his condition but successfully covered her impression. She led him upstairs, where he settled in on the couch and picked at a loose thread on the cushion between his legs, keeping his eyes on the task. Katlyn sat in the armchair.

"Do you want me to go?" Dwayne finally said.

"Of course not."

"You must hate me."

"I don't hate you, Dwayne."

"What do you want me to do? I'll do anything."

"Just relax."

"This is so hard to explain."

"I don't want an explanation, at least not yet. I probably know the reasons anyway."

"You know everything."

"That's simply not true."

"I want to know. Everything. About you."

"You will, in time."

He looked up at her. "I'm not going to jail. That isn't a certainty, but my lawyer told me I'll probably get off with a fine and community service. The community service will be good."

"Your mother thinks that's what you do now."

Dwayne laughed weakly.

"Seriously, how is she taking it?"

"Predictably," Dwayne said. "My mother is so entirely convinced the world is populated with criminals and lunatics that she's outraged the authorities have singled me out." He paused. "And she's my mother. She loves me."

They sat quietly awhile and Dwayne felt a lot of his anxiety slipping away.

"I've been thinking," Katlyn said.

Dwayne didn't seem to hear.

"The basement at The Workbench. I bet we could fit tables and chairs for seventy or eighty people down there. Carpet the floor, fix up the walls, a small stage. No need for a separate bar — we could serve from upstairs. The whole thing could be done cheaply."

"Yes," Dwayne said. "It's understandable that you're focused on your job. I've hardly given you reason to be concerned abut your private life."

Katlyn ignored him, plunging on. "There should be lots of comics available with The Laugh Chance closed. And you told me you're on intimate terms with all the talent in town. You could manage the downstairs while I run the bar upstairs. I think we'd make a pretty good team."

"Team? Us? A business partnership?"

"I was counting on more than a business partnership."

"You're not throwing me out?" Dwayne cried. "That is, I was never in, but the night we . . . the evening that we . . . ?"

"I told you that I love you. I've never said that to anyone in my life and I'm not about to take it back. I love you, Dwayne."

He stood to his full height, swaying from the shock of it all. The end of his belt flopped down from the new hole he had punched into it and a moan escaped from deep within his shrunken belly.

A comedy club — of his own! Dwayne saw it all before him in a second: him wearing a beret, reviewing tapes of rising comics, occasionally deigning to appear on stage but mostly offering paternal advice and avuncular encouragement to the other comics, the lesser ones. He'd ask Harold to help him get set up. Harold had a good eye for such things. Dwayne's plans raced ahead of him into the distance. By now he was planning a syndicated TV show to be taped at the club. He'd have to start a file, interview prospective talent and crew and makeup girls and . . . O! this was how the universe was meant to unfold. His eyes widened. He could see, actually see his name on the door, on the stationery. Dwayne Feller was a new man, reborn. This was fulfilment, vindication, triumph.

It was the Mfecane! The crushing!

He jacked back to the present and there she was, the one responsible, his own Katlyn. All this and love to boot. His heart was aching and tears streaked his cheeks. For the first time he knew why love confers power. All true power is simply being in a position in which no one else can bring their power to bear against you. It has nothing to do with money or glory or fame or prestige. It could even be held by him, by Dwayne, by virtue of just not reacting to the pressure. With Katlyn to love, and her loving him in return, Dwayne was one bulletproof sonofabitch.

"I love you," he croaked.

He leapt the coffee table and she rose to meet him. They slammed together into the ficus.

"I love you," she whispered as they fell to the floor. Then she had to beat her tiny fists on his chest, trying to free herself before she suffocated. "Dwayne!" she said. "Dwayne, hold on!"

"*La Pasionaria!*" he breathed.

TWENTY-FIVE

Monigan knew the healing was well along when he felt his impatience returning. The surgery was behind him and so was the hospital, as he sat in the warm June air on the front steps, waiting for Katlyn. He had never realized how much his life held until it was nearly taken from him, and even the post-operative recovery time had accentuated the richness of simply walking the sidewalk and reveling in what the world dumped on his ugly head. He didn't need to be a hero. He had plenty.

"Why don't I call you a cab?" The nurse looked down at him on the steps.

"It's nice waiting," he said.

"I have to get back to work."

"I been abandoned before. Only try to collect up my parts after the raccoons finish with me."

She put her hand on his shoulder and he covered it with a paw. "Take care," she said.

Katlyn arrived in a cab and walked to meet him.

Monigan stood up and took her by the waist. "You look so good," he said. He drew her close and put her head on his shoulder. "Lemme just hold you a sec."

Back at The Workbench, Dwayne was downstairs hectoring the renovation crew that was slapping up the new comedy club, a farrago consisting of pub regulars working for draft beer. So often had Dwayne changed his mind about details that the men had adopted a shambling, desultory approach to the job, though that might have been the draft cutting in. There was little left to be done at this stage. When Dwayne heard Katlyn's voice up in the bar he picked up his copy of *Leadership and Exchange in Formal Organizations* and climbed the narrow stairs. He didn't hear the clatter of tools hitting the floor behind him.

With three steps to go he stopped. He could hear his father. Dwayne had been to the hospital eight times while Monigan was in there, and on each occasion he had done no more than pace outside and drink pop from the machine in the lobby. He didn't know where to start, what to say. But he was a club owner now, or manager at least, and was in love; he had authority and responsibility. He gripped the bannister firmly and continued his ascent.

"Monigan," he said to his father's back.

Monigan turned and looked him up and down. "You lost more weight than me, even."

Dwayne shrugged.

"Looks good on you," Monigan said.

"I came by the hospital," Dwayne said.

"Sure."

"I couldn't come in. But I came by."

"Don't need to explain to me," Monigan said. "Only I was sleeping all the time anyhow, so it wouldn't have been any use. No sense beating yourself up."

Dwayne faltered. "I don't know what to say."

"Nothing's fine," Monigan said. Then he added, "For now."

Dwayne smiled. "For now."

"I guarantee you the construction stopped when you come up here," Monigan said. "Gotta keep on top of the workers around here. Six-incher wouldn't hurt."

"Right," Dwayne said. "I'll go check up on them."

Katlyn was behind the bar, watching.

"Monigan," Dwayne said as his father turned to go.

"Eh?"

"It's good to have you back."

"Yeah," Monigan said. "And thanks for the hammer."

Dwayne nodded. They didn't linger on the moment.

Monigan banged his hands together and approached the bar. "First thing is slide a pitcher of draft my way. Then me and old Bill are gonna skin everybody at the pool table."

"Monigan . . ." Katlyn said.

"What's up?"

"We wanted to wait till you were better."

Monigan deflated and he looked her hard in the eyes. "How'd it happen?"

"He just went," Katlyn said. "We found him upstairs on the floor. At first we thought someone might know something — there were two bowls of soup and two cups of tea on his dresser — but they had been there a long time. He just went."

"He didn't seem so bad," Monigan said. "I mean, it wasn't like he was all there or nothing, but he could still do stuff, and he had a bit of a life here."

"I know," Katlyn said. "At least he had a friend."

"Some friend."

"You were."

He held out his fingers and Katlyn stuck a cigarette between them.

"I was gonna say he run outta time," Monigan said. "But time for what? I guess Bill had done all the stuff he was supposed to do."

"I'm so sorry," Katlyn said.

"Aww, Bill," Monigan said. "Fuck a fullgrown duck."

TWENTY-SIX

Saturday, Opening Night.

There had been a certain amount of apprehension on the part of the comics but their fears had been allayed, at least to this point. The room looked good, if tiny, and Katlyn seemed to have a handle on advertising, at least judging by the number of people Harold had talked to who had heard about the place. Besides, with The Laugh Chance boarded up, they weren't exactly floating in stage time, so any club was welcome. But who could have predicted this?

Dwayne Feller, Club Owner Dwayne, was firmly in place atop a pedestal of self-importance. He had taken to wearing a tweed jacket with leather patches on the elbows, a carefully knotted club tie, good stout walking shoes — apparel that represented a casual yet professional approach to his work. And Dwayne actually had mastered, at minimum, the impression of professionalism. Mature and particularly calm, more in control than any of them could remember.

"Maybe it's his girlfriend," Reba said.

They were all at one table at the back of the club in the basement of The Workbench on opening night. There were no customers yet, but it was still two hours before showtime, and Dwayne had assured them they would have a full house. The inaugural meeting was over, Dwayne had given them two free pitchers of beer and now they were waiting to strut their stuff.

"Probably," Harold said. "She has a lot on the ball, and she's affected *some* type of change in Dwayne."

A well-frayed trio of the building's lodgers hit the bottom of the stairs and froze. They weren't sure what to make of the alterations and clustered together, afraid to reconnoitre.

Harold snickered. "If that's an example of the crowd, I can throw out my act."

Dwayne arrived and testily pushed his way through the three men. Then he turned and had a few words with them. They looked at one another, each shrugged a why not, then sat together stage left. Dwayne wandered over to the comics. He greeted Harold and Reba personally and gave the other performers a brief nod. He didn't have it in him to be an ogre, but he did find it effective to avoid intimacy with the hired help. Harold and Reba were friends but with the others Dwayne wrapped himself in contemplative mystery, a man pondering great truths.

"How does it look?" Harold asked.

"Oh, we'll be fine," Dwayne said as if placating a worried child. "Just fine."

Harold bit his tongue and watched Dwayne mount the stage and fiddle with the microphone. Harold had been in the business long enough — he'd keep it to himself till he got paid.

Meanwhile, Monigan was hustling along as quickly as possible. He had promised to be there for opening night and he'd be in right royal shit from both Dwayne and Katlyn if he was late. It wasn't really his fault, he figured. Who could have known that he'd make it all the way through the wedding? He released a sharp, triumphant bark of laughter as he recalled leaving the reception early to great protests from the other guests. He had buffaloed them all.

A dust devil flung grit and leaves at him so he stopped and shook himself and smoothed down his hair. A man wearing a tuxedo can't just let himself go. It defeats the purpose. He glanced up at the sky that was partially blocked by a web of multicolored leaves overhead. He spat. Could use a cigarette. He patted the pockets of his tuxedo but no luck.

Monigan was wobbling a bit from the drinks his new friends at the reception had urged on him and skittered off the path that bisected the small inner-city park. Somehow his feet got tangled and down he went. He was pretty comfortable and he still had a couple of minutes to kill before the opening night show. He wondered if he would be allowed to bring the mutt into the club.

He checked again for smokes and noticed his tux was grubby. He'd put it in with Katlyn and Dwayne's laundry when he took it over Monday. Monigan still found it weird to be doing favors for his son.

He looked up the other pathway but there was no use in thinking about him too hard. Bill had been a friend and a good man and now he was gone. Old Bill could play pool, and Monigan had never met anyone so good at fixing things, but that was about the extent of it. Maybe Bill hadn't needed any more time.

Monigan got up and crunched through the leaves, setting a good pace, and reached the sidewalk. The Workbench was a few blocks away and he'd be fine when he reached there. A little chili, couple beers, a laugh or two and he'd be fine.

That was a pretty good wedding, he thought. Up ahead he could see the sign on the tavern sticking out over the sidewalk.

Saturday.